FREDO'S
DREAM

SEAL BROTHERHOOD

Revised Edition featuring Fredo's Secret Novella

SHARON HAMILTON

This is a work of fiction. Names, characters, places, brands, media, and incidents are either the product of the author's imagination or are used fictitiously. In many cases, liberties and intentional inaccuracies have been taken with rank, description of duties, locations and aspects of the SEAL community.

I support two main charities: Navy SEAL/UDT Museum in Ft. Pierce, Florida. Please learn about this wonderful museum, all run by active and former SEALs and their friends and families, and who rely on public support, not that of the U.S. Government.

www.navysealmuseum.org

IF YOU GOT ANY CLOSER, YOU WOULD HAVE TO ENLIST

I also support Wounded Warriors, who tirelessly bring together the warrior as well as the family members who are just learning to deal with their soldier's condition and have nowhere to turn. It is a long path to becoming well, but I've seen first-hand what this organization does for its warriors and the families who love them. Please give what your heart tells you is right. If you cannot give, volunteer at one of the many service centers all over the United States. Get involved. Do something meaningful for someone who gave so much of themselves, to families who have paid the price for your freedom. You'll find a family there unlike any other on the planet.

www.woundedwarriorproject.org

SHARON HAMILTON'S BOOK LIST

SEAL BROTHERHOOD
SEAL Encounter (Book .5)
Accidental SEAL (Book 1)
Fallen SEAL Legacy (Book 2)
SEAL Under Covers (Book 3)
SEAL The Deal (Book 4)
Cruisin' For A SEAL (Book 5)
SEAL My Destiny (Book 6)
SEAL Of My Heart (Book 7)

BAD BOYS OF SEAL TEAM 3
SEAL's Promise (Book 1)
SEAL My Home (Book 2)
SEAL's Code (Book 3)

BAND OF BACHELORS
Lucas (Book 1)
Alex (Book 2)
Jake (Book 3)

TRUE BLUE SEALS
True Navy Blue (prequel to Zak)
Zak

NASHVILLE SEAL
Nashville SEAL (Book 1)
Jameson (Book 2)

FREDO
Fredo's Secret (novella) Book 1
Fredo's Dream (Book 2)

NOVELLAS
SEAL Encounter
SEAL Endeavor
True Navy Blue (prequel to Zak)
Fredo's Secret
Nashville SEAL
SEAL You In My Dreams (4/19/17)
SEAL Of Time (Trident Legacy) (3/28/17)

BOXED SETS
SEAL Brotherhood Box Set 1 (SEALs)
SEAL Brotherhood Box Set 2 (SEALs)
Ultimate SEAL Collection Vol. 1 (SEALs)
Ultimate SEAL Collection Vol. 2 (SEALs)
Big Bad Boys Bundle (SEALs)
Immortal Valentines (Paranormal)

FALL FROM GRACE SERIES
Gideon: Heavenly Fall

GOLDEN VAMPIRES OF TUSCANY
Honeymoon Bite (Book 1)
Mortal Bite (Book 2)

THE GUARDIANS
Heavenly Lover (Book 1)
Underworld Lover (Book 2)
Underworld Queen (Book 3)

FREDO'S
SECRET

SEAL BROTHERHOOD NOVELLA

CHAPTER 1

Fredo was not sure how Mia would take the results of his doctor visit, but his training taught him to just be direct with it, tell her that he could not father children. They had little Ricardo, who was not his biological son, but the son of a lowlife now in prison. Fredo and some of his team buddies had rescued Mia from this evil man and his gang. So, Fredo told himself he already *had* a son. Ricardo would grow up thinking of Fredo as his father in every important sense of the word. But he wanted to give Mia more sons, and perhaps a daughter or two.

God had other plans.

An inner city kid growing up, Fredo had been like a lucky penny, associating with both street kids and gang members, as well as the pretty girls who played volleyball and went out for cheerleading in high school. After high school, he escaped being caught, unlike some of his friends; not for doing bad things, but for being in the wrong place at the wrong time. It was the custom that once a youth got into the system, they rarely escaped. Fredo was sharp and lucky enough to never get into the system in the first place.

He thought Cooper would have some solid advice on his parenting situation since he and Coop were still two of the tightest buddies on SEAL Team 3. Cooper now had two children, a boy and a girl.

The Scupper was nearly empty, but that was probably because it was barely three o'clock in the afternoon.

He found his old friend sitting at a long table, as if they were expecting their usual cadre of regulars from Kyle's Team. Fredo hoped Coop hadn't invited anyone today.

"How's it hanging, Fredo?" Coop asked as they fist-bumped.

"Not complaining." Fredo motioned to their usual waitress, and she acknowledged his need for a beer. Cooper sat behind his mineral water, chewing on ice, and making his usual noise.

"You know, Coop, I'm not sure your dentist is very happy with you. You gonna crack all your teeth."

"Nothin' wrong with my teeth, Fredo. My great-grandfather was a horse. We got great teeth."

"I'm not talking about how well you are endowed. I was talking—"

"Well, that, too, if you must know. But then you seen me in the shower, so this should be no surprise. So you wanna tell me why we're talking about my dick?"

Fredo adjusted his defense mechanism. He was going to spout off something offensive in response to Coop's remark, as was their pattern, but he reeled himself in. Part of him was so angry, he wanted to punch something. If Cooper got in the way, it wouldn't be good.

"Okay, well, I just came from the doctor, and he told me I'm sterile. I'm fuckin' shootin' blanks. No little *zarapes* or baby *sombreros* in my future, Coop. No father of the bride walking down the aisle shit for me."

"Borrow one."

"Borrow a sperm? You mean let Mia get a sperm from someone else?"

"No, asshole, that wouldn't be borrowing one. That would be making one a part of your family." Cooper's half smile and partial frown were hard to read. "Borrow a kid," he said, nodding.

"Just how the fuck do I borrow a kid? Besides, Mia wants her own kid. She wants my kid."

"No, she doesn't. She wants you, and if she doesn't, she's hopelessly crazy."

"I think I know my Mia."

"Sure you do. What I'm sayin' is you adopt. Nothing wrong with that. Hell, I'd have done that if it happened to us."

"But I want my own."

"You honestly think you could tell which fuckin' sperm was yours if you looked at them under a microscope? What the hell difference does it make? That's like saying you could never love a woman because some other man got there first. That makes no sense at all."

Cooper did have a point. "I think, in this case, I would be able to tell mine from others. Mine would be with dented heads and wouldn't move."

"Dented heads, huh? What kind of a doctor showed you what your sperm looked like? That does no fuckin' good. I'd

3

have nightmares if they showed me that shit. Like a science fiction freak show or something."

"I wanted him to prove it to me."

"Oh. Well, then, that explains it. You dumb shit. You didn't need to see that."

Cooper nearly finished his mineral water, sucked on the lime until his cheeks caved in, and then chewed on ice. He looked at Fredo like a cow chewing hay, watching the cars go by and not keeping up with the movement. "I don't care what mine look like."

"Yeah, well, yours swim."

"Apparently." Cooper swallowed and went for the last gulp of ice. Before he could set his plastic glass down, the waitress brought him another mineral water and lime with tons of ice.

"I don't know what to say to Mia." Fredo wanted to be honest with his best friend. He was still trying to reconcile the fact that beautiful Mia, who could have been a model or a beauty queen if she'd chosen that path, and was the most stunning of all the SEAL wives, had chosen him. And Fredo knew he was generally thought of as the least handsome of the bunch. He'd had to work long and hard to win her love. He worried that perhaps this would disappoint her. Ever at the back of his mind was the concern that she would one day leave him.

"I can hear all that Mariachi music rolling around in your head, Fredo. Don't get your cart before the horse. You're worrying about something that might not exist."

"But what if it does? What if she's angry? Coop, what if she thinks I'm not right for her?"

"Fredo, you dumb shit. How can you say that? You think she's that shallow? Mia's a strong and beautiful woman, inside and out. She loves you, Fredo. When she finally got it, she was hooked, man." Cooper nodded to a couple of young tadpoles who had entered the bar. "God almighty, they make 'em younger every year. Did we ever look like that?" He nodded to the new recruits.

"I think I was born with hair all over my body. Someone who knew my mom said she called me a little gorilla. Not sure I ever looked like a little boy."

Cooper was laughing. "That's a visual I need eye bleach to get rid of, Fredo. Why did you have to go tell me that? Now I won't be able to think, seeing this little gorilla boy running around the streets of LA."

Fredo began to get steamed. "Okay, asshole. I can see this was a big mistake. I come to you with something serious, and you get me all talking about my childhood and sperm and stuff." Fredo knew it was an unfair argument, but he couldn't hold it back.

"Okay. Calm down. Seriously, Fredo. You just tell her the truth. You ask her what she wants to do, okay? And then you do whatever she wants. If she wants to adopt, you adopt. If not, you stay good with that. If she needs to think it over, you give her space, let her know you're here to discuss it if she wants. But let her decide. We don't make those decisions, they do."

Fredo figured it was probably the best advice he'd get tonight, or any night. He did dangerous things every day, especially when he was overseas. But today, this sitting down and talking to Mia about the doctor visit was the hardest thing he'd have done in over a year.

"You guys have plans for Christmas?" Coop asked.

"Getting together with her mom and Mayfield. What about you?"

"We're going up for a couple of days to Libby's folks' cabin at Big Bear. You should come up."

"I'll ask her."

On the way home, Fredo stopped to buy Mia's mother some items he knew she'd want for her Puerto Rican traditional Thanksgiving feast. The little supermercado was in a seedy part of town where every bar, restaurant, house, and school had bars on the windows. Even the windows at the public park were barred and locked at night with large iron grates.

Fredo only knew the shop owner as Jose, since that's what Mia's mother called him. Recently, Mayfield had insisted on accompanying her. Fredo knew some of the gangs in the area were not opposed to robbing an older military type, even a retired cop, which Mayfield was. So, Fredo tried to do the shopping for her mother as much as he could. Mia almost never cooked. Mama Guzman insisted on doing all of it, so there was no arguing with that. Ever.

He picked up some corn husks and specialty tomatillo sauce, the hot sauce she liked that was made in her hometown in Puerto Rico, and some good rum that Felicia loved to mix with her coconut milk to celebrate anything that required alcohol.

Outside the mercado, he found a couple of pre-teen boys looking for someone to buy them liquor.

"*Jefe*, you maybe wanna help us out some?" the kid with the blue eyes said. Fredo remembered seeing him before, since it was so rare to see a Mexican kid with blue eyes.

"I told you boys I wouldn't do it last time, but what the hell. It's nearly Christmas. You tell me what good deeds you done this week and I'll think about it."

His two friends swore and snuck around the lamppost, walking in the opposite direction, disgusted. But blue eyes stayed behind.

"Punched a kid at school who was being rough on a girl," the boy blurted out. "That good enough for you, frog-man?"

"Where'd you get that name, son?" Fredo asked.

"Because that's what you are. You got webbed feet. You got tats, and you're a fuckin' swaggering asshole frog-man."

"Asshole? This the guy you expect to buy you some booze and you call me an asshole?"

The kid grinned. Fredo saw something different about him. It was either something dangerous or dangerous for the environment. He was eager. Maybe too eager. Fredo adjusted his stance, moving his package to his left arm so he could retrieve his gun from the holster in the small of his back with his right.

The boy's eyes half-lidded. That made Fredo even more nervous.

"I hate you frogs." He ran off.

Fredo stood for a moment and surveyed the alarmingly calm street. It was always like that overseas, too. When it was quiet, that's when you had to worry about getting picked off. That's when the shit hit.

Or maybe he was getting paranoid. Fredo rolled his shoulder, checked both sides of the street again, squinting into the sun and still not seeing anything that gave him a reason for all the hair on the back of his neck to be stuck at full attention.

But something was definitely wrong. He couldn't find any of the three boys he'd seen. He began getting into his beater four-door truck. He heard the ping of the windshield before he felt the shot to his chest. He was surprised it didn't hurt more than it did. But he couldn't breathe. He felt the blackness all around his eyes as he began to lose consciousness. It was fuckin' hard to breathe. That meant the shot hit a lung, and he was not going to survive if the blood was fast.

The street was a tunnel when he felt the tug at his pants. His wallet was taken. He did hear swearing, an altercation, and some choice words in Spanish. He wanted to get up and stop the fight, but couldn't move for some reason. Someone was still upset. Then a lady screamed. He slumped over in the front seat, trying to stay on his back so he wouldn't expose the gun he had at his waist. Just before he passed out, he saw a pair of blue eyes and focused on them until everything was black.

CHAPTER 2

Fredo awoke and thought he was in heaven. The beautiful angel hovered above him, light all around her, just like the pictures he'd seen at Sunday school when he was a kid. Her long brown hair fell around her face and over her shoulders. Then he realized the angel he was staring at was his wife, Mia.

"Mmm—" He tried to say her name.

"Shhh, Fredo. My love, oh, I'm so hoppy to see you're awake."

His eyes must have looked wild.

"You were shot, Fredo. Do you remember who shot you? You were shot doing Mama's shopping. I'm so sorry. They robbed you, but thank God, they did not rob you of your life."

She smelled clean, from fresh soap. Her large almond-shaped eyes were framed with worry lines on her otherwise flawless smooth forehead. He used to think he could see his soul in those eyes when he first fell in love with her, before he heard it in her breath, in the way she talked to him. Her full lips were ripe and did wonderful things to his body. Right now, she was talking to him, and he was only hearing every other word.

"Someone did some quick medical attention on you, Fredo, or you would have died. Oh, God, I couldn't have taken that!" She threw herself onto his chest, her hair tickling his chin and neck. He looked to the ceiling of what he assumed was the hospital, as if God was leaving him a message in clouds that weren't there. Her moist tears stained his chest. The vibrations from her sobs gently rocked him. He tried pulling his right arm up and couldn't, so bent his left arm at the elbow and placed his palm gently at the small of her back. Immediately, her sobbing stopped. She arched up to him, just the way she did when she made love to him, her beautiful face bordered by her wild natural curls. He could never look at her, even after two years of marriage, and not be stunned.

"Mia, I'm glad I didn't die, too." It was stupid, and it wasn't what he really wanted to say, but his words were sparse.

"Oh, my love. You have to promise me you will never go to that supermarket again."

He smiled. "I promise." He was rewarded with a relieved smile on her face, just about the most beautiful thing he'd ever seen in his life.

Then he remembered his doctor visit that morning, and sadness fell upon him.

"What's wrong? Are you in pain?"

"No," he said, but he avoided eye contact.

She insisted he look at her, holding his jowls between her red fingernails. Her fingernails were always red, and her hands always smelled like the vanilla hand cream she used, just like today. She adjusted his head and peered down at him. "Tell me, Fredo. Tell me."

She was hard to lie to. She was hard to do anything but love as often as he was allowed to love her, any way he could love her. She was hard not to do any little thing for. Even taking out the trash was an homage to this beautiful woman who owned him more than he ever thought possible. But today, he would lie.

"It makes me ache to see you so worried, Mia, my love." Then he thought of something he could say that would be plausible. "Did they get my gun?"

"No." She arched back, the top of her cotton vee-neck shirt revealing her soft breasts. Her forearms were on his torso. It was his favorite way to watch her, when she was naked, resting her body against his, her legs between his, feet and sheets entangled. This was coming close. "Your gun was still on you when the paramedics arrived. They got there in just a minute. Happened to be nearby. Otherwise, Fredo," her lower lip began to quiver again, "you would have died. And I would have died alongside you."

That made him laugh. Always so high strung and over-the-top dramatic, Mia was like the ancient Mayan women who used to throw themselves on their dead husband's funeral pyre. His laughing made him begin coughing.

Mia was off him, dashing out the door. Fredo still smelled her beautiful body and felt the moistness and warmth of her even after she was gone. He was left aching.

A very homely nurse with a reddish horse face was the next person he saw. She had a wide nose, nearly Fredo's width. No unibrow, but her eyes were small, and her jaw was prominent, like a man's. Seeing her made him inhale, and he stopped coughing.

"Glad to see you're awake, Mr. Chavez. How do you feel?" Mia stood behind her.

He wanted to say something like, 'Can she stay with me tonight?' but he knew that wouldn't fly.

"Hurts when I cough."

"Yes, well, you've got a tube in there, for drainage, and to keep your lung inflated. They'll probably take it out tomorrow, if everything goes well. You were in surgery for nearly three hours. You'll be sore for a while, but you were lucky it was a small caliber bullet."

"I want to go home."

"No, I'm sorry. You're spending Thanksgiving here in the hospital, I'm afraid. You're not cleared to discharge until the Navy doctor gives the okay."

"Can he have food? My mother will be so disappointed—" Mia was chirping like a little bird at the woman's side, her hands flying everywhere.

"Nope, I'm sorry. You're going to be on clear liquids for twenty-four hours. Closest thing I can get you is perhaps some turkey or chicken broth. That's it, I'm afraid." She checked his IVs and made some notes to his chart with a computer at the side of his bed. "I've alerted the doctor that you're awake. Not sure what his plans are, but I think he'll be in to see you later. Are you in any pain?"

"Just when I cough."

"Let's see what he says first. Be thankful you don't need a ventilator. Welcome back. We're all glad you made it alive, Mr. Chavez."

Fredo realized that, for all the times he'd been overseas, he'd never been shot before. He'd been stabbed, butted with a rifle, partially blown up, thrown from a second-story roof that collapsed under him, pushed off a third-story balcony, and nearly poisoned by one of Coop's health drinks, but never shot.

Kyle, Cooper, and T.J. stopped by late that evening.

"You get a good look at who shot you?" Kyle asked.

"Nah. I was coming out of the market, and these three thugs were there. But they all left before I got shot. Then I saw one of them before I lost consciousness, but not shooting me. No. I got shot through the windshield, which was the opposite direction they'd run off to."

"What did they want? Did they say anything?" Kyle asked.

"Looking for someone to buy them beer or something." He hesitated, but decided he needed to tell Kyle about the blue-eyed kid. "I said no."

"That was smart, doing that in this neighborhood," added Coop.

Fredo considered his comment carefully. Something about the timing seemed off to him. "There was this one kid I recognized. I've seen him before, I think hanging around. But they were never violent looking, you know?"

"You're gonna have to talk to the police now that they know you're awake," T.J. said. "You think they did it, though?"

"I don't think so, but that's just a gut reaction."

"Maybe he's the one who did the first aid," added Coop.

"First aid?"

"Yeah, someone stopped the bleeding. Found a rag and duct taped it to your chest at the entrance wound. I think it saved your life." Coop began examining his IV drip and the monitor on the computer screen at Fredo's bedside.

"You're kidding. So that's what hurts like a son of a gun." Fredo scratched his chest, moving aside his gown and finding a large band of hairless skin cutting him in half at the level of the bandage and drain. "Holy shit, I've been waxed."

Kyle, Cooper, and T.J. chuckled.

"Thank God you always carry that shit around everywhere."

"Duct tape is the bomb." Fredo didn't try to hide the reverence he felt for the stuff in his voice. He worshiped it.

"Too bad they didn't put a piece between your eyes. You'd have gotten your unibrow fixed finally." T.J. could hardly get the words out.

The SEALs laughed again, and Fredo delivered T.J. the finger.

Even Mia had begged him to have his eyebrows tweezed, but he'd always told everyone it was unmanly to alter his physical appearance, even if it wasn't a handsome one. "I'd rather get cut."

What he'd meant to imply was that he'd get his manhood cut, a vasectomy, but that had already been done for him without the surgery. The pain of his doctor visit came back. He glanced up at Cooper, who, thank God, didn't say a word. Instead, Cooper grabbed his hand, and they clasped.

He hoped Coop hadn't told anyone, and the handshake was acknowledgement of that, Fredo thought.

"Okay, well, you look like you'll pull through. But you were damn lucky, Fredo. You don't try to go do anything heroic, you hear? Just stay in bed, try to watch some T.V., and get yourself right. We need you back." Kyle squeezed his shoulder, and then gave him a swat to the side of his face. "Won't be by tomorrow, with Thanksgiving and all. I have to help Christy mind the hellions so she can do her cooking thing. But Mia will take good care of you."

"Thanks," Fredo said. He said goodbye to the three SEALs and as he watched their backs exit the doorway of the hospital room, knew they were going home to wives and the sounds of babies and toddlers at home.

It was something he wouldn't be hearing much longer in his own household. He never knew he missed it until the possibility was taken from him.

CHAPTER 3

Something about the boy's blue eyes kept haunting Fredo. He tried to push it out of his head when Mia came by late the next morning to hand feed him turkey soup that Felicia Guzman had made special for him. She'd gotten approval from the nurse's station. The way his wife's delicate and smooth arm rose and fell with each spoonful, her mouth opening and closing with her tongue licking her lips, was giving him a hard-on. He'd sit there forever if he had to. If she'd just keep feeding him, fussing over him, he could stay there for the rest of his life.

Her small talk, the way her deep brown eyes sparked up at him, sometimes hiding behind her shiny black hair charmed him today just like every time she did it. The, woman would be beautiful at eighty, he just knew it. She'd cause accidents everywhere she went. She'd cause a riot in any nursing home she'd wind up in.

But he kept seeing the boy's blue eyes, which triggered something deep and painful. And then again, he'd remember the secret he could not tell her. He did not want to tell her he was less of a man. He didn't want to admit sometimes he felt like nothing without her. Was it wise to love someone so much that you were so afraid her life would be snuffed out and you'd not be able to survive? The world was a dangerous place. He couldn't be everywhere to protect her or little Ricardo, whom she doted on even more than she did Fredo. She was the best mother he'd ever seen.

"So, *mi amore*, you are feeling better now?" Her warm smile bathed him in the glow he felt all the way to his toes.

"Yes, *mi amore*. I feel much better now that you have revived me, as no other woman ever could." He puckered his lips. It hurt to lean forward, yet he tried.

She answered him by mating her lips with his, carefully, so as not to cause him pain. His finger found the vee of her opening in front, so he could stroke the top of her left breast there. His tongue slipped past hers as he drew her deeper into his mouth. He felt her little giggle, the gentle way she told him she liked him touching her there, liked that he was needing her.

"If they'd let me stay over, I'd probably get you in trouble, *mi amore*," she said, as she let his hand slip under her skirt, over her pantyhose.

"I'd like that very much. Sneak in. I won't tell a soul, Mia."

"You're so cute, Fredo, my love." She pulled away. He was mesmerized by the flowery scent of her, mixed with what he knew to be her natural pheromones. Her eyes sparkled as his hand was prevented from finding flesh under her skirt because of the pantyhose.

"Ah, these things. I don't like these things. This guy who invented them never knew how smooth and beautiful your legs are without them."

She arched back, looking at him with half-lidded eyes. "I am swelling inside for you, *mi amore*. I am needing release. Would we be able to do this before your next nurse examination?"

"My God, Mia. Lock the door. Be quick about it."

She ran to the hallway, searched both directions, and then closed the door, locking it behind her, leaning against it, and showing him she'd placed her hand under her skirt. She removed her pantyhose in one quick, sexy peel. Fredo was instantly so hard he forgot he was in the hospital and nearly tried to climb out of bed.

She left her dress on, but hopped up on the hospital bed, turned around, and presented her rear end to him.

"God, it is such a sacrilege what you do to me. Jesus himself would have never been able to resist the temptation of your beautiful body," he whispered. His hands pushed her skirt up over her tanned smooth ass, and although it hurt like a son of a gun, he leaned forward, tongue out for a drop of her golden juices.

Mia looked at him around the side, her hair covering half her face, and widened her knees at the sides of Fredo's prone frame covered in tape, tubing, and blankets. The bottles hanging at the sides of his bed began to rattle as she inched her pussy closer and closer to his mouth. She was nearly an inch away, and taking her time, when Fredo reached forward, grabbed her around the waist, and smashed her warm lips to his face, where he drank, making no effort to stop while loud slurping noises bounced off the walls.

"Mia, you make me want you more each day. This is so unfair, being here. I want to fuck you all night long."

"Let's do it. How long before you think they'll call security? I'm so hot; I might come twice before they break the door down. Satisfy me, *mi amore*. I am in need of your brand of satisfaction. I ache…"

The green light she gave him as he sucked and lapped had him confused. Once again, he forgot he was in the hospital and tried to get to his knees so he could properly mount her, but he was held back by IVs he was close to tearing out of his arm.

She pulled the blankets back over his engorged dick, as it bobbed and glistened with precum. She spread her butt cheeks wide as she angled herself so her opening covered the crown of his shaft. She sucked in her belly, tightening her muscles and drawing him inside her. Fredo felt like she could pull his whole body inside her.

"Fuck, Mia. I cannot fuck you proper."

"Oh, Fredo, you are doing it; my love, you know I like you deep." She clutched and spread her butt cheeks farther apart, grinding herself down on him and pressing him hard against her cervix; then she moaned with the contact. "More, *mi amore*."

He tried, but he was limited.

"Fuck it." At last he decided he'd had enough. He pulled the IVs out, removed the heart monitor that instantly started sending off little alarm signals. He got himself up on his knees, and covered her from behind, ramming himself inside, lifting her body with his thighs, and the thrusting of his cock. He held her chest down into the bed, one hand at the back of her neck, with her rear in the air as he pumped her. The bed shook, the equipment over the bed started to fall down, tubing began to slap against the sides, and then the IV fell over with a loud crash. The plastic bottle bounced on the floor several times before landing at a stop. Again, a big thrust in as they both heard pounding on the door. Someone was shouting, but Fredo needed to spill inside her as if it was the last act of his young life.

Mia was trying to thrash, grabbing the sides of the bed as he kept thrusting and lifting her. He pulled her back against him, one arm under her waist. Finally, after several long strokes, he began to come. He felt her begin to shudder. He let loose of her neck as she rose up, squeezing her own breasts through the cotton fabric of the dress.

The pounding on the door got louder and louder until he heard some keys clanging.

"They're coming," Mia said.

"Oh My God! So am I, Mia. So am I."

CHAPTER 4

The boy's blue eyes came to Fredo in the dream he was having. For some reason, he kept seeing the boy in an ill-fitting suit, the top being black and the pants a dark brown. He saw blue clouds in the sky, and a couple of sea birds flew above them. There was the sound of something else, cadence calls. Someone was softly crying. The boy in blue stared him down, his eyes scarred with anger, looking so out of place on a young boy. Behind him, a diminutive gray-haired woman was accepting a folded flag.

Fredo was jolted to attention and nearly fell out of the hospital bed as the sounds of a gun salute cracked the easy afternoon in San Diego and made the sea birds scream for cover and disappear. The boy didn't flinch, but Fredo could feel the sweat dripping down his own spine right now as he sat staring at the black screen of the sleeping TV that was mounted on the wall in front of him.

He oriented himself. He was still in the hospital, and it was late morning. He'd had a difficult night, not due to the pain, but his lack of being able to take a deep breath. Mia would be here soon. With any luck, the nurses would let him take a shower. He'd like it if they'd let her do it. Maybe they'd even let him go home. That would be an unimaginably wondrous gift.

He'd seen those eyes at a funeral. For whom? He pushed the grit of confusion from his brain, rubbed his eyes, and shook his head, but it did no good. He'd been there. He'd been to that funeral. This kid was there, too, and hated him. Maybe it was because Fredo lived and someone this boy cared about didn't.

The nurse came in, busying herself with details that didn't require they speak, and Fredo was grateful for this. Her lips made a sneer as if she had smelled something unpleasant. He watched the ever-blue sky outside and just waited until he was alone again to think. He really wanted to remember more.

"Can I go home today?"

"Not sure, Mr. Chavez. Maybe another day or two. You just sit back and be comfortable; relax a bit."

Did she know how fuckin' stupid she sounded? Sit back and relax? What the fuck was up with that?

"How about a shower? I need one," he scowled, crossing his arms over his waist, giving her a squint. "My wife can help me."

That cracked her veneer. Her lips arced up, and she winked at him. Her gruff demeanor melted enough for him to see a kinky side to the greying woman with the man's voice. "I can only imagine."

She scurried around the bed to the window.

"I'm not on any real pain meds."

"You want these drapes pulled a bit? Sun will be coming in here in about an hour."

"I like the sun. I come from a place where it never sets." His chin jutted out in defiance. He scratched his arms.

"That so?" She raised her painted eyebrows up, her forehead skin making accordion folds above her considerable unibrow. At the sight of it, he swore to himself and tossed his torso back into the bed.

"I know it's hard on you guys. You like to be up doing things. No fun lying here in bed, watching the world to go by. Of course, that doesn't stop all of you from being…creative."

She gave him a fat-lipped smirk and wiggled her eyebrows up and down, telling him she'd known what he and Mia had done the day before. No doubt, they were the talk of the floor from the looks on everyone's faces.

Detective Clark Riverton had come by the previous day, on Thanksgiving, which told Fredo the man's love life hadn't improved. He'd arrived while the door was locked, and with the flurry of activity going on around him as the staff worked to get Fredo reconnected to all the monitors, Riverton had given up and made the date to come back.

Clark Riverton was one of the good guys. But his lifestyle dictated that he live somewhat in the shadows. Never married, his luck when it came to women was better with professionals; that he could pay to be silent. He made a point to tell Fredo on one occasion that he didn't pay for sex. He paid for discretion.

Riverton had been known to date an old girlfriend of Coop's, Daisy, the tattoo artist all the SEALs on Kyle's team went to. Although she didn't look the part, she was extremely selective, so that gave Riverton an added dose of respect.

Fredo didn't think he had many regrets. He wasn't the kind to stay at home, retired, raising someone else's kids, either. Fredo wondered if that would be his fate. One big difference between them was that Clark never seemed to covet a family lifestyle; Fredo did.

When Riverton entered the room, he tossed Fredo a chocolate foil-wrapped turkey from one of the famous candy stores.

"Someone dropped a whole basket of these off at the office, so don't think I went out of my way to shop for you, Fredo." Riverton rarely smiled. His eyes drew down smaller as he took quick furtive glances at the tubing and equipment, now thankfully at rest.

"Thanks." Fredo began peeling the foil and taking a bite out of the tail.

"You should probably ask them." Riverton held his thumb over his right shoulder.

"These things are so sensitive, they'll start beeping. Then I'll stop. Chocolate is a food group in Puerto Rico."

"May I?" Riverton gestured to the straight-backed chair in the corner, removing a newspaper before he sat. He crossed his legs and brought out his small vest pocket spiral notebook and pen. "I wanna ask you about who you saw at the grocery store."

"Supermercado. They don't say grocery store in that part of town."

"Duly noted. So Kyle says there were three of them?"

"Yes. Why did you call Kyle?"

"He called me." Riverton wasn't going to reveal anything else until he got his questions answered. "So tell me about those boys. Three? Is that it?"

"Yes, there were three. I know I've seen one of them before several times. Even had a dream about him last night."

Riverton stopped his chicken scratches and looked at Fredo, slightly tilting his head to the side, a worried frown consuming his ruddy face. "We're dreaming about boys now, are we, Fredo?"

"Shut the fuck up. More like a nightmare." Fredo couldn't believe how stupid he'd been to reveal the dream.

"So which guy we gonna talk about now. The one in your dream or the one who accosted you outside the *supermercado?*" Riverton showed his disdain for the Spanish he was forced to speak in California.

"Funny. I remembered him from somewhere. There was a funeral, I think."

That made Riverton pensive. Fredo was careful with his words. Most obvious in the room was the fact that there had been way too many of them recently. The Special Forces were experiencing casualties unlike ever before, and for a war that hadn't escalated in the public's mind, but one Fredo knew was brutal and deadly and still in its infancy. Fredo knew it would some day be called the hundred-year war. Or it would until someone had the guts to stop it by being more brutal than the enemy. Fredo and his buddies on SEAL Team 3 were the spear of that miniscule fighting force.

"You remember which funeral it was? Someone on Team 3?"

Fredo focused on the birds outside his window, swirling in a small swarm. Starlings or some other small birds that traveled in clouds, pulsing like the beat of a human heart, morphing into different rounded shapes.

Everyone's connected.

Here he was, sitting in the hospital bed with a gunshot wound to his chest, unable to be over at Mama Guzman's Thanksgiving feast with Mia and her mother fussing all over him like he was a boy of ten.

And then it hit him. He'd seen this kid a few years ago.

"I know who he is now."

"Enlighten me." Riverton's deadpan was even deader. The only way Fredo knew he was interested was the speed with which he answered.

"We had this kid, came from the projects here. Tried out for the teams and washed out during the underwater phase. He couldn't swim. Afraid of water and all that."

"How'd he get a shot at trying out if he couldn't swim?"

"Well, he'd gotten some training all right. He was a big, physical kid. Family from Mexico. We used to see them bring food and things they weren't supposed to. Hung around the parking lots, the beaches where we trained."

"So he washed out. Whose funeral was it, then?"

"His. He begged for a second chance. But the Navy grabbed him, and he was off to the Pacific fleet. Family was devastated when he got shot. He was home on leave. Just a random thing, like this," Fredo said as he pointed to his chest.

"You guys attended the funeral, I take it?"

"Yeah. We all did. Kyle had taken a liking to him, too. We were going to try to help him. Had a tough life. They were very poor." Fredo studied Riverton's face to find a trace of compassion there and found none. "A lot of us came that way."

Fredo remembered the big kid with the wide smile. In uniform, he could have been a kid from a middle class family in Santa Monica. Fredo had felt the instant bond between them, due to their backgrounds.

"Go on. Was he involved in something he shouldn't have been?"

"Yeah, there was a girl he knocked up." Fredo faded to the place where this young man was dead, a man who could father children, and he was very much alive, but not able to add to his own bloodline.

Get yourself away from this pity party you're having, Fredo. Makes no difference. Makes no difference.

He found Riverton sitting at rapt attention, his pencil poised on the little notepad. He didn't know how many seconds he had been daydreaming about life and the meaning of life—all very dangerous stuff. Stuff that could get you killed. Or worse, get a buddy killed. Fredo jerked his mind out of the clouds and continued.

"Had a ton of brothers and sisters, too. All of them had moved away. Who could blame them? He came back to help his mom with his younger brother. This kid with the blue eyes. The kid idolized him."

"And the girl?"

"What girl?"

"The girl he knocked up."

"Last time I saw her she was as big as a house, but she wasn't allowed to sit with the family, not that she wanted to. She moved away, and no one ever saw her again. Too bad, too. I think the grandmother would have liked to have her here."

"Can't say that I blame her. She gets a way to get out, she takes it. End of story. There's a different concept for a family here in these streets."

"Yeah. I grew up knowing that, too. You stick together, and you're safer than on your own."

Riverton sighed and leaned back in his chair. "Well, that's one helluva story, son. Not sure it does me much good. Unless you think the kid, or one of his little buddies, did you."

"I don't think so. I'd be surprised."

"He recognize you at the store?"

"Oh definitely. Most definitely."

"What makes you say that?"

"His friend asked me to buy alcohol for them. I usually decline. But it was almost Thanksgiving, and, hey, I was a kid their age, too, once."

"No kidding. We all were."

"So I messed with them a bit. The two of them ran off to go look for another asshole to buy their booze. This kid played my game."

"Game?"

"I asked him what kind thing had he done." Fredo stared directly into Riverton's eyes to make sure he got the point. "He told me he'd stuck up for a girl. I think I embarrassed the kid, and he had second thoughts."

Riverton shrugged. "This is leading nowhere. How do you know he knew you?"

"He called me a frog-man. And then he took off before I could figure out who he was. Now that I know, I doubt he was the shooter."

"You got a name for this kid?"

"His brother had a strange name—Ephron Hernandez. We just called his little brother Blue, *Azul*, because of his blue eyes. All the kids had brown eyes, and the mother had brown eyes. But this kid had the bluest eyes you've ever seen on a Mexican kid."

Riverton closed his notebook after getting a further description of all three of the boys, especially Blue. "Well, I think this helps. How many blue-eyed Mexican kids from this part of San Diego are there? Can't be that many." He stood, shaking Fredo's hand. "My best to Mia."

Riverton was clean-shaven today, but his clothes were wrinkled, like they always were. Fredo watched him shuffle out of the room, like he was some ghost of lost souls, dressed in ashen rags. He figured Riverton's job, studying and solving mysteries involving bad things people did to each other, usually life-ending things, was a calling. But it sure wasn't one Fredo had any attraction to.

CHAPTER 5

Three days later, Fredo was released from the hospital. They began shopping for Christmas. Mia took him to an upscale children's clothing and toy store. He spent most of the time there squinting, examining price tags so small he thought perhaps he might need glasses.

"Geez!" Fredo growled, noticing the price on a pair of little girl's socks with lace trim around the ankles. "I don't even pay that much for a hundred percent wool." He held the tiny pair of pink socks high in the air, between his index finger and thumb.

Mia bestowed a broad smile, following up with a wink. She rescued Fredo from the lethal clothing fashion statement. "You don't wear lace, do you?"

"Well, I like lace. I like lace very, very, much, Mia. Just not on me."

She giggled, her warm cadence lightening his heart. Anything was fun with Mia, even shopping for socks for little

Ricardo or Mia's cousin, who was about the same age. As she approached him, she allowed her tits to brush against his chest, and on cue, his dick got hard so fast he nearly doubled over.

"You know, you been filling my belly with come so much, Fredo, I think you gonna give me a little present one of these days. I want a little girl, sweetheart. Can you fill my belly with a little girl, hmm? Please?" She reached into his pants and squeezed his package while Fredo searched the boutique to make sure no one was going to see her actions.

"Oh my God! Fredo. I never knew shopping for baby clothes turned you on so much!" She purred up close and personal to him, her little pink tongue darting out between her red lips as she moaned. "I want you to fuck me until I am big with three children."

"It doesn't work that way, Mia," he could barely say.

"It could. You are the magic man, Fredo. Nothing you cannot do." She grabbed his hand and shoved it down her considerably tight blue jeans. "Just touching me makes me come."

Her half-lidded eyes lasted only a few seconds, as they heard the bell of an incoming customer with a string of little ones in tow. Fredo counted three. All boys.

"See, that could be us, my lover. *Let's do this.* Isn't that what you guys say?"

It was what they said all right. It was the doing part that bothered him the most. The practice was fine, but the filling her belly with little ones—that wouldn't be happening. Fredo thought that by now it would have gotten easier.

Riverton wanted Fredo to take a stroll with him around the neighborhood where he'd gotten shot. Fredo agreed on one condition—that they both wear Kevlar.

He felt like the Michelin Man as he waddled down the nearly non-existent sidewalk overrun with weeds springing up defiantly between concrete cracks. He was used to walking this way, his swagger from side to side usually accentuated by his hands on his H&K, in a walking shooter's stance: right up top, finger on the trigger, left down on the barrel. If need be, he could swing his weapon up, balancing it on his hip if there wasn't something else he could use to prop against. Without the gun, he still found himself holding his hands in that position just from force of habit. In a dangerous neighborhood like this one, having a semi-automatic made sense, even though it was illegal as hell.

Riverton was nervous and not used to wearing the heavy Kevlar. It was also due to the fact that someone had underestimated his girth, the detective's arms exploding out the sides like growing eyes on a potato. But it was the constrictive breathing Fredo could hear that caused him the most worry.

"Clark, you wanna stop breathing through your mouth? You're making too much noise."

Riverton rolled his eyes and pulled his neck up and out of the protective vest, resembling a turtle coming out of its shell.

"You want me to loosen it? I can, you know."

"I'm fine."

"Breathe through your nose. You won't scare so many people."

They came to the little neighborhood store, and Fredo took the lead, striking up a conversation with the clerk, who appeared to be from India. Fredo was going to speak in broken Spanish until he saw the young kid's dark face and wire-rimmed glasses.

"*Amigo*," he started. "I was here a week ago, before Thanksgiving."

The lanky teen nodded.

"I got shot, right outside your doors there. This here's Detective Clark Riverton from the San Diego P.D. We're looking for a couple of kids. One has real blue eyes, blue like the sky."

"I'm sorry, haven't seen them today."

"Okay, so you know who we're talking about, then?"

"Sure. Sure. The kid with the blue eyes. I see him just about every day."

Riverton pushed Fredo to the side. His considerable girth took up most of the counter space. "You know where we can find them? Know where they live?"

"No, sir. They come in, buy stuff, and then leave. They're no problem."

"They use a credit card or pay by check?"

The clerk returned a face to Riverton, looking like he was sucking on a mouthful of lemons. "No checks. We never take checks. Cash. We take cash only. Food Stamps. They use Food Stamps."

"Food Stamps?" Fredo asked.

"Yes. The one with the blue eyes has an older sister with a baby. They buy diapers sometimes. Baby things, cereal." He drifted off, naming items Fredo didn't recognize.

"Any idea where they live?" Riverton asked.

"No. I'm sorry, but I don't pay attention. They pay; they leave. I don't want to watch or get too curious. This is a terrible neighborhood."

"Tell me about it," Fredo mumbled under his breath. He knew his instincts were good in not allowing Mia's mother to come to shop here anymore. In fact, he'd tried to get Felicia to sell her little bungalow and move some place safer with Mayfield. But if Mayfield couldn't change her mind, Fredo and Mia, and Mia's brother, Armando, would never convince the stubborn woman, who had lived in the same house for over twenty years. It was her piece of the American Dream, purchased with the settlement money from her husband's murder in Puerto Rico.

Fredo took a turn at the clerk. "What does the sister look like? How old?"

"She's not much older. I think she's still in school."

Fredo swore and shook his head. He remembered his first encounters with Mia, who also was a wild child and had run with the wrong crowd. The son he was raising as his own was, in fact, the biological son of a man in prison for gang violence and drug dealing. Mia had nearly cost Armando his life when he tried to defend her.

"Do you know where the kids here hang out?" Riverton asked.

The clerk gave a smirk. "You mean like a library or public pool? A park?" He wrinkled his brow. "If we had a park, it would be filled with druggies. If we had a library, they'd be setting fire to the books or the paper towels in the bathroom."

"What about sports? Any basketball courts around?" Fredo watched as the clerk suddenly had a bright thought.

"Yes. I've seen them before. St. Rose Middle School. It's abandoned now. Boarded up. But the basketball court still has the rims. No nets, nothing but blacktop and those big poles. No lights, either, so you don't want to go at night."

That was a start. The two of them got directions and found the abandoned school, covered in graffiti, some of it rather colorful and well-done. Scenes depicting jaguars, large spotted cats, and panthers hiding in bushes with big eyes made him feel like he was walking through a museum of modern art.

"Shit, this is good," Fredo remarked.

"No kidding." Riverton was viewing the landscape of abandoned houses, car hulks, and upturned garbage cans in the middle of the street. The neighborhood was deserted.

"Reminds me of some places in Syria and parts of Iraq."

"That's a statement," answered Riverton. "Come all the way back here and find districts like over there."

"Oh man, you should see some of the hill country, though. Beautiful. Snow, trees, not hot and dusty like the cities. Baghdad was a beautiful city at one time, was legendary for its beauty. Hard as that is to believe now."

Fredo caught a glimpse of a pair of teens rounding the corner of the school, heading straight for them. Riverton braced himself and stiffened. But the kids, when they saw Fredo, turned around and ran away.

"That's him, blue eyes," barked Fredo as he took off after the pair.

They wound around several alleyways, avoiding loose dogs in fenced yards and lines of laundry, swinging a whole street away from a group of nearly a dozen youths, all with gang colors. Someone in a flat black, lowered, seventies model muscle car with darkened windows and custom paint drove slowly by, trash talking rap music making the insides of Fredo's chest rattle. Fredo noticed Riverton had pulled out his badge, wearing it on his belt, and he'd unclipped his holster.

"I don't like this at all, Fredo. This was a bad idea."

"I thought you was smoking something to even suggest it. We don't want to stop these guys or mess with them in any way. We should head back."

Riverton followed behind Fredo, turning every few yards to make sure they weren't targets. They hung close to trucks and large-trunk trees, and next to wooden fences and the sides of buildings so they weren't out in plain sight, just like they searched the neighborhoods in Ramadi and Fallujah. What surprised Fredo most was that he felt safer there than he did here, in his own country, only fifty miles from where he grew up.

He saw movement out of the corner of his eye and caught a flash glimpse of two teens running around the corner of the abandoned school building. Riverton was going to run after them, and Fredo held him back.

"We don't want to put too much attention on them. Not in their best interest to be talking to a cop."

"Just didn't want them to get away. They're suspects."

"No way, Riverton. We take this one slow." Fredo knew well the damage an angry street gang could do to a kid's house, his parent's car, or one of his friends. If blue eyes didn't want to talk to Fredo, he sure as hell wouldn't want to talk to Riverton.

Easing along the backside of a wall perpendicular to where the kids had run, Fredo checked the streets, listening for sounds like a safety being released, rounds loaded with a metal clip, a whisper, or a scared dog barking his lungs out. The chopped vehicle was gurgling down away from them, two streets over. Birds were chirping in rhythm to the white noise of a freeway nearby. Fredo led them to the end of the building and then quickly turned the corner without making a sound.

He caught the tail end of a screen door being shut, as if someone had entered hurriedly. He motioned to Riverton, and the two walked across dead lawns, past three abandoned houses with plywood covering non-existent windows, until they found a light pink home that reminded him of his mother-in-law's place. Flowers in bright colored pots stood to either side of the front door. The front lawn and shrubbery that lined the walkway to the front door were casualties of the California drought. Residents were not allowed to water their front yards, but the half-dozen colorful pots stood in stark defiance of that order.

Fredo was going to knock on the front door, but Riverton barked behind him, "San Diego P.D. Open up!" It made Fredo jump and his ears ring.

"Dammit, Clark. Don't you do anything quiet?"

Riverton gave him a wolfish grin. "Not a damned thing. I think being quiet is unnatural, don't you?"

Fredo was ready to make a sharp jab back at the detective when the front door swung open and they were staring into the barrel of a long-nosed Colt. He was just about to say something to himself like "how could anything get worse?" when a shaking thumb cocked the hammer back.

She was a girl, trying to sound like a deep-voiced boy. Trying to sound older than her maybe sixteen or seventeen years. That told Fredo there wasn't anyone older in authority in the household. He knew Riverton had to be careful, so Fredo made use of his training, quickly grabbing the gun, wresting it up and out of her hands; then he held her arms behind her back with a quick downward jerk, which he knew to be painful. And if she screamed, he'd yank her arms up so quickly he could nearly bust or dislocate her shoulder. He stowed the pistol at his back, out of reach of the girl.

Riverton made a quick entry into the house, leaving Fredo with the girl near the front door.

The girl was struggling to get away, but could not let out a call for help because Fredo's huge hand covered her mouth and lower cheeks. "Don't want to hurt you, missy. You behave."

The girl ignored him. Girls were always ignoring Fredo, though, so he was used to it. She was making growling sounds Fredo found oddly sexy, especially given the circumstances.

What's up with that?

Fredo dragged her behind him while she struggled without success to get out from under his grip. "Where's your little brother, Chica?"

"None of your fuckin' business," she managed before she bit the palm of his hand.

"Fuck!" Fredo was in serious pain, and her quick action scared him.

Glancing down the hallway of the house, he saw Riverton standing at a bedroom doorway. The detective raised his pistol with both hands on the stubby grip, and kicked the door open. Fredo knew Riverton had already seen one gun, which meant there could be more. He wasn't taking any chances.

Fredo grabbed the struggling girl, dragging her with him as he tried to follow Riverton. She was showing incredible strength. If he didn't get a hold of her soon, he'd be forced to do something he didn't want to do.

"Julio, run!" the girl shouted to the occupant of the bedroom. Fredo didn't want to, but he gave her a backhanded slap across the chops, and she collapsed, unconscious. He needed to aid Riverton in case the Detective faced hostiles. He laid her down carefully and rushed to Riverton's side.

The drapes were pulled, making the darkened room impossible to navigate. Riverton tripped over something and was on his knees with a groan. Fredo heard the unmistakable thud of Clark's gun falling to the wooden floor. Following the sound, he lurched forward, clutching for what seemed like thin air before he felt clothing and a mop of stiff hair. His nostrils scented teenage sweat, and he heard the heavy breathing of a young man not nearly as strong, while Riverton groaned in the background.

He felt the metal of the gun, grabbed it toward his chest, and stiff-armed the youth away from him. He shoved the gun into Riverton's chest until the detective could grab hold of it then found the front of the kid's shirt and yanked him to standing position.

Riverton scrambled to stand, gasping.

"I got it," Fredo barked.

Riverton pulled at the drapes, letting in some light just as they heard a baby wail in the room next door. The kid was still wiggling to get loose from Fredo's iron grip.

"Quit it. I don't want to hurt you," Fredo whispered. "We just want to talk. Cut it out, you little motherfucker!"

It did little to stop the youth. Riverton threw handcuffs on him from behind then pushed him onto the mattress sitting directly on the floor. The bright blue eyes stared back up to Fredo, revealing a cocktail of hatred and fear.

"Anyone else here?" Fredo asked.

The teen shook his head slowly, resigned.

Fredo bent over the girl as she began to regain consciousness. He noted she'd have a bruise over her left eye and cheekbone. He felt awful about hitting a woman, but his overwhelming concern for other occupants of the house who might have weapons caused his quick and violent reaction. It was part of his training that would never leave him alone. He was forever expecting and being prepared for deadly force.

The baby wailed again. Fredo and Riverton shared a look. The unspoken call to action fell on Fredo's shoulders.

"I'm good with the kids here," Riverton said.

The bedroom next to the darkened room was also pitch black. He followed the sound, nearly running into a crib in the corner. He leaned over the wooden rails and instinctively picked up the frightened child.

"Shhh. Shhh. You're okay," the SEAL said, as he bounced the toddler, pressing him against his chest. To the top of his curly head, he whispered, "Everything's fine now. Don't be scared." Then he kissed the small warm head and heard the huge inhale as the child settled.

Fredo shuffled in the dark over to where he saw a thin crack of sunlight, pulled back the drapes, and let the room flood with light. A single bed was made up in the corner opposite the crib. An old dresser with a cracked mirror was the only other piece of furniture. The top was fashioned with a plastic pad for diaper changing.

The two of them, the warrior and the toddler, took stock of each other briefly before the child's lower lip began to quiver and he started another series of mournful cries. This time, the bouncing didn't help, as the boy realized he was being held by a stranger.

Fredo brought the baby into the other bedroom. The girl was sitting next to her brother, unrestrained, so Fredo handed her the child.

Riverton cleared his throat. "We just want to talk. First, I gotta ask you, do you guys live here alone?"

"No," the girl said. Her face was swelling. Fredo felt horrible about the pain it must cause her. She put the baby to her breast, and it seemed to ease everyone in the room as the unmistakable sounds of feeding began. "Our mother lives here, too. But she's at work."

"Okay, so missy, we have some questions we want to ask your brother here. This *is* your brother?" Riverton asked.

She nodded.

"He's Julio?"

Again, she nodded.

"And you're?"

"Lupe. Lupe Hernandez."

"Okay, thanks. Now, we think he saw something we need to find out about," Riverton added.

She nodded again and turned to frown at her brother.

"I didn't do anything. He's a frog, Lupe. One of those." The kid was sneering at Fredo.

"Yeah, and I'm a fuckin' monkey. Don't get smart. We just want some information, son, and depending on what you tell us, we'll be on our way." Riverton checked with Fredo and then continued. "This the man whose life you saved, son?"

Riverton's thumb curled back in Fredo's direction.

The boy didn't want to answer. Fredo changed his stance, placing his fingers on his hips, and it made the boy flinch.

"Yes."

"Where'd you learn that?"

Traces of an evil smile appeared on the kid's face. "If you spend much time here, you learn about things like this. And my brother taught me a few things."

Riverton turned to Fredo, asking for advice to proceed. Fredo took his cue.

"He the one who tried out for the teams?"

Both brother and sister solemnly nodded.

"We're sorry about that. Your brother was a good man. The Navy lost a good Corpsman." Fredo could tell the boy didn't trust him. He looked around the room.

"You kids home alone a lot here? In this neighborhood? Your mother leaves you alone like this?"

"Sometimes we have someone else come in. I work, too. Julio does—"

"I'm a student," Julio said defiantly, cutting off his sister.

"I take the baby with me to high school. They have an after school program for girls like—me." She looked down at her baby, her palm smoothing over his curls. "There's a neighbor lady friend of our mother's who sometimes looks in on us. Not like we're children," she added.

Fredo knew Mia and Armando were both kids raised under similar circumstances. Felicia Guzman had worked cleaning motels and doing laundry. It wasn't legal, especially with the baby. They were wise to be cautious. Fredo could see the girl didn't want to give up her baby.

"Look, we're not here to get into all that," Riverton reassured them.

"You see who shot me?"

Julio looked away immediately. It was just as Fredo suspected. He knew who had shot him.

"You know someone who owns a small caliber gun? Like a woman's gun. Did I get shot by a woman?"

The kid shrugged. His non-cooperation was pissing Fredo off. Plus, he was getting increasingly uncomfortable in the neighborhood where they were easily outnumbered and outgunned.

"You were a target. I think you popped someone's cherry." The kid grinned, enjoying Fredo's pain.

Riverton was familiar with this scenario and told him so. "They get the kids to go shoot someone, usually kill someone, or someone's pet, as an initiation to become one of the members. And with all the witnesses, you gotta rely on them not to snitch. Nice family bonding experience." Riverton's face reflected the disgust Fredo knew he felt inside.

The kids had no future. It saddened him.

"So who do you run with?"

"I'm clear."

"I find that impossible to believe."

"I don't want to go that way. Trying to stay out of it. I wanna go to school. Maybe work in a hospital."

"Yes. Ephron was teaching him all kinds of first aid. He's actually saved some lives already at his young age," said Lupe.

"You saw him get shot, didn't you?" Riverton was also losing patience.

"Nah, I didn't."

Fredo knew the kid was lying. His heart still ached that the boy had to do this to survive. Patch together some scumbag so he could go terrorize the rest of the neighborhood another day. He decided the kid had less of a future than he initially thought. He prayed no one knew Julio had seen the shooting.

They kept asking questions, and the boy dodged them smartly, being used to dealing with law enforcement. Something became apparent to Fredo the longer they stayed in the home; the kid was brave. His medical skills were helping to keep the family under the protection of someone; but for how long, Fredo wasn't sure, although he could understand Julio's thirteen-year-old logic.

Riverton gave both kids his card. Julio looked at Fredo as if he wanted his card, too, which Fredo found touching. "We don't do that shit. Sorry, man." Then he had an idea. He grabbed Riverton's card and wrote his cell on the back, handing it to Julio, and then did the same to Lupe's card. "You call me if something's going down."

Julio gave them a smirk. Fredo decided it was his most common form of expression, those half-lidded eyes telling everyone in the room he didn't take shit from anyone and he didn't believe anyone was there to help him, either.

"You think somethin's funny?" he asked Julio.

"Yeah, the fuckin' SEALs. Bring in the SEALs. Now that would be something to watch."

CHAPTER 6

Fredo thought about the kid's remarks for the next couple of days as he helped Mia get the house ready for Christmas. He helped Mayfield and Armando string lights around Felicia Guzman's front porch. He replaced a window for her, fixed her dishwasher, and picked up a new mixer for her holiday cooking.

He bought a miniature plastic tool set for Ricardo that came in an authentic-looking plastic tool case. Felicia made the toddler a carpenter's apron with numerous pockets, embroidered with the outline of a particular tool. One afternoon, while making repairs, Ricardo followed him around, wearing his apron, the pockets stuffed with Fredo's plastic tools.

"You do this, Ricardo," Fredo said as he helped chubby fingers wrap around a red screwdriver, pushing it into the window sill. Ricardo did it several times, and squealed with delight.

"Now, look at this. You're gonna love this!" he said as he whacked a piece of scrap wooden window trim with his hammer. Ricardo got out his plastic screwdriver and raised his arm over the wood.

"No, no, no! Ricardo, you need to pay attention." Fredo showed him the hammer, with the flat nose and arched backside that matched his own. "See? This one."

Ricardo screamed again and hit the wooden piece several times, nearly falling down in the process.

Mia came up behind Fredo, lovingly melting into his back, whispering in his ear, "You are soooo good with him, my lover. He's going to grow up to be a carpenter because of you. Look how he can use his tools already."

Fredo chuckled. He was sure Mia didn't understand the double entendre she'd used. While thinking about tools, he got hard again.

Mia was always easy to be around, so beautiful, making every excuse to touch him, rub against him, and keep him in a state of continual arousal. She'd brought up the subject of getting pregnant, again, and Fredo was close to letting her know the truth about his doctor's visit. Coop even asked if he'd talked to her yet.

"No, and I'm waiting for the right time. Maybe I should do it after Christmas, Coop."

"You better tell her."

"Why, did you go and fuckin' tell Libby? That what you're sayin'?"

"No. I wouldn't do that. Who do you fuckin' think I am?"

"Oh, I get it. When you get all aroused and you're pumping her, you feel the need to unload all your burdens, and you tell her about my little tadpoles with the dented heads?"

Coop laughed. "Man, you're twisting this all out of shape, Fredo. No fuckin' way I would tell her. I'm just sayin' Mia will be pissed if she finds out you've known for a long time."

"I'm getting adjusted. I got shot, for Christ's sake. Give me a fuckin' break."

Fredo knew Coop was right. The wives had a circle of communication that was faster than being hard-wired. Almost like they had a hive mentality. If a word was mentioned about his sterility, everyone would know within a matter of hours, perhaps minutes.

He thought about the kids living in that little house. He even drove past it on several occasions when he needed to pick up things for Felicia. He thought about them when he gave money to the bell ringers by the Post Office. He took it upon himself to get a couple of nice thick beef sandwiches to carry around in the truck so he could stop and feed some homeless men. He brought cans of dog food for some of their dogs that probably ate by scrounging garbage.

It was the Christmas spirit, filling his heart. The season was about doing good, taking care of each other. The team took up a collection for a simple wedding for one of their froglets, a new guy on the team. It was uncommon for the SEALs to come from well-to-do families, so collections were always being taken so they could help each other.

One day, he had an idea.

Kyle, T.J., Cooper, Danny, Lucas, and several others were passing time at the Scupper.

"You hear some of the guys on Team 5 are building a brewery?" Kyle asked.

"Well, we got us a winery up in Sonoma County," said Coop.

The team and several others, including Libby's parents, had invested in Devon and Nick's winery a couple of years ago. It wasn't yet a profitable venture.

"What are they calling it?" someone asked.

"Brotherhood Brewing Company."

Of course.

Fredo decided the time was right for discussion of his idea. "I've been thinking about the kids we met, you know, living in the neighborhood where I got shot. I was thinking, because it's Christmas, maybe we could take on a family, you know, adopt them?"

"We do that at church," someone said.

"This is different. I'm talking about doing a community improvement project."

"What did you have in mind, Fredo?" asked Kyle.

"Well, they basically have a dying neighborhood. Houses boarded up, even the Catholic middle school—" he leaned over and nodded to Armando—"You and Mia went to school there, I think. Right, Armani?"

"Yes. Used to be a decent school."

"You want to open up a school, Fredo?" asked T.J.

"No. Just a basketball court. A place for the kids to play. Fenced, maybe with some lights so they are protected at night."

"Basketball? You don't play basketball, Fredo."

"Doesn't matter. What else is there for the kids to do? They have to take a bus to go to any Boys or Girls Club. No one wants to teach there, so the school closed. If they had a place to play, a safe place, maybe some good could come out of it. Maybe we could start something that could grow into something nice."

Like any task the Team did together, they started making lists of all the things that needed to be done. It took nearly ten napkins to write down the thirty or so important things that would have to happen before the project could be launched.

"What do we call it?" Coop asked him.

Fredo scratched his head. "How about "Operation Freedom: A Place to Play?"

They set up a meeting with the Archdiocese, who agreed to allow them access to the old school so they would have a place to store tools and materials for the project. A donor's list was started, beginning with a fence company who donated all of the chain-link fencing. One of the wives found a small private school that was going to be demolished. The basketball court lights were donated to the project. The Archdiocese agreed to pay for the water and electricity to run the property, and to have a functioning kitchen, and bathroom facilities.

They found a road grading contractor who agreed to re-blacktop the whole playground. The courts were painted and re-striped. Hoops were replaced.

Fredo and Kyle got on the City Council agenda, in an emergency session, asking for the city's support for the project; they were given a community block grant of over fifty thousand dollars as seed money, with local banks and other businesses providing matching funds in exchange for promotional rights. A local news station got wind of their project and did a series of stories, which were picked up by crews from Los Angeles. A couple of professional players from the Warriors agreed to donate time, do television spots, and help set up and run basketball clinics.

Christy Lansdowne and several of the realtors from her company donated a work day. Boarded up houses were painted and re-opened. The properties that had been abandoned had reverted back to the City of San Diego, so work crews and several contractor firms took on projects, house by house, donating labor and materials. Julio, Lupe, and their mother were able to move into a newly refurbished rental home run by the San Diego Housing Authority, overlooking the basketball court.

By the time the New Year had started, the old school had been inexpensively converted to a club house that the Archdiocese agreed to run, in partnership with one of the local service clubs. There were plans to install computers and classrooms teaching painting and creative writing, as well as other crafts.

Fredo's project took on a life of its own. But of all the things he enjoyed, they paled in comparison to the relationship he was building with little Julio, who had learned to be quite the community organizer, and became the "grass roots" unofficial spokesman for the project. Lupe and her mother helped with bookkeeping. In essence, Fredo had created gainful employment for the entire Hernandez family.

"Why you do all this, man?" Julio asked him one day.

"Just because we can. Because someone has to do it."

"I'm not complaining. Just why doesn't our government do things like this?" Julio asked.

"Oh, who knows? Probably trying to defend against lawsuits, trying to manage the media, all that shit. This is just simple. We get people to help us because it's fun, it feels right, and everyone likes to work together. Maybe these sorts of things should never be government-run."

"You could have a lot more free time with the Mrs." Julio pointed out. "Can't imagine you'd want to do anything else, you understand what I'm sayin'?"

Fredo put his arm around Julio. "Oh yes, there are times when a man's got to do what a man's got to do. I manage to get some time in there for Ricardo and Mia."

Mia had been reminding him of the same thing, but Fredo didn't want Julio to know. She'd been fretting a little over not getting pregnant and even went to the doctor about it, without telling Fredo.

"So now you go, Fredo. It's not me. You go and get checked."

He started to agree when he got a phone call that completely shattered his day.

CHAPTER 7

"Calm down, Lupe. Where is he?" Fredo listened as Lupe told him they'd taken Julio to Scripps.

"How bad is it?

"He's looking like a piece of hamburger. He tried to stop them. Fredo, the school, the club house—everything is destroyed. They even shot out all the lights."

Fredo was furious, but he knew there would be time for that later. Right now, he wanted to go to Julio's side and be there when he got out of surgery. Mia watched as he disconnected his phone. He might have thrown it against the wall if Mia hadn't been standing there.

"Fredo, you go. But please, don't do anything stupid, my love. You call and let me know what's happening. You call more than you usually call. No going dark, hear me?" She ducked down to capture his gaze. It was hard to say no to Mia, and it always would be.

"I will," was all he could muster. She sent him away with a hug that hurt his still-sensitive lung cavity.

Riverton agreed to meet him at the hospital. The detective had a female officer posted over at the Hernandez house. The Department was doing a house-to-house search for a group of armed thugs, kids wearing black sweatshirts and masks, claiming they were "taking back the neighborhood." Pictures of the partially burning building and twisted piles of chain-link fencing that had been literally ripped from its roots began to surface on the local and national news service wires.

While Fredo waited for Riverton, Mrs. Hernandez arrived. He was glad Lupe and the baby had stayed behind.

"I am just sick, Fredo. I should have never let him go over there by himself. He saw the boys, I think recognized the boys. Actually, he said there were a couple of girls, too."

Fredo hugged the small woman who reminded him of a younger version of his own mother-in-law, Felicia Guzman.

"This will not go unpunished." Fredo worked to keep his anger between the lines. Part of him wanted to throw the waiting room furniture.

While they waited together, holding hands, he viewed the news reports, fisting and un-fisting his left hand while seeing live camera shots of the destruction on TV. Materials and contents of the school building were dumped on the blacktop, much of it set on fire. One of the light standards was lying on its side, having been rammed with a large truck of some kind. Several of the houses, even those with occupants living in them, were spray painted "Take It Back" with black letters.

Fredo thought they were nuts.

Riverton joined him. "I'm just racking my brain, wondering who would do this and why?"

"One reporter said someone was disgruntled because they weren't hired on. Another said they heard the complaints that it was "outsiders" who tried to take over their neighborhood, and they wanted it back." Fredo shook his head. "But that just makes no sense at all. I mean, ninety days ago, they could care less what went on there."

"So maybe we disrupted their operation. That's what I'm thinking."

They sat in silence. Fredo took it as a personal attack against himself. And he understood now that the Hernandez family, just by virtue of being friends of his, were vulnerable. He'd caused this just by showing kindness and doing the right thing.

Dr. Patterson came out into the waiting room, his weary eyes telegraphing something tragic. Fredo embraced Mrs. Hernandez, and they both inhaled, waiting to be told the news.

"I pulled out five slugs. Small, luckily." He rubbed his eyes together with the tips of his fingers, forming a tent over the bridge of his nose. "I cannot get the last bullet right now at the base of his skull."

Fredo felt like he'd been gored.

"Base of his skull? He was shot, like an execution?"

"I'm afraid so. If they had anything bigger, he'd be dead. Right now I can't do anything more until some of his brain swelling goes down. Then we'll worry about the spinal cord injury."

"Spinal cord injury!" Mrs. Hernandez screamed. "My Julio. Oh my God, Julio!"

Her voice echoed throughout the emergency room and probably beyond.

"I need those rounds," Riverton whispered to the doctor.

"You got it."

"So when will we know?"

Dr. Patterson's long face didn't look hopeful. "I'd prepare for the worst. He's already had two seizures. We can do certain things for the swelling or it will cause further injury, both for his ability to be mobile as well as for the health of his brain. My biggest fear is infection. We'll have to play it out. Good news is that the kid's healthy and young. Young tissue heals fast and responds to treatment. And thank God he has no drugs in his system."

"Of course he has no drugs in his system." Mrs. Hernandez barked her protest to the young doctor.

Patterson shook his head. "We *always* test. This age group, high percentage of even casual drug users. Affects what we can do. We gotta know, especially with stimulants."

"Is he conscious?" Fredo asked.

"I'm afraid not, and that's good. I want him to heal. He needs rest. Not going to wake him up right now. It could risk his life."

Fredo was numb. All the good he had been creating for the neighborhood wasn't worth the news about Julio. What was he thinking? He didn't miscalculate like this usually. Why didn't he see it coming?

He withdrew from Mrs. Hernandez, who sobbed against the doctor. Dr. Patterson lovingly extricated her from his chest and handed her over to Riverton, who stiffened at first then accepted his role.

"I gotta go. Unfortunately, Julio wasn't my only GSW tonight."

Riverton helped Mrs. Hernandez to a seat next to Fredo.

Evil exists when good men do nothing. Fredo wanted to blame himself for this. It was indeed his fault, or at least part of it. But as a SEAL, he was more prepared for paying the price with his life, his health. He hadn't counted on a youth of thirteen who'd already lost his older brother and a mother who had lost one son to the violence of the neighborhood—hadn't counted on them having to pay that price, as well.

But pure evil worked that way. Preyed on the innocent. Fredo knew it wasn't a good idea to plan a counter when he was in the heat of loss and grief. But he knew that somehow he'd get even. He searched his options. None of them were viable, not if he wanted to remain a SEAL.

"Kyle, you see the news reports?"

"Yeah. Knew you were busy with the family. What can I do to help?"

"I'm gonna get these bastards."

"Roger that, Fredo; and I didn't hear it, either."

The pause on the phone between the two warriors was awkward.

"Don't go taking any of our guys down that hellhole, Fredo. You choose to hang up your career, don't drag anyone else with you. This isn't our fight here."

"I understand, LT. But this is my fight. This is why we're doing this. No way this should have happened. I was completely shit-faced stupid."

"Don't bear that one. You can't be everywhere. Besides, your job is elsewhere. You do understand your real job, don't you, Fredo?"

"Yes, I do."

"And yes, this sucks. But we live in a land where there are laws. I wish the police could do what we do over in the arena. I wish they had the firepower, the training we do. But that's for another day. Today, you fight to stay sane, Fredo. I don't want to lose one of my best men." After a brief pause, when Kyle didn't hear Fredo's response, he sighed and said, "I'm sending Coop and Jones, maybe T.J. too. They're gonna stick like glue to your ass until you get yourself back home. You hear me?"

"Yes."

Fredo was already trying to figure out how he could give them the slip, do his own reconnaissance, find the guys—or at least the leader of the gang who did the destruction—and do him in; painfully, slowly, with relish. He'd look into the face of the man he was going to kill, and he'd take that life. Perhaps the last time, he'd take a life. And he'd make damn sure he enjoyed every second of it.

His dark thoughts scared him more than some of the dark dangerous streets in Iraq or Syria.

CHAPTER 8

As word of the destruction of the project spread, the out-pouring of sympathy and help from the community in San Diego, especially the SEAL community, kicked in big time like a high-level tactical operation. Just like always happened when they lost someone on their team, the guys got busy. Work always made horrible things seem less horrible. This wasn't a time for smack talk, play, or joking around. This was as serious as the protection of all of the country. Someone had violated the normal boundaries of their SEAL community, and that wasn't anything that would be allowed to stand.

The activity did give Fredo minutes here and there when he could get lost in the neighborhood. At first, Coop, T.J., and Jones let him go on short errands, but when he was gone two hours without checking in, they remained one link away from his person.

Taking at least one Team guy with him, Fredo discussed the project with the leaders at the Archdiocese. He talked to several of the volunteers who worked at the center. While no one gave him a name, a pattern developed. Older kids, kids who used the vacant buildings as drug houses, kids who hung out in the dark and dirty regions of the neighborhood, had begun to ask questions. Fredo could see that this had been a planned and coordinated attack designed to fill them with fear so they'd give up.

Well, they didn't know the half of it.

Because of the high profile nature of the violent event, police and community resources were being used. No one wanted this attack to go unchecked. No one wanted the haters to win.

A couple of non-local news media erroneously reported a terrorist connection. Fredo doubted that, but four days into the rebuild and cleanup, and after canvassing the neighborhood, he still needed to speak to Julio. Fredo knew the kid would be able to tell him who did this. He knew he had to get the mystery solved, or at least help the police get it solved, while everyone's attention was still there. Once another shooting or event overseas eclipsed the news, the spotlight would be silenced, and then it would be harder to catch those responsible.

Every day, he came by the mercado and asked if the clerk had seen anyone of interest or heard anything. Today, he had Jones with him.

"I'm glad you came by today, Mr. Frodo."

"Fredo, asshole."

"Pardon. I overheard something. I didn't get any names, but several new guys showed up and bought energy drinks, snack foods, and lots of alcohol. They were talking about some big party going on very soon. Some big gang leader was getting out of jail. They were going to celebrate and have a 'do-over,' they called it."

"When is this happening?" Fredo asked.

"Sounded like very soon. Like this guy was pissed they didn't wait for him."

"Okay, thanks. You stay safe."

"I'm going to close up early tonight. I've told the owner I'm not well. He doesn't have anyone to cover me, so I think we'll be closed."

"Probably smart. You call me if you see anything." Fredo wrote his cell on a piece of paper for the clerk.

Fredo called Riverton and let him know what he'd been told. Riverton confirmed what Fredo had been told. "We got fuckin' Sonny Alvarez getting out of Pelican Bay this afternoon or maybe tomorrow. Got his conviction overturned, and I'm sure there will be a retrial, but the Feds are cooking something up, and he'll get re-charged, but we don't know when. He's a total scumbag, Fredo. He'd gotten twenty-five years to life. He's not supposed to return to the neighborhood, per conditions of his release, but sounds like he has other plans."

"Maybe that could tack on additional years, then, if he gets caught."

"Could be. It's the catching him that's the problem. Takes a lot of resources, and we've got our hands full with budget cuts."

Fredo knew it might be a long shot, but this was the connection he needed. He and Jones started asking neighbors if they knew where the Alvarez family lived. He got an answer from an unlikely source the next day.

Mrs. Hernandez told Fredo some of Sonny's junior lieutenants, boys still in high school with clean records who could move in and out of society without notice, had been harassing Lupe.

"Ephron knew it. I couldn't be sure, but I wondered if that's what got him shot," she mumbled. A fat tear traveled down her cheek.

"You tell the police this?"

"Oh yes. That was almost two years ago. Fredo, the police did nothing, really. Just called it a random shooting. But I know my Ephron. He wasn't a Navy SEAL, but he was still a corpsman, and he'd have been like you, not willing to let it go."

"So did the harassment stop after his death?"

"Lupe said so. But by then she was pregnant, and out of school for the summer and then later to go have the baby."

"Did Julio know these guys?"

"I don't know. But if I was to guess, I'd say yes."

On the way over to the hospital, T.J. asked Fredo several questions. "So Jones says some big gang guy is getting out of prison, and he might have a connection to all this? That right, Fredo?"

"Yes. Riverton thinks he gets out today."

"So you think Julio knows him?"

"No, I don't. But I'm sure there's a connection."

"So why are we going over there?"

"I wanna see if Julio is any closer to waking up or can talk. I need a little bit of something more, T.J."

"Not sure that's smart, Fredo."

"Gotta try. We're running out of time. If they're planning on something else, we better be ready."

"But you just can't wake up a patient like that. You could cause brain damage."

"I know that. I won't do that. But I gotta try. Gotta do what I can."

A few minutes later, Fredo was arguing with the head nurse, in hushed tones, at the foot of Julio's bed in intensive care. As if hearing the voices, Julio's eyes began to trace beneath his closed eyelids.

"Holy shit, Fredo, he's regaining consciousness," T.J. said as he grabbed his buddy's arm, pulling him to the bedside.

"You don't touch him. I'm going to get the doctor." The nurse shut off her attitude, turned, and ran to the hallway.

Fredo leaned over Julio. "Hey there. You still at home, little Corpsman?"

Julio's eyelids fluttered in response to Fredo's words.

"I don't got a lot of time. No problem if you need to chill some more. I need to get some intel, but only if you can. Can you help me, buddy?"

T.J. was looking down on the patient with a frown, concern all over his face. "You be careful, Fredo."

They could hear someone running down the hallway, equipment jiggling.

"Think they're bringing a cart. You only got a couple seconds, Fredo."

All of a sudden, Julio mumbled something.

"What?" Fredo put his ear right up to the boy's lips. "Tell me again, son."

"Diego Mora. He shot me."

Fredo squeezed his shoulder, got out his cell, and turned on the voice messaging feature. "One more time, my man."

Julio repeated the words just as the heavy-set nurse, an orderly with an equipment cart of some kind, and a young intern entered the room.

"Out!" the intern pointed to the door behind him. "You're not family, and you get the hell away from my patient."

Fredo slipped the phone in his pocket as he and T.J. exited the room then ran down the hall to the outside.

CHAPTER 9

Fredo made the quick call to Mia, which was hours overdue. "You know you're glad I'm a big girl and got Ricardo and lots of projects to keep me busy, with all this cleanup. And of course I got your other SEAL buddies beside me nearly twenty-four-seven, you hear what I'm sayin'?"

"Yes, dear."

He rolled his eyes at T.J., who gave him the thumbs-up. Fredo got her caught up on Julio's near-awakening.

"That's wonderful. Answer to prayers, I'd say. Better tell my Mama. She's been prayin' every hour, holed up in that little house of hers."

"Mia, we're gonna have to convince her to get out of that neighborhood. I think the time has come for that fierce talk."

"Good luck with that. I'm not gonna be anywhere near you when you try to tell her that. Maybe you and Armando and Mayfield can get your heads together, and after all this violence, maybe she'll finally be ready."

Next call he made was to Riverton. "Got a name from Julio. Diego Mora."

"Julio awake now?"

"Barely. Here, I'll send you the voice clip. He said it clear as day." He did the phone playback and heard Riverton swear.

"Okay, I'll pull in the Feds right now. God, I hope it doesn't take them a week to get their shit together. You got an address for this Mora guy?"

"Nope. But I'm sure someone knows him. We were asking the wrong question. And, Riverton, put a guard on Julio's door at the hospital. It's too open there; makes me nervous."

"I'll get a uniform on right away. Now Fredo, you stay out of it, you hear? You wait for us to get the plan put into place. In the meantime, just sit tight, and if you get an address, well, I want to be the first one you call, hear me?"

Fredo made screeching noises into the cell phone, rubbing his mouth with his hand, imitating a bad connection, then pushed the red button to disconnect.

T.J. had his hands on his hips. "You dumb shit."

"You'd do the same, and you know it."

"Okay, so now there's *another* thing I don't wanna know! Fredo, Kyle told you *not* to get involved, Riverton just told you the same thing. And yet you're fuckin' gonna jump in anyway, aren't you?"

"What the fuck to you think, T.J.? Wouldn't you do the same? Come on, you know you would."

T.J. was about to crack a smile, but stuffed it. Fredo didn't want his friend to know he'd noticed.

"So here's what I'm thinking. I'm thinking Kyle asked you and Jones and Coop to keep an eye on me."

"Yeah. Impossible, but yeah."

"Let's go get 'em so you can do your jobs."

"Unbelievable," was T.J.'s only response.

By the time Fredo and T.J. gathered their gear and got over to the club house, there were ten SEALs waiting for them. Their team leader, Kyle Lansdowne, was one of them.

"Now that's what I call boots on the ground," Fredo said with a big high-five for his LPO. It was the first time Fredo had felt like smiling in four days. "You're one slimy bastard, Kyle. You played that one really well, asshole."

"Just makin' sure enough people heard me and wanted to see if you really had the balls to carry it off. Officially? We're not here. We get caught, we're screwed. Way I see it, one of us gets busted, we all do." Kyle addressed all of the men. "We got two things we gotta do and one thing we most definitely don't want to do." He walked in front of the group like they did at their Team building in Coronado, walking that straight imaginary line in the floor. "We find these bastards. And I'm talking about the Mora kid and his cronies. We turn them over to the Feds or San Diego P.D."

Fredo knew what the one thing was that they weren't going to do before Kyle had a chance to say it.

"We don't, and let me repeat, we don't suffer any loss of life. I mean if you should run over a small dog or cat, our mission is screwed. Certainly no women or children and abso-fuckin-lutely no bad guys."

"What about us?" Luke asked.

"That goes without saying. That's *always* the rule. No heroics, just get in and get out. So first we find them. It will be your basic fan out and reconnaissance. We go door-to-door. We ask questions, and look for nervous people. They're gonna think we're cops anyhow, unless they remember us from the project."

Lupe appeared in the doorway, holding her baby in her arms, and Kyle nodded to her, which made every one of the SEALs turn. Unlike a mission overseas, they didn't have their long guns or strange unicorn hats with the scopes for night vision, but they were stowed across the inlet on the island at the Team building if they needed them. Fredo also knew that every one of the SEALs had his own personal shooter, along with a KA-BAR or some other ugly kind of knife, and they were wearing Kevlar. From behind, they might have looked like a bunch of hikers readying themselves for nasty terrain.

"Ma'am?"

"I know where Diego Mora lives, or where he used to live."

"Holy shit, Lupe. That's a streak of good luck," Fredo barked.

"I'll take you there now."

"Whoa, just give us the address, and you can stay protected."

"No. This is what I must do. I hold myself responsible for Ephron. He was trying to help me, and it cost him his life. Besides, you won't get anywhere close to him without me there."

"I can't let you or the baby go with us, Lupe. I just can't do that. Sorry." Kyle tenderly put his palm on her shoulder. Her seventeen-plus years of hard living didn't mask the admiration she showed Kyle as she drank from his gaze.

"If it weren't for me, Ephron would be one of you. I know he would."

Fredo could tell from the fidgeting in the room the Team wasn't in favor of getting Lupe near the kill zone.

Kyle's voice was low and authoritative, like he was talking to a child of five. "No. I said no, and that's final."

"You don't understand. He doesn't care anything about any of you, or even me. He wants to see his baby." She held the toddler up, his dark eyes scanning the faces of the men all around him. His fat pink cheeks and curly dark-brown hair made him look like a real-life cherub. As Lupe bounced him gently, she added, "He has never seen his baby."

None of them were happy about it. These were the types of situations they'd rehearsed over and over again, the kinds of times when extreme care would be taken to protect the innocent, even if it meant their own personal loss of life. There was background chatter as Kyle finished laying out the plan. Fredo knew, as he watched everyone check their weapons, test their Invisios, tighten their straps, flatten their extra Velcro custom pockets, and double check their extra clips, If he asked any one of them, they would all tell him they'd take a bullet for her and the baby without thinking.

Unlike overseas, they had the added restraint of not being able to shoot first, which was always the safest. Hostage negotiations worked out badly over fifty percent of the time because someone on the other side either got scared or had thought that perhaps they couldn't trust one of the SEALs, and often it cost them their lives. Adding to the fucked-up situation they were in, some of the local gangs had acquired cop-killer rounds that would slice through their armor like a curling iron through a popsicle. So they could shoot to defend themselves, but only to wound and not to kill.

But none of the bastards deserved to live.

Fredo was beginning to get tired, and realized his stamina hadn't built up. Breathing hurt a little. He wasn't getting enough sleep. He'd work on that, after they finished their mission. Until then, he would just have to put it out of his mind.

After they got all their gear together, Kyle called a brief team meeting, going over the strategy and Lupe's description of the compound Diego lived in one more time, just like they always did. Rehearsing, over-rehearsing was always the plan. It increased the odds they'd have a successful mission.

Fredo called Mia again, this time letting her know they were "doing something," their code for "don't ask, I'll never tell."

"Fredo, you stop all that playing around and come home. I don't like you running around with your buddies so soon after you were in the hospital."

"I'm fine. No need to worry." He did experience a little shortness of breath. He made sure she didn't hear it.

"That's when I worry the most! Oh, Fredo, come home and fuck me, okay? Wouldn't you rather do that than run around with—you have guns with you?"

Again, he couldn't lie to her. She'd know it.

"Mia, of course. We have to protect ourselves. Going after the guys who did all this shit. Would be stupid not to go in armed, my love."

She purred some favorite words to him, and sure as heck, his unit came to full attention.

"Mia, you're making me hard."

"Good, then you can just tell Kyle and the boys you gotta come home and service me proper. Fredo, please."

"I'll be home. Just hold that thought." He was grateful for the sexual banter, which took his mind off of the stress and apprehension he was feeling. But all too quickly, he realized if it went bad, this could be the last time he'd talk to her. It was strange, because he'd never felt this way at home before. It was always when he was leaving to go overseas. He decided it might be a good time to tell her what he'd been trying to tell her all this time.

"Mia, just in case, I want you to know—I wanted you to know—how much I love you."

Mia became unhinged on the other end of the line. Fredo was silently cursing himself for not being more careful to not worry her.

Fuck it.

She didn't need to know about his little sperm with the dented heads. There was nothing wrong with his equipment. Compared to some of the larger issues at hand, whether or not he could make babies seemed less important.

"Mia, we'll have a good time when I get home. We can stay in bed all day. Or go somewhere, okay? You like that?"

She settled down. "Be careful, Fredo."

"Of course. I'm with ten other guys. We got this. This is what we do. All you gotta do is be ready to see me when I get home."

Lupe was grinning at him when he hung up the phone. She'd caught every implication, and he didn't feel embarrassed in front of the young mother.

"Lupe, you'll have this some day. I love being married. We're gonna help you find a real man, not just a sperm donor." The word did stick in his mouth, and he nearly stumbled on it.

"Maybe, Mr. Fredo. Maybe someday." She picked up her diaper bag and jacket.

He didn't know how Lupe had gotten mixed up with someone like Mora. He could never understand why Mia had run with Caesar and his gang before Fredo was able to convince her of his love. He knew what kind of woman she was, and he loved every part of her, even her flaws. He did not know the woman who had tormented him those first few years they knew each other, making fun of him, teasing him, and driving him wild. It didn't matter how many times her brother, Armando, tried to talk him out of it, Fredo could not give up on her. He would have gone to his grave loving her, if that's what it took.

Now he had that life, that perfect life. He tilted his head, smiling down at the toddler, placing a palm on his curly locks, and realized that he could love someone else's baby like he loved little Ricardo, the child Caesar had fathered. He could die for a child some low-life like Diego had fathered without a thought. It didn't matter if he or she was his flesh and blood; it was who he was as a man.

So it was time to make sure someone else got a chance, got the time to think about choices and perhaps make different ones, like Mia had eventually done. Without the SEALs, without this project, without all the people who wanted these kids to grow up safe, none of them had a chance.

And that just wasn't acceptable.

CHAPTER 10

The house Diego lived in didn't look anything like a home. It looked like a prison. Razor wire was generously rolled along the top of ten feet cinderblock. The entrance to the compound was heavy and metal, and it rolled to the sides, rather than opening like a normal gate. It could have been stolen from a cell block, just like a guard tower or entrance to a maximum security prison. Behind the walls, Fredo could hear dogs barking as they approached.

"Lupe," he stopped to talk to her before they approached. "If this goes bad, it will all be over fast. If it goes good, it will all be over fast. These things never linger on for days and days, or even hours, you understand? There will be no hostage situation here, and there will be no hesitation. If I yell down, you go down on top of the baby, okay?"

"You give me the signal, then?"

"No, sweetheart, I'll just yell. You won't be confused at what I ask you to do. But pay attention, okay? And watch everyone around us, know where they are and what they're doing all the time, okay?"

"What if Diego isn't here today?"

"Well, if he's not here, he's dead. I doubt he'd be allowed to have free time when the boss has just come back to town. It wouldn't be very good for his longevity."

She nodded, and together, they resumed their walk, heading directly toward the complex. This had all been arranged. The rest of the Team was in hiding at various places. He knew Armando was some place high up so he could get off shots if it came to that. Danny Begay, the Navajo SEAL, was ready with his slingshot and throwing knives. He was the fastest and quietest killer on their team in hand-to-hand combat.

Normally, Fredo would be making little IEDs and small explosive charges or smoke bombs. But they'd decided he was the target once and could be the target again. This time, however, he wore the Kevlar. Lupe wore a vest, as well, and a plate was strapped around the baby's back, hidden under the blanket she carried him in.

They were damned lucky Lupe knew so much about the complex. Her showing up today was probably the last thing in the world they expected.

The two of them walked down the center of the road, aiming for the gate. Though armed, Fredo held his hands up, indicating he was not packing. It might give him the precious few seconds of safety he'd need if things started to go wrong.

A guard appeared at the top of the gate, holding a semi-automatic. He wasn't afraid to brandish it, even though it was illegal as hell in California. But with the stiff gun control laws, and those laws becoming more strict by the day, the gap was widening between the bad guys and the people who just wanted to go about their lives without interference.

"We only want to talk to Diego Mora. We're here to negotiate some kind of a truce," Fredo shouted with authority.

"Well, asshole, I speak for fuckin' Diego Mora. And I doubt you have anything I want that you can negotiate with, except that pretty little mama there."

Fredo understood that he was probably gazing at the fighting form of Sonny Alvarez, looking refreshed and ready for all-out war, having just recently returned from his vacation at Pelican Bay. Fredo guessed Sonny hadn't been informed Diego had knocked up a local girl.

"Well your man Diego might have something different to say about that. Why don't you just tell him, and we'll wait right here?" Fredo felt Lupe shaking next to him.

Alvarez nimbly jumped down off the wall behind the fence. A few seconds later, the gate was rolled back, and out stepped Alvarez and two other lieutenants, armed to the teeth. Clearly, no one was concerned about violating parole, least of all Sonny.

The man was covered in prison tats, faded and milky, caused by unsanitary implements and skin that wasn't properly attended to during healing. He sported a ring of skulls around the base of his neck. With his ruddy complexion and large craters from acne, he was probably the ugliest man Fredo had ever seen. His skinny chest showed a breastbone that pushed forward, a childhood deformity that was never fixed. Only about half the teeth remained in his mouth. The crowd of three stopped nearly ten feet away. Too far. He had to find some way to get closer.

Fredo saw recognition crest on the face of the young man to Sonny's right. The man was fixated on the baby.

"Can I hold him?" the man asked Sonny, not Lupe.

"No," said Fredo as he stepped in front of the girl and the baby. "We got issues to discuss first."

Sonny searched the surrounding area, as if sensing the rest of the team. "You got a lot of balls, little man, or are your friends out there in hiding?"

"I got one man who will call the cops if something should happen to any of the three of us. We got 911 on speed dial."

Sonny's arrogance was his downfall, Fredo surmised. He also guessed the man wasn't terribly bright. It looked as if thinking actually caused him some pain.

"You're probably wondering why we're taking such a risk." Fredo tried to act casual, but it wasn't working. And he wished Lupe would stop shaking because it was making him nervous, too.

"I'm a reasonable man. I'll listen."

"Way I hear it, you're not supposed to be hanging around here. You're required to move off somewhere else, good riddance and all."

Sonny laughed in Fredo's face, his guffaws markedly loud.

"I'm not going anywhere. Didn't you hear? I'm free. Thinking of settling down, finding a nice woman," he said as he nodded to Lupe. Fredo quickly assessed it wasn't going so well with Diego, who flinched as if he'd been slapped.

"Well, maybe we can sweeten the pot a bit. We want the center left alone. We want to fix it back up. We don't want the walls tagged or the windows broken again. The Mayor wants to be able to come down here without fearing for his life."

"That can happen anywhere, and you know it."

"How much money would it take for you to leave and never come back?"

Fredo watched as Diego's eyes grew to be saucer-like.

"How much we talkin'?" Alvarez asked.

"I don't know. What's it worth to you?"

"Well, if I'm gone, then you still have to work with these dudes."

Fredo was running out of options. He saw two other men on a catwalk above the walls to the right of the open gate. He made sure he and Lupe were not an open target. With Sonny and the two others in the way, no one inside was going to start shooting.

He had to get closer. Fredo saw something glint in the sunlight off in the distance to his right and realized Danny had pulled out one of his knives. He hoped Diego or Sonny hadn't noticed the glare.

"Look," Fredo said as he took two steps forward. To his surprise, Sonny let him. "We've brought the baby as an act of good faith. We want you to relocate your enterprise. Just think what a couple hundred thousand dollars could buy you."

"Why don't I just make the same deal with you? You and your buddies leave my town, and I'll agree not to kill you." He chuckled slightly, aided by his two helpers.

Fredo judged the distance carefully. Sonny wasn't used to holding the assault rifle, and he certainly wasn't ready to fire.

He slowly turned, keeping his peripheral vision tuned to the rifle in Sonny's hands. That assault rifle could cut him in half if the man knew how to properly use the weapon. He noted Diego was covering the butt of his handgun with his left hand. The other lieutenant looked like he was window dressing, his eyes rheumy and his breathing ragged. "Lupe, honey, show them how cute the baby is." As he turned toward her, he also took another step closer to Sonny and Diego.

Lupe's eyes were filled with panic. Fredo motioned for her to come toward him, and as she did, everyone either looked at the baby, or at her lovely face and sensuous low-cut cotton top. Fredo made his move. He grabbed the AK from Sonny's hands and hit his nose with the butt of the deadly weapon. Immediately, Sonny doubled over as blood began spurting everywhere. Fredo gave red-eyes a swift kick to his kneecap and heard a satisfying crack. Then he heard the dull thud as a throwing knife hurled out of the shadows and hit Diego between the shoulder blades, sinking in nearly to the hilt. Diego screamed and fell off to the side.

"Down," Fredo yelled as part of their cover was gone. He kicked Sonny again in the face, and this time, the man fell unconscious. Fredo immediately trained the rifle on the two guardsmen. Kyle and T.J. appeared from the opposite side of the opening, both yelling, "Drop it."

Seeing their friends completely disabled, they quickly made the decision to cooperate and take their chances, rather than starting a gun battle. As their rifles dropped to the ground below, Fredo felt the tension completely leave his body. He was left with a sense of peace and calm he hadn't felt since that day back at the hospital when Mia had visited him.

And fuck it, yeah. He was rock hard again.

CHAPTER 11

Riverton was not happy when he and several other detectives, as well as a number of regular uniformed policemen arrived after getting the 911 calls. The huge SWAT Team vehicle completely blocked the entrance to the complex. Two ambulances and a fire truck also converged on the scene. Some news crews had also found the complex, and there was a helicopter overhead broadcasting live shots. Speculation was rampant, some even calling it a terrorist cell broken up by the project organizers. Riverton was busy making communications. The Feds were still on their way, which meant San Diego P.D. was bearing the brunt of the costs.

A handful of gang-affiliated youths were arrested inside, all of them younger than twenty. Sonny Alvarez was taken into custody and escorted to the medical center where Fredo had been just days before. There were mountains of evidence to collect, catalog, and haul away. Neighbors and curious onlookers had to be kept at bay.

Riverton wouldn't look at Fredo. He wouldn't say more than two words to anybody. Finally, Fredo asked him.

"You got the bad guys. Caught them with all their stuff," Fredo reminded him. "The good guys won, for a change, Clark."

"You're not to interfere. You're a fuckin' SEAL. Stay off my lawn!" Riverton looked like he was going to burst a blood vessel. Fredo didn't understand the intensity of his fury.

"I don't get it. Please clue me in."

"I'm gonna have my ass handed to me. You don't make the Feds look bad, Fredo. You make nice; you take their resources. Our county now has to pay for all this shit," he said as he waved his arm over the beehive of activity. "You just couldn't stop yourselves from interfering."

"Fuck no, not after what they did to Julio. Not after what they were planning on doing to what was left of the neighborhood."

"You stupid macho kids. You gonna be around for the trial or will you be half way around the other side of the earth? Some defense attorney's going to have a field day," Riverton said, his face beet-red.

Fredo rolled his shoulders and puckered his lip with a frown. "Not what I do. That's your department, Clark." He knew they had evidence—too much evidence, in fact. They'd toured the complex and found black hoodies, spray paint, and items stolen from the school.

He figured Riverton just wasn't going to get to the same page, so Fredo retreated to the company of his brothers on the Team, where the mood was considerably more jovial.

Armando grabbed Fredo's arm. "You better get hold of Mia. She's going into full-tilt panic mode. She and my mom have been on the phone non-stop, watching the news and everything."

"I got it."

Fredo was able to get signed out, and before he left, he gave a hearty thanks to the guys who had helped him. The rescue and fire crews were enjoying doing some smack talk with the SEALs. Normally, Fredo would kick back and wear some accolades like beads in New Orleans, but now, he had another mission to run.

Her cell phone was going straight to voicemail. Mia was continually forgetting to charge her phone then forgetting where she put it, sometimes going two days without it.

Fredo stopped by his favorite florist and bought some deep red roses. He wanted a shower, but didn't want to keep her waiting.

He felt himself getting teary-eyed. Maybe he should not even tell her about the testing, but he tossed that idea out the window. She'd see right through him.

He remembered what Coop had told him way back on the day he'd been to the doctor.

Let the woman decide.

Hell, she could do anything she wanted with him. She could put him chained in a holding cell for all he cared. If it made her happy, he was all for it. But this, this one thing she wanted, he couldn't do for her. He mentally told himself, whatever her reaction, he'd love that too about her. She'd be disappointed; he knew she would, but he'd love her even more for it.

Before he got to the house he got a call from Dr. Patterson.

"Hope this is good news." Fredo said. He noticed the little soreness in his chest was not present any longer.

"Very good news, and I'm calling you before I call his mom. Julio's got feeling in one foot. Still not out of the woods, and we have to get that slug, but I'd say this is about the best sign we've had. We can work with it."

Fredo wanted to kiss the doctor through the phone.

"Well, you go enjoy your evening. Just thought you'd like to know."

"Thanks, doc."

"And thanks for helping with the cleanup today. It's all over the news."

He rang the doorbell instead of using his key and stood to attention with the roses at his chest. The door swung open. Her beautiful face was framed in curls cascading down over her shoulders. He could barely see part of one large golden hoop earring brushing against the fine texture of her long, flawless neck.

The spark and fire that was Mia, even when she was calling him names and insulting him, was there in her eyes, as it always was. But today, she was filled with relief, as well. Her abundant lips colored in red smiled at the sight of him. She looked straight back at him before she acknowledged the roses. Like she knew Fredo by his heart and not by the wrapper he came in.

"*Mi amore.* Oh, thank God you are safe." She slammed into his arms, crushing the roses, but he didn't care. He allowed her to pull him to her, hold him. He found peace in her scent, and the warmth of her soft body. He whispered in her ear how much he loved her. He didn't want to cry, so he kept holding her until he could compose himself.

Her red fingernails pawed over his back as her breathing grew deep, and he could smell her arousal. It would always be this way, coming home to Mia. Whenever they were apart, there was a celebration of epic proportions when he returned, that almost, but not quite, made the parting worth it.

"You are so bad not to call me."

"Where is your cell phone, Mia?"

"I lost it about two hours ago." She pulled herself away from him, slammed the door shut at her back, and grabbed his hand. She flicked her long hair up over her neck and then let it drop.

"How could I have called you? I tried. I really did."

"You need to try harder, Fredo," she said over her shoulder.

And, oh baby, yes, he was harder already.

"Punish me, if you like, but I am yours for the next twenty-four hours, Mia. You can do with me whatever you like, and I won't complain." He was mesmerized by the sight of her tight ass swaying back and forth. He liked her exaggerated moves for his behalf. She peeled off the cobwebs from his dark brooding nature with the way she manipulated him, and he so willingly took it. She was, and would forever be, his wild child.

"Wait!" She suddenly stopped, and he ran into her backside. "The roses. You brought roses."

"Yes, my love, but they're all over the floor by the front door. We smashed them."

"Then they are the best, all fragrant and moist!" She winked at him and licked her lips, and Fredo nearly came to his knees. She ran back to the living room and picked up the bouquet, with most of the roses hanging their heads, broken at their delicate necks.

Fredo frowned at the ruined bouquet.

"I read in one of my books where the hero and the heroine crashed into each other, and she was carrying a huge bouquet of red roses, and they fell all over them. Their first touch. He fell in love with her right then and there."

He was all in. "Yes! I've fallen in love with you, Mia. I fell in love with you again, just now. These roses are magic," he said as he stepped to her. He saw in her eyes that she was game for a little foreplay. Although he wanted inside her peach so bad, he could withstand a few moments of play, especially if it heightened her pleasure.

Mia acknowledged his idea silently with a smile, and then a kiss. She pulled away when he went deeper. Shedding their clothes, they frolicked down the hallway to the bedroom. He didn't feel as graceful as she looked, bending over so he could watch her jeans slide down her smooth ass. Mia removed her bra and pulled her hair up over her head, giving him that sideways sultry look before she licked her lips.

She handed him half of the roses. "Come, we must prepare the bed, yes?"

Well, of course! Absolutely!

Grabbing the bobbing heads of the fragrant roses, she yanked and beheaded each one, throwing the long green stems over the bed and away from them. Her delicate fingers crushed the petals nearly to the point of squeezing liquid from them. She sprinkled the gloriously scented red petals over the mattress. He was standing before her, naked, with a hard-on the size of the Chrysler Building. But he had forgotten to do his part with the roses.

"Fredo, you have a one-track mind. Shame on you." She put her finger in her mouth and returned a coy expression.

His heart was light. He loved watching her do anything, especially when she got in one of her playful moods like today, welcoming him home to her open arms, and smothering him with her free spirit and lightness of being. He even liked watching her sleep, brushing her hair, and helping her do the dishes in the kitchen sink and getting water everywhere.

How could he have been so lucky? He felt unworthy of the reward of being permanently mated to the one thing he was truly addicted to and could never get enough of: Mia.

She crawled up on the bed, lay on her back, filled her palms with petals, and sprinkled them all over her body.

He dropped the roses at his feet, climbed up on the bed and let his fingers travel up her smooth thigh. Mia arched up, her breasts looking luscious with petals falling from her nipples and into the cavity at her belly button. He explored the pink flesh between her legs. Mia let out the most luscious moan he'd ever heard in his life when she spread her knees and gave him deeper access.

Kneeling before her writhing body, he bent over, lapping her arousal and savoring every drop of her wonderful elixir. He played with her little bud, chasing it around with his tongue, letting it be elusive like the woman who played with his soul every day. He brushed the bunch of petals over her smooth abdomen, around both breasts, and up under her chin and around her neck. He was nearly on top of her now. She gave him the needy look he dreamt about when he was overseas and missing her the most. Her arms were lying against the white cotton pillowcase, her red fingernails toying with her curls.

He kissed her neck below her ear, a place he knew was her favorite spot.

"You bring new meaning to the word *homecoming*, my love."

"Ah, Fredo. We will love each other's bodies forever, won't we?"

He hesitated, faltering on her words a bit, not quite sure where it was leading.

"Of course. Forever and ever."

"We are good for each other, Fredo, aren't we?"

"Yes, my love. We are the best." He brushed a petal over her cheek, up around the side of her eye, and across her forehead.

She moved her palms to his butt cheeks, bent her knees, and arched herself to receive him. Her fingers deftly encircled his cock as she rubbed his tip over the fleshy petals of her sex and then pressed him inside her.

"This," she said in a hiss, "is what I live for."

"Mia. Beautiful Mia. You are everything to me." The heady aroma of the crushed blossoms filled his nostrils as he pressed his lips against hers and felt her melt into him.

They traded slow kisses and nibbles, tasted each other in a long, slow love-making session that wasn't urgent. He let her orgasm build, watching her for little signs of things she liked. Having this exquisite creature explore and taste him was nearly more than he could handle. She pushed and pulled him to pick up the rhythm until she was pressed against him, holding herself and then letting herself go. Against her warm insides, he gave her what he could. He filled her with his seed.

And no one needed to know they had dented foreheads and didn't move. It would remain, as long as it could be, Fredo's secret.

* * *

FREDO'S DREAM

SEAL BROTHERHOOD NOVEL

CHAPTER 1

Special Operator Alphonso Manuel Esquidido "Fredo" Chavez knew he was dreaming but he liked the subject matter, so coaxed his fantasy a bit longer, willing to keep his eyes closed. In his dream, he had just landed and was carrying nearly a hundred pounds of gear, stumbling out of T.J.'s new Hummer, yet propelling as fast as his legs could carry him up his front walkway and into the arms of his wife Mia. The sound of her soft breath was the first part of her that began the conversion from fighting man to lover. She never failed to make his homecoming spectacular, and today was no exception.

"Ah, Fredo, my love. I have missed you terribly," she whispered as he nuzzled into her hairline, kissing her long beautiful neck and licking the space between her breasts. If he had to die, he hoped he could take his last breath with his face buried in her cleavage. Even better if he was rooted deep between her legs.

His hands slipped over her warm, bare ass. The dress she wore melted to the floor in a colorful puddle of orange and yellow flowers.

He'd dropped his duty bag somewhere. Now he dropped his pants and absorbed her laughter as he showed her his pink boxers. This made him nearly wake up. But soon she was kneeling in front of him, completely naked, searching for his shaft, clutching his butt cheeks and moaning in that soulful way only Mia could do. She was beside herself with need and he aimed to satisfy that need tonight and keep himself hard for as long as she wanted it. Only in a dream could this be. He felt the chuckle in his belly vibrate against her forehead as she worshiped him on her knees. A better homecoming could not be had.

The scene changed and he was now in their large bed, her hot sweaty body calling to him. He had tasted her all over. He had lapped the sweat from her forehead and the juices between her legs, hungry for her still.

He carefully lifted her knees over his shoulders then undulated forward as he sought oblivion deep inside her, rubbing against her delicate channel from several angles, first slow, then fast, then slow again, drawing her kisses long, pulling her up to him by gripping her hips. Her shoulders lay back with her black hair splayed over the pillow, her enormous tits shaking as he stroked her quickly, then stopped to let her luxuriate in his powerful thrusts.

This was what made the deployments worth it. Homecomings were always done in bed. He usually gave her a head's up the instant he landed on either coast, so she could arrange a play date for little Ricardo with one of the other SEAL families who had not just come home. Everyone in the community understood how important that first day was when they got home from deployment. They all knew about their men's need to be intimate and why. It was the first thing they'd all do on their home country's soil, an unbroken ritual to melt the stink of war off them all. There was purity in it, a long beautiful cleansing as he made love to Mia, as they all loved their wives—the vehicle to getting fully back home. It never changed.

He leaned back to watch the beauty of his penetration, see how her pink lips fit so snug around him and accepted his girth. It wasn't fair she couldn't see it like he could. Burying himself inside her was truly one of the miracles of being alive.

"Fredo, my love, make me grow a baby inside. Please. I want your baby."

Even in dreamstate, there was a dose of reality there, piercing like a hot surgical steel blade in his heart. He saw the picture of his sperm, unmoving, with dented heads. He couldn't look at her as his seed began to burst from him, filling her. He closed his eyes, and felt himself pulse, rocking her, giving her everything he had.

When he opened his eyes, her belly had grown. It grew larger still as he pumped his last. His eyebrow knitted and his forehead puckered above it. He scrambled off her, smoothing over the taught skin and inverted belly button of her tummy.

"Mia!"

"Oh Fredo, thank you! Now I can give you back what you've given me for so long. Thank you my love."

She arched her back, her knees bent, and he saw something move in her belly. Was it an arm, a leg or the head of his child moving there inside her? He felt the movement as it responded to his gentle touch on his wife's flesh.

Her face was in ecstasy as she bore down, contractions coming, her eyes fixated on him, a hungry smile on her lips as she bit herself. "Oh, Fredo, I do this for you!" He saw she was in pain, but at the same time it was pure pleasure to her. "Take my baby, Fredo. Take our baby."

He quickly scanned the liquid space between her legs, now flushing blood and red-tinged fluids. In the sea of birthing fluid came blood of his blood, a baby born, still attached to her. As he picked it up, miraculously the skin pinkened and he held it in a soft blanket that had also magically appeared. The infant gazed up at him. The child was older than a newborn all of a sudden.

His attention was drawn back to her body again as another child appeared. He lay the first two into Mia's bedside as she cooed and kissed them both. When he delivered yet a third infant, the first two had grown large enough to crawl off the bed of their own accord, chubby arms and legs scrambling. The toddlers righted themselves, their laughter and squeals again pulling at his heartstrings. They ran out the bedroom door like chubby-cheeked cherubs from Heaven, black curly hair covering their heads.

The new baby was placed at Mia's side. His concern was growing, but Mia's face was in full repose, enjoying his look of shock and awe.

"What is this?" he asked, as another baby presented itself to him. He barely had time to give this new child to Mia when another appeared.

"Our family, Fredo. Our family is growing, Fredo. You are strong in seed and you have given me many children, just like I wanted."

"No, Mia, something isn't right. The children—" He stopped because the two toddlers at her side suddenly made their way off the bed and joined the other two somewhere in the house. The sounds of happy play, laughter and beginning speech patterns filled his head.

He presented the newest baby, wrapped and cleaned as if some mysterious midwife had prepared him, to Mia who accepted the new child with kisses, even as she arched to deliver yet another.

Fredo had to stand up. His heart was pushing limits toward emotional overload. He searched the bed, his hands, and found no traces of blood. A child stared up at him again, again cleaned and pink, kicking arms and legs and cooing, from between Mia's legs. Mia was releasing yet another child to the bed sheets, and Fredo picked up the toddler to make room for another. The little boy wiggled his way out of his arms, and slipped to the floor, running off in the direction of the others.

Now worry began to tug at his belly. He looked back to his wife who seemed unconcerned, her breasts engorged with milk, nursing a child as another one was delivered. Her sultry smile filled him with fear.

"Mia. This is too much. This isn't—"

"See how strong your seed is, my love? You unleash your manliness inside me, just like I've always wanted. You cause me to bear enough children for the whole world. You make me the earth mother I always wanted to be. Thank you, my love. Look at the evidence of our love!"

He turned and saw a crowd of toddlers at the doorway.

"Hello, Papa," they started to say, one by one. Some waved to him. Some smiled. Some looked down shyly at their toes.

"How can we afford all these children?" he asked her. He fell back, sitting on the edge of the bed as the children came over to hug his legs, putting their heads in his lap, on his knees. He worried about his nakedness, but suddenly realized he was fully clothed. With joy, his fingers touched the heads of these cherubs, stroking their curly hair and feeling the warmth of their little bodies, cupping their cheeks and drawing them to him, one by one.

Mia threw her head back and laughed, her long neck arching, her breasts leaking milk all over her belly and the bed sheets at her sides.

Earth mother indeed! She had transformed into a baby-making machine. He was being overridden with flesh of their combined flesh, children who wanted a piece of him. He could only hold one or two at a time, while the others pouted and asked for attention. He allowed himself to be overcome, letting the children crawl, covering him as he lay back at Mia's feet, now confident this was the limit to the birthing.

He had suddenly gone from a dad raising another man's child to a father with almost a dozen children. They pressed against him, kissing his neck, tugging at his hair, and whispering words of affection like Heaven's little angels.

He woke up. There was movement around him. The familiar scent of his woman came to him first, her lips whispering something. He wanted to ask her about the babies, but when he opened his eyes and scanned the room, they were alone. Mia had grabbed his hand and placed it between her legs, moaning with her need. He wasn't so sure he wanted to repeat what had just happened, so he sat up.

His back and shoulders were soaked with sweat. He had trouble breathing. Mia scurried to her knees, her beautiful naked body jumping to action.

"You are not well, my love?"

"No. I—I just had a dream, I guess."

"Oh, sweetheart, tell me. But are you okay? Everything okay? You dreamed about overseas? Something that happened to you?"

She was thinking he'd had a nightmare about his time in the war zone! But was it a nightmare? It was something he knew could never happen, and yet he experienced it just like it did. His heart raced. Should he tell her? Or should he just let her think it was some form of PTSD? And was this kind? Was it honest? But if he told her he knew it would never happen, couldn't happen, then he'd have to reveal to her his secret.

That he was sterile! His sperm did have dented heads and no movement. He'd seen it with his own eyes in the doctor's office.

The worst day of his life.

He met Coop at the Rusty Scupper, their favorite Team hangout, later that morning. He had already downed one beer and was working on his second, and it wasn't even lunchtime.

"Whoa! What's up, Frodo?" Coop's lanky frame deposited across from him as gracefully as a giraffe in heat. He'd recently gotten over being offended at the nickname Coop gave him from *The Hobbit*, since he was the short, stocky one, and Cooper had the height and litheness of an Olympic swimmer. But today it felt like a kick in the gut.

"Did I ever tell you I hate it when you call me that? Don't do it any more."

"Never?" Coop asked casually, not taking him seriously. He sipped on his mineral water and ice chips, checking out the room for people he knew.

"I said fuckin' never! I don't like that shit."

"What the fuck's gotten into you?"

How could he tell Coop? The dream had been so powerful, he was still sweating, his heart pounding like a funeral dirge. Maybe they needed to get to Gunny's for a workout. Maybe he needed a five-mile swim in the inlet. Maybe three or four more beers or some scrambled eggs and the hottest chilis he could find.

Something had to happen to erase the images of toddlers calling him *Papa*, hiding in closets and cupboards when he opened them, crawling over his duty bag, throwing the laundry all over the room, and chasing little Ricardo, who was older, but barely old enough to stop them from overrunning them. These visions plagued him even though he was fully awake. And he couldn't tell Mia what he was seeing, or rather, imagining. Was he going crazy?

Maybe it was PTSD!

"Hey, man. Libby and I were doing just fine this morning in bed, and the kids are over at Kyle and Christy's for a sleepover. So you got me here, but I'd rather be in the arms of the most beautiful lady in the whole world right now. So tell me the fuck what's so important I gotta sit here watching you piss your pants and drink beer before noon."

"Coop, something's wrong with me."

"Well blinding flash of the obvious, Fredo. With what you eat every day—a diet straight from hell, man—what do you expect? You think you'll be thirty years old forever? You'll feel young and invincible the rest of your life?"

"What the fuck does that mean?"

"It means that your old fairy godmother over here," he thumbed at his own chest, "is telling you you're gonna die if you don't start watching what you eat. I make jokes about it all the time."

"Tell me about it." Fredo wouldn't look at him. He noticed a couple of high school hotties intent on landing a nice SEAL enter the bar with barely anything on. This also wasn't like him, but this morning, he checked out every luscious detail. *He* had the most beautiful wife on the Teams, not Coop. Mia, the Puerto Rican bad girl bombshell had become his sex kitten and wife, totally devoted to him, totally loving doing all kinds of nasty things to him that blew his mind on a regular basis. Why in the world would he be looking elsewhere? But today, he was.

Coop noticed. "You're an asshole, Fredo. You guys have a fight? Am I here to give you an alibi so you can go fuck some frog hog? That it?"

Fredo stood to lean over the table, toppling his beer and trying to grab Cooper's polo shirt. Coop, too quick for him, backed up two steps. He returned a gaze Fredo was ashamed to admit made him feel terrible.

Coop threw down five dollars and turned to leave.

"Wait." Fredo was hyperventilating. "I need some help."

"Fuckin' A you do, Fredo. Is it your time of the month? Or did Mia cut you off? What the hell's going on?"

Fredo looked at the mess on the table. "I need to get out of here. Let's go."

"Sure."

Just before he ducked going through the doorframe out to the Strand and the bright street in Coronado, Coop added, "We gonna hold hands now and make up?"

Fredo kicked him in the butt and followed behind. They ambled down the block, then crossed the street and headed toward the neighborhoods at the approach to the beach. Cooper was taking his lead from him, searching everywhere else but not looking his way, which Fredo was grateful for. The two close friends knew each other well. Coop knew Fredo would eventually come out with it. Problem was, Fredo didn't know how to put words to what he was feeling.

A block away from the sand, Fredo found his voice. "I had a bad dream."

"Really." Coop stopped, putting his hands on his hips, and stared back at his best friend. "This is all about a bad dream?"

Fredo sighed. "Yes. I think so. Maybe something is wrong with me, but this dream was a total nightmare. I just don't know how to explain it."

"Just fuckin' breathe, asshole. And try. I need to get back to Libby. I'd much rather be there, but I'm here for you, man, as long as you don't take too much time."

They approached the sand, which was already warm. Fredo's flip flops allowed the white grains to calm his toes. At least that part of his body was soothed.

"I'm dreaming about babies."

"Now I've heard it all," Coop said as he sat down abruptly. "You. Dreaming about babies."

"Yes, *my* babies. Lots of babies."

"So where's the nightmare aspect of this? You've been obsessed with babies ever since you had that fuckin' doctor's visit. I told you it was unhealthy to look at your own sperm. A man should never do that."

"I know, Coop. This has nothing to do with that."

"Oh, yea? I imagine Mia dreams about babies, too. What's the matter with that? Maybe it's God's way of telling you that you need to come clean with her, let her know the truth. You guys are young and healthy. You should look for kids to adopt that need a loving home like yours."

"Well, maybe I'm not so healthy after all."

"Now, there's no fuckin' surprise there."

"Maybe it's up here." He pointed to his temple.

"Like you're going batshit crazy, Fredo? That what you mean?"

"Or something like that." He shrugged and sifted the sand with his fingers. He liked the warmth on his butt. Now his fingers were warm, too. Being here was helping. It was making it easier to tell Coop the impossible details of the dream. Or so he thought.

"I've never had this dream I had last night. It started out okay. I'd just come home from deployment, and Mia and I were—you know the routine."

"I sure do. Best part of being a SEAL, in my opinion."

"Right. Me, too."

"And?"

"Well, we were making love, and the next thing I knew, her belly was getting big right under me. I was pumping her up like over-inflating a bicycle tire? A balloon."

Coop looked at him like he'd looked at the camel spider they'd dug out of the garbage on one mission overseas. "I can't say as I've ever had that image before, Fredo. I've fucked my pregnant wife plenty of times. It's not a nightmare. It's a fuckin' beautiful thing. Seeing her big belly and all."

"No, when I was—she wasn't pregnant. But right in the middle of it, her belly became distended, and she began to have a baby."

"While you were having sex? I can't see how that's possible."

"Not while, well, I pulled out, I guess. I—I just watched as she delivered a baby, but then she delivered another, and another and—"

"Excuse me. This is not making sense, Fredo."

"It makes no sense to me, Coop. My house was suddenly filled with toddlers."

"Like zombies? Day of the Dead sort of thing?"

"Oh no! They were beautiful children, all smiling, curly haired."

"Boys or girls?"

"What the fuck difference does it make?"

"I thought maybe it could be a Freudian thing, you know." Coop's turn to shrug. "Libby's dad could help with this, you know."

"I have no idea. I wasn't looking at their sex, man."

"Hard to miss that one. But you're right, that's a fucked up dream all right."

"It was like that Disney movie where he kept getting the buckets of water and they wouldn't stop. You know that one?"

"Fantasia?"

"Yeah. The kids kept coming. Right in front of me, they grew to walking size. They started talking."

"What did they say?"

Fredo looked hard at his best friend. "Hi, Papa."

"You mean like in Dracula?"

"Fuck no. Like a little kid would say to his daddy." Fredo noted the worried look on Coop's face deepened. "You *do* believe me?"

"Of course I do. That sounds exactly like the kind of dream I could see you having. With all the shit you put into your body, no wonder you dream about birthing babies. I'm surprised you don't see tamales with little arms and legs running around your house and beans and tortillas floating through the air. Your diet, man, sucks."

"It's gotten better. I'm trying to eat vegetables."

"Um hum. Don't lie to me, Fredo."

"No tofu. I refuse to eat tofu. The traditional Mexican diet is healthy."

"Lard. Corn meal. Cooked goat. Sure."

"Haven't you ever studied anything about cultural anthropology, Coop? Our traditional diet is actually healthy."

"Fuck, Fredo, your ancestors were eating human sacrifice."

"And yours were eating Englishmen and fucking their wives. Those Viking assholes smelled like fish all the time. Something major wrong with that."

"They conquered the known world with their kippers, Fredo. They battled the cold, each other, the rough seas, pirates. And yes, they ate fish."

"And drank like hell, too."

"That they did. But just what does this have to do with your dream?"

"I'm saying we each eat what we are culturally predisposed to eat. What's natural for you isn't natural for me."

"Except your diet gives you sperm with dented heads."

"I don't think that has anything to do with it. Just the way I was made."

"So if you're so perfect, why don't you tell her, asshole?"

Fredo didn't have an answer for that one.

CHAPTER 2

G unny's gym was crowded today. Timmons was doing a circuit training for several of the "silver foxes" as Fredo called the former SEALs and lifers from Marines and regular Navy. Older gents with beer bellies and huge arms covered with tons of tats—more so than the younger military men. Used to be full sleeves were the norm, but now it was somewhat discouraged. BUD/S instructors made life hell for the new recruits who came loaded up.

Grunts, groans, and loud expulsions of air were common during these sessions. Timmons could bark just as effectively as he did when he communicated what the Head Shed had in mind for SEAL Team 3 back when he was the Team liaison. In his retirement, he found new love and a purpose in life, but he could slip back into ordering everyone around like he used to. The more he drilled fitness into the older guys, the more he began to sound like Gunny, Amornpan's first husband who had passed some three years prior. He'd even taken on the role of being father to the half-Thai youth and only offspring Gunny knew about, Sanouk.

As Fredo began his own PT, he noted how everyone in the community had a place. No two men on the Teams were alike, nor were they supposed to be. They all came from different cultures and backgrounds. Some grew up privileged, but most of them came dirt poor with nothing else agenda-wise but becoming an expert killing machine. It was a coat of armor that was common to all of them, forged from resentment and their upbringing. Every one of the Team Guys was completely and nearly religiously comfortable with it.

The difficulties came when the Teams were home, so intense PT was required. Routine travel to specialized trainings often broke up the long weeks between deployments, which was especially helpful if some of them were having trouble adjusting to "normal" life. But life was anything but "normal" when they came back, based on what they'd seen.

Single guys found it hard to keep up with their ladies and often lost them while on deployment. Married men struggled, too. The SEAL Community came first in all respects. They blended their families into the community, not the other way around. Some wives, like Lucas' ex-wife, Connie, went completely nuts over the rotation. Her world wobbled and eventually tilted, sending her completely away from the whole scene. But Lucas had demanded and eventually got custody of his three kids.

Fredo was raising another man's son, little Ricardo, Mia's baby born to a gangbanger now serving time. And he still mentored Julio, the at-risk teen who helped them weed out a predatory gang intent on keeping the community park project stymied. One of their other Team Guys, Danny Begay, was also fathering a little orphaned Iraqi boy, Ali, whom they rescued on their last mission. Their little community was becoming quite international.

Julio, *Old Blue Eyes* as he was teased, was now fifteen and had successfully stayed out of the San Diego gangs. The Center project was completing the rebuild, with classes starting again, and Julio was considered to be Fredo's eyes and ears to the neighborhood, his right-hand man. Ephron, Julio's older brother, had nearly made it to the Teams as a first rate medic before his murder. Fredo and other volunteers from Kyle's SEAL Team 3 felt they owed a debt to Ephron's family, as well as his whole neighborhood. It was working. Fredo was proud that the violence was dropping and more and more kids were showing up at the after-school Center, instead of wandering the streets and getting snared by trouble.

Amornpan, Sanouk's mother, came up to Fredo as he was dropping his hand weights.

"Mr. Fredo, Chief says I should talk to you about starting a dance class at the Center. You think the girls would be interested?"

Fredo found her charming, quiet demeanor very alluring, although she was old enough to be his mother. She cowed her eyes as her mother no doubt taught her growing up. Fredo knew this is what had snagged Gunny's heart and also kept Timmons a very satisfied retired Master Chief.

"Dancing, as in the Thai dancing your group does?"

"Yes. I can get donations for the costumes from the Thai community. If I have the girls who want to learn. Do you think it would be…appropriate?"

"Why wouldn't it be?"

"Well, they know nothing about my culture, my language. Not sure they even know where my country is." Her pretty eyelashes covered in tiny silver specs fluttered demurely like a young girl's. "But I can teach them to dance. Give them something to think about outside of what they see every day." She angled her head to the side, like one of her dance moves and unpeeled her palm, her fingers with long white fingernails curving up to heaven. Her graceful motions were part of the way the woman moved every day. And it was downright distracting. More than one gruff SEAL had dropped a weight on his foot due to his lack of focus.

Fredo examined his fingers, opening and closing them slowly before he looked up at the exotic beauty in front of him. "You will need Timmons to come with you, or one or two of the SEALs. Still a little dangerous there. Not a good idea to have you there at night, either."

"But that's when they'll be free to dance. Daytime, girls are in school. At least that's what I want. I want them to learn. Sanouk said he'd help me as well."

Fredo suspected Sanouk had his own reasons for wanting to be down at the youth center, and he suspected it had more to do with the young Latina girls than anything else. Fredo and other Team Guys devoted a fair amount of time to raising funds for the Center's computers and some first-rate tutors. It was one of the most popular classes and was jammed with participants, especially the young girls.

The lines between language and culture were blurring more and more every day, he thought, warmly. The transgression Gunny had in Thailand and the birth of his son, Sanouk, was now bearing fruit thousands of miles away in a community reeling from an oppressive culture that wasn't giving the neighborhood a chance. In a way, Gunny's seed had begun to liberate children halfway around the globe, which was as it should be, he thought.

"If you can get adequate backup, I say, why not?" Fredo grinned and noticed how Amornpan's face glowed with joy.

"Oh, thank you, Mr. Fredo!" She grabbed him in a bear hug before he could discreetly step aside. Her exuberant displays of affection erupted often and without much warning. She did remind him of his wife, Mia, in that way.

"Can I ask you something?" Fredo whispered after she released him.

"Sure. What is it?" She glanced over at Timmons who was scowling, having caught a peek at the bear hug.

"Is Julio okay? Has Sanouk said anything about him to you?"

"Sanouk doesn't talk much about him. I just know he's interested in the computers."

Fredo was careful with his words. "I'd love to see those two become closer. I think it would be good for Julio. Sanouk can be an older brother type to him."

"I agree. I will ask him. May I tell him you suggested he try to work more closely with Julio? He thinks so much of you."

This tickled Fredo a bit. He hadn't noticed it in his dealings with the polite young man who wanted to become a SEAL one day. And because Sanouk was Gunny's flesh and blood, the Team was going to do everything possible to get him ready for a tryout at some future date.

Fredo knew he needed to spend more time at the Center, but with Mia on the mission to get pregnant, he was somewhat hampered for time. He would have enjoyed it more if he knew he could give her more than just a good time in bed. He wanted to give her a child and could not.

Thinking of his dream, he shuddered.

"You are not feeling well, Mr. Fredo?"

"No. I'm fine. Just a little tired." At least part of that was the truth.

Her wide and knowing smile decorated her pretty face. Almost as if she knew what had been keeping him up late nights.

A bell rang at the top of the front door. Cooper's massive frame hesitated for a second, drowning out the sunlight, then came over to Fredo and the Thai woman. "Yo, Amornpan. I see Fredo's got you distracting him so he can cut corners on his workout today."

"Always my fault, see?" Fredo said to her. "I never catch a break."

"We were talking about Center things. I think it was a worthwhile conversation," she said in her heavy accent. "I approached him about teaching a dance class there."

Coop's eyebrows rose. "Fredo. You Thai dance?" he said as he rolled his neck around and juggled his arms and hands at right angles, like they'd seen beautiful Amornpan do during several recitals.

She laughed easily. "Coop. You so funny! Such a funny SEAL."

She abruptly whirled around and wafted away from the two SEALs mesmerized by her graceful movements. Everything the woman did looked like a dance to Fredo.

"Now that will be something to watch. Seeing those little Latinas doing all those dances with the anklets and finger cymbals."

"Christy and Libby will want to join in. You ready for that?"

"And not Mia?"

"Well, she dances all day long with Ricardo. She dances when she does housework."

He smiled and picked up his hand weights again. Cooper fell in beside him and after a brief warm-up, the two of them began alternating on the equipment.

Cooper hung his head so he could speak more in private. "You tell her yet?"

"Tell her what?"

"Fuck sake, Fredo. You know what the fuck I'm talking about."

"I just told you yesterday, no. No. I'm not going to say anything. It's our secret." He peered into his friend's blue eyes. "Fuck better stay that way too."

"I feel you. It won't come from me. But Fredo, she's gotta find out some day."

"I'm not ready."

"You are having sex, right?"

"Shut up, Cooper."

Fredo's voice carried louder than he'd intended. Several of the silver set looked up from their concentration, frowning.

"For the record, Fredo. I've told you over and over again. Tell her. Don't string it out. Tell her."

After a grueling PT, Fredo begged off the stop for yogurt and decided to shop for something for dinner. Mia had said she'd be home a little later than usual since she had to take Ricardo for a well baby checkup and shots and had some shopping to do for one of the new SEAL babies born that week. He'd begged off accompanying her, not wanting to discuss the topic of having children.

At the gourmet deli, he wandered down the meat counter aisle and selected a thick New York steak he and Mia could split. He searched the store, making sure no one he knew was watching him, then he made his way over to the produce department. He picked out a bunch of carrots, their long green tops flopping in his paws. After the carrots, he selected a colorful bag of medium chilis in red, green, orange and yellow colors.

He saw a woman selecting some string beans, and he joined her, picking out those that were uniform and unblemished. He bought strawberries for dessert, passing on the other sweets nearby. On the way over to the cash register, he passed by the juice bar, which smelled to Fredo of freshly cut grass. It turned his stomach.

The juice machine was screaming. A frothy orange-green plastic glass was handed to a patron next to him.

"Would you like one, too?" the fresh-faced youth said cheerfully.

"I don't like it. Smells awful," Fredo mumbled, waving his hand in front of his nose for emphasis.

"Oh, no way. I guarantee you'll like my juice. We have the sweetest carrots in all of San Diego County."

"That doesn't look like carrots." Fredo was referring to the greenish tint.

"That's spinach and a little celery. But I put apple in it too. Very yummy." He began throwing things into the blender, and before Fredo could respond, handed him a greenish-orange mixture.

"No, thanks, man." He attempted to give it back to the boy.

"Oh, come on. You chicken? This will curl the hair on your butt and grow your pecker a whole inch. Promise."

Fredo chuckled at the kid's sense of humor, delivered straight.

"I don't need hair on my butt," Fredo laughingly answered him, handing him back the glass.

The boy wouldn't take it. "Just one sip. I dare you. You don't even have to pay for it if you don't want to finish." The kid leaned in for a shared secret. "But if you go home and find your pants are fitting just a little snug, well, you can thank me either before or after you see your wife."

Fredo did think of Mia. Despite his doubts, he took a generous gulp, so as not to appear weak. It actually tasted good. The two men shared a conspiratorial moment of understanding.

"You come back tomorrow for one, and I know you'll want to, and that one you'll have to pay for. This one? It's on the house."

Fredo tried to frown, but didn't have the heart to lie. "Thanks."

He left the juice bar and found fresh nine-grain bread with the heavy seeds, the kind Mia liked to toast for breakfast. He also bought eggs, some tortillas, some cheese, and diapers for Ricardo. He selected a nice bottle of red wine and two six-packs of microbrew beer. At the checkout counter, he found some male enhancement vitamins and discreetly added them to the conveyor belt with his other purchases.

Maybe tonight he'd serve Mia a nice steak dinner with string beans and green salad. She'd be impressed with that. He had lettuce and fresh tomatoes, and strawberries for dessert with whipped cream he'd snagged on impulse. Over the glass of wine after dinner, he'd gently tell her of his dilemma. He'd tell her he was sorry for keeping something so important from her. He'd ask for forgiveness.

And no matter what her reaction, he'd love her just as much and hope that she loved him back with the same devotion. He thought she would. But the little niggling doubt at the back of his brain made him slightly nervous. He'd proven so much to her. He'd delivered on every promise he'd made her, except this one.

He could love another man's child. But he still could not give her one of his own. He hoped that was enough for her.

The dinner was everything he'd expected. Mia was delighted with his attempt to put more greens in his diet, eat more healthy. She savored everything he prepared for her. He'd even told her he'd like to start cooking more, relieving her of some of the burden.

Her mood was upbeat and grateful. Fredo poured the wine and thought he could talk to her about the test results. But before he could say anything, Ricardo began to whine and she excused herself to put him to bed. Fredo followed with a kiss to the youngster's forehead, his chubby arms wrapped around his neck. He got three kisses back for every one he gave Ricardo.

When he returned to the dinner table, Mia handed him his wine glass.

"I like this new change in you, *mi amore*. You ply me with good food and wine. I intend to show my appreciation." She gave him a sultry smile under heavily lidded eyes and delicately touched his glass. He watched her swallow her wine, the soft muscles in her neck looking so delicious. She licked her lips and raised her glass again. "Come on, my love. Drink up, and then I want you to fuck me all night long."

He was powerless to resist her. The wine was good, the ambiance perfect. He couldn't wait to experience how she loved him.

He'd decided so many times before to wait to tell her. What was one more night? Surely, he deserved being able to worship her body one more time, before he had to tell her the truth.

CHAPTER 3

Fredo woke up with a start. A loud explosion had rocked the little house. Ricardo started to cry, and though Mia jumped out of bed, Fredo beat her to their son's bedside.

After verifying the noise had nothing to do with the condition of Ricardo, he went about checking on the house. Nearly a minute passed before he heard sirens, and then he heard several more. He padded out to the front door and saw a grey plume of smoke rising into the pre-dawn morning air. Dogs barked all over the city as people came out of their houses in their bathrobes and slippers, runners stopped and checked their watches. Some checked their cell phones.

Fredo grabbed his, seeing the panel light up.

Bomb at the Center. Don't come yet. The notice came from Kyle. Fredo knew he'd disobey that order without question. He nearly ran into Mia holding the still-crying Ricardo as he dashed to the bedroom to get his clothes on.

"Fredo, my love. What is it?"

"Bomb at the Center. I've got to go over there now."

"No, not alone. You get Coop, or call my brother, Kyle, or someone. Not alone, Fredo!"

She had a good point. He dialed Coop first and didn't get an answer. He'd already taken the man out of his wife's bed once this week. He decided not to leave a message. He dialed Mia's brother, Armando, one of the snipers on SEAL Team 3. Gina answered.

"Hey, Fredo." He could hear their little one crying in the background. "What's up?"

"I need to talk to Armani."

"He's out for a run."

Fredo knew he'd have heard the explosion and was probably already on his way over to the blast site. "If he calls you, let him know I'm going over to the Center. There's been a bomb or something that went off this morning."

"I heard that. Wish I could be more help. Want me to call the station to see if I can get any details? I'm not without friends still on the force." Gina had retired nearly two years prior to raise a family with Armando.

"Do that, and call me back if you've got anything."

"Sure will."

Fredo dialed Cooper again and again got voicemail. This time he left a message. "Coop, there's been an explosion at the Center. I'm heading down there to check things out. I think Kyle's on his way, but he told me to stand down. Hell, as if I'm going to do that. Just wanted you to know. I think Armani's on his way as well."

Danny Begay had done a special training on bomb making, so he left him a message too. He grabbed his keys and was nearly out the front door when Mia screamed at him.

"Fredo! Your pajamas!" Her face was contorted in shock as she pointed to his groin area. He'd nearly left the house in the red, white and blue striped pajama bottoms he'd taken to wearing lately. And his navy blue slippers with the anchor stitched on top she'd given him for Christmas last year.

He muttered his frustration to the floor as he kicked off the slippers, and jumped into a pair of jeans, leaving his white T-shirt on then stepped into his canvas slip-ons. At the door, he turned around again and headed for the closet, uprooting the carpet to find the gun safe. He quickly worked the combination but had to do it twice, then pulled his duty bag out quickly and slung it over his shoulder. He was out the front door all in less than two minutes. It was just like what they were used to over in camps in Afghanistan and East Africa, where time could mean the difference between life and death.

His green beater backfired but groaned until it picked up speed and rounded the corner in a squeal of rubber. He didn't have to check the rearview mirror to know he'd left a smoky trail.

Fire crews had arrived on the scene and were dousing the whole area with water, sending a sooty mist over everything. There was little fire that remained, but a lot of smoke as the classrooms at the old St. Rose School smoldered from the inside out. Fredo knew the paint in the arts room and paper in the computer learning center would be highly combustible.

He also knew even if the computers hadn't been touched by flame, the heat and smoke from the fire would claim them. Not to mention the water damage.

A ragtag group of neighbors, many of them also in their bedclothes, huddled just outside of the chain link fence that "protected" the grounds. After he parked the truck, he saw Julio come running over to him. The youth grabbed him, clutching at Fredo's shoulder blades and sobbing into his chest in an unusually emotional show of frustration and what Fredo picked up as fear.

"It's okay, Julio. We'll get those sons of bitches," he said squeezing the kid to him tight. Fredo had cycled into attack mode big time.

Julio trembled. "Why? Why do they do this?" His bright blue eyes shone in the evening moonlight like he was lit from within. He sniffled and wiped his nose and eyes on his jacket sleeve. Fredo took out a foil packet Warrior Wipe he always carried around with him.

"Because they're assholes," he said, ripping open the towelette and handing it to the boy. "All they want to do is tear down what they can't build on their own." He tousled the teen's hair as the kid cleaned dirt from his face. "Come on, let's go see what we can find out."

Fredo wondered how Julio had gotten so much soot on his face. He slung his duty bag over his shoulder, not daring to leave it in the truck. As they ran side by side, he glanced over to Julio to ask his question. "Did you see anything?"

"Nah. Nothing, man. Just been a lot of punks hanging around."

"Punks you know or new guys?"

"New guys. And they're like new gangbangers. And there was this other weird guy."

"Weird? How do you mean weird?"

"I don't know, he just gave me the creeps."

"He hang out with the others?"

"No. All by himself. The others I think are cashing in on a turf war."

"Explain."

"Because they fucked up Lorenzo, one of Sonny's guys. Cut him all up and shit. Cut off his little finger, man."

"Who were they?"

"I didn't want to get too close to find out. I stay clear of that crazy group." Then he abruptly stopped, grabbing Fredo's arm. "Word on the street, Fredo, is Caesar is getting out of prison soon."

Caesar was the father of the boy Fredo was raising as his own, Mia's former boyfriend. The timing of his release couldn't have been worse. If there was a confrontation between the two of them, Fredo knew only one of them would survive.

"When?"

"Christmas? Maybe after New Years. His boys are getting testy, too. Taking over Sonny's corners. I gotta get Lupe and Mama out of this place. Now with this, it's gotten worse. It's all fucked up, man. Feels like the place is falling apart."

Fredo wanted to ask more questions, but he needed to get to the scene first. Now he knew why Julio was so afraid. It was just like some of the places he'd seen overseas. The innocents never knew from which direction their enemies were coming, or whom to trust.

There would be time for gathering information later. He completely agreed that Julio's sister, who had a child by one of Sonny's men, needed to find some other place to raise the baby. Julio's mother was old enough to make up her own mind. Like Mia's mother, Felicia Guzman, she was just as stubborn about leaving the old neighborhood.

The two of them slipped through a breach in the fencing, which may have been the way the bomb makers had either arrived or escaped. Two units were pouring water on the old administration building, which had taken the brunt of the blast. A large brass bell from the tower fell to the pavement below as the structure collapsed on itself. The clanging noise could be heard over all the sounds of generators and equipment.

A crew was breaking through the heavy metal doors and the gate that blocked the classroom hallways since the rooms were fully engulfed with flames licking up the sides of the two-story building. Fredo watched in horror as smoldering boxes of papers, printers, and computers were dragged out onto the blacktop and then doused with water.

Danny suddenly appeared at Fredo's side, making Julio jump with surprise. "I'm thinking they packed the admin building with the biggest charge, which makes no sense," shouted Danny over the din.

Fredo considered this. "You mean because the classrooms are what held all the valuable equipment and stuff?"

"Yes. Almost like they didn't know." Danny squinted.

"You think there could be more set to go off?"

"Nothing that hasn't already caught fire, unless they light up one of the surrounding houses. What a mess." Danny shook his head in disgust.

Fredo's heart pounded. Revenge bubbled in his gut like thick black oil. He wanted to kill something, make someone pay. "Fuckin' waste of time and money. Scum of the earth. They destroy their own community," Fredo grumbled.

"It's a signature blast, Fredo. A calling card. Not meant to do anything but get TV time."

Julio had moved away, heading to the windows of the computer lab, trying to look inside. He was quickly detained by two huge San Diego police until Fredo could get there. Danny again appeared out of nowhere.

"He's not involved. I'm Special Operator Chavez. This is SO Begay. Our Team has sponsored this Center. This place is a SEAL Team 3 special project for the community. Julio here is one of the good guys from the neighborhood who helps us look after this place. Our eyes and ears."

One of the uniforms asked for identification and was shown both Fredo's and Danny's military IDs, which raised eyebrows. Julio wiggled his way loose to produce his library card, which was ignored. The officer holding him released the youth.

"I'm Lieutenant Corcoran." Without the formality of shaking hands, he continued. "The bomb squad can't work the scene yet, so I'm afraid I can't let you any closer."

"Understood." Fredo noticed the bomb squad logo on the side of a white van parked nearby. "You think it started in the old admin building? Looks that way to me."

"What we have here, Mr. Chavez and Mr. Begay, appears to be one large device planted over where that tower dropped. We think the seat of the blast came from there. But looks to me like little explosive charges were also placed in the class-rooms and were detonated by the main blast."

Fredo's shoulder was gripped by a hand he recognized. Kyle Lansdowne, his LPO, was at his back. "Thought I told you to stay away, Fredo."

Fredo turned and gave him a defiant grin. "And you were dumb enough to think I would, right?"

"At least you brought backup." Kyle winked at Danny, and then addressed Corcoran. "Kyle Lansdowne. These are my guys. We're just here to help, not interfere. What can we do for you?"

Corcoran shook Kyle's hand. "I was just saying we can't let anyone in until the bomb squad finishes their investigation. You boys have any idea who would do such a thing?"

"We've had some trouble with the local gangbangers," said Fredo. "But we've sent a couple waves of them off to the University. The neighbors are your best bet. No one stays here on premises."

"Anyone with a grudge?"

"Just punks," said Danny.

"Julio, tell them what you told me," barked Fredo.

The boy cleared his throat. "We seen new guys hanging around, you know, harassing. One of them cut up a local guy real bad."

"Who was that?" The officer was making notes.

"I don't know who the dude was, but Lorenzo Freitas only got nine fingers left."

"I remember that. Freitas, you say?" the officer asked.

"Yes, sir."

"Where is Mr. Freitas now? Would he have reason to believe this Center was somehow responsible for his trouble?"

"He took off, man. No one's seen him since."

"So where do these new guys live?"

"No idea. They just come in, push their way around, stole a couple bikes, harassed the girls."

"You need to tell me, Julio. I didn't know any of this," scolded Fredo.

"I'm telling you now." Julio had developed a bit of an attitude.

"Who else has seen these guys?"

"Carla, and I think they came after my sister, Lupe."

"What did they say?"

"Mostly they whistle and laugh. Ask around. Maybe someone knows. Ask my sister, Lupe."

Corcoran was being summoned back toward the smoldering ruins. Crews were beginning to put away their equipment. Water was being applied in one area, but several investigators descended over the scene. A couple FBI jackets were recent additions to the mix.

The three SEALs were joined by Cooper. Then Fredo's brother-in-law, Armando Guzman, showed up in his running clothes. The little squad watched in silence, hoping for an update that never came. Members of a local news crew appeared with their bright lights and cameras. The Team Guys slipped off into the gray early morning San Diego dawn as if they'd never been there in the first place.

CHAPTER 4

A month passed and although the repair and reconstruction to the Center began, Fredo's anger hadn't dissipated. Mia had tried to cheer him up, but for the first time in his SEAL career, he was having difficulty controlling his negativity. This was the second attack on the Center. Although the Archdiocese had the buildings insured, it was mostly for liability in case someone got hurt there. As an abandoned school, the improvements hadn't been updated to the policy. That meant they had to raise money for the rebuilding which could have gone to more computers, more teachers. The loss wasn't Fredo's loss, but he took it that way.

Mia had been attentive and careful, which Fredo appreciated. She didn't attempt to draw him out in a discussion about his feelings, which was a blessing. She just used her feminine powers to distract Fredo. At this, Mia was qualified expert.

But Fredo had his biggest difficulty sleeping at night. At first he thought it was the vivid dream he had, as if he was afraid he'd have another one. His stomach was upset, and although he worked out nearly every day with Coop, he found himself losing weight. He'd always had the opposite problem. He doubled up on the vegetables and green spinach health food drinks, but it still left him restless and unable to properly sleep. He kept the worry to himself.

Fredo continued to take his vitamins, doubling them until his pee was bright yellow and smelled like Kim Chi. He drank from the juice bar daily, adding garlic and more greens to his mixture, learning to tolerate the taste. He even incorporated tofu into his diet, finding some stir-fry dishes he could tolerate. He was proud of the changes he was making. But he wasn't feeling healthier. Though Mia never complained, he smelled like garlic all the time.

But even with all this, sleep was still a problem for Fredo. He finally resigned himself to the fact that perhaps he needed to talk to Doc Brownlee, the unofficial Team psychiatrist. He made the appointment without Coop knowing, since Brownlee was Coop's father-in-law.

"Do you wake up in fear you'll have that dream again, Fredo?" Dr. Brownlee asked him one afternoon.

"I don't know. I really don't know. You tell me, Doc."

Brownlee laughed and crossed his long legs. He placed his fingers to his temple while loosely holding his pen. His handsome face erupted into a sly smile. "I like it when my patients have confidence in me, but that goes beyond what I can do. Just being perfectly honest. So let's explore deeper. Do I have your permission?"

Fredo wondered if Coop had told the doctor about his visit to the lab. "I do have something I need to tell Mia. I was going to tell her, but then the fire at the school happened, and we've been distracted."

"What do you have to share with Mia?"

"Well, in fact, it does have something to do with my dream. I'm sterile, doc."

"How do you know this?"

"I got checked out. My sperm are dead. They have dented heads, too."

Brownlee chuckled and stopped with difficulty. "I'm sorry. Just the way you say that—you're a funny guy, Fredo." The doctor reeled himself in quickly.

"Yeah, funny, but my lot in life is to raise someone else's kids."

"Fredo, I owe you an apology. Please forgive me for seeming to make light of this. I understand how important it is. That was not appropriate of me."

Fredo shook his head, not even registering what Dr. Brownlee had said. "Those lazy motherfuckers, lying there, like they'd run into something or had some vampire suck the life out of them." He snuck a look at Dr. Brownlee who was now nearly covering his whole face. He knew the guy was going to split a gut. It *was* kind of funny, if it wasn't so pathetic.

A minute ticked by, neither man watching the other. Fredo decided to be gracious and give Brownlee a chance to compose himself.

"I've known people who were raised by adoptive parents who felt very special because of that. They felt they were *chosen*, not just 'hatched' as they say."

He knew what the doc was trying to do, but Fredo felt defiant. "Doesn't work for me, Doc." He didn't want to go further into some of his fear Mia would find him unworthy. Hell, he felt unworthy of the beautiful woman who made his life complete. He couldn't imagine life without her.

"So what would it look like if you told her, Fredo, and she didn't take it the way you fear she might. Tell me what that would look like."

"I don't want to tell her."

"I get that. But if it did go well, how would you tell her, or what would you say?

"Honey, I'm sterile."

"I admire your honesty. You want to role play that?"

"With you?"

Brownlee smiled but didn't laugh. "I realize I'm a sorry excuse for your beautiful wife, but humor me. Let's role play."

"My sperm are dead, Mia."

"Does that feel better?"

"No."

"Then how else would you tell her? Or maybe, why is it important to tell her?"

"Because she asks me for a baby every time we make love, or nearly."

"So could you bear that, not telling her, and having her ask you all the time? If that was the only price, would that work for you?"

"No."

"And why not?"

"Because it's not fair to her. It's not the truth. I'd be play acting."

"Again, I admire your honor. That is a most admirable quality, Fredo. Answer me this, then. How would you feel if Mia couldn't have children and was hiding that fact from you?"

"I wouldn't care. I'd love her anyway."

"Don't you feel maybe she might react the same way? You just said you'd still love her if it were reversed. Why do you think her reaction would be any different?"

"I guess I just don't want to take a chance."

"A chance at what, Fredo?"

"A chance that she might find me lacking."

"So, how would you feel if you found out she wasn't being honest with you, had hidden this fact from you?"

"I'd feel like shit."

"Okay, and wouldn't you prefer knowing the truth, even if the truth wasn't something you wanted to hear?"

"What if she doesn't want me anymore? What if she thinks I'm damaged, not good enough for her?"

"Does she ever give you any indication of that? You pick that up from her at all?"

"No." Fredo's heart began to melt. He knew the time had come for him to come clean with her. But he still felt it was too soon.

"When you love someone, don't you love them, flaws and all?"

"But my wife *is* perfect. She has no flaws." Then Fredo grinned at the ridiculousness of his situation, meeting Dr. Brownlee's smile halfway. He actually used to believe this. He knew the doc would make a special note in his little book.

Brownlee was gentle. "I can appreciate a man who thoroughly loves his woman. I have thought the same of my wife for many years. She is perfect. Perfect for *me*. I couldn't bear not loving her, flaws and all, which is why I'll love her forever."

Fredo looked into his cool bright blue eyes and saw respect. Brownlee was indeed a man who understood his devotion to his wife.

"Don't you ever doubt yourself, Doc?"

"All the time."

"So how do you deal with it?"

"I got some great advice in medical school from one of my mentors. He said, '*If love doesn't solve the problem, then the cure for it is apply more love.*'"

"I don't think I could ever love her more."

"Love is trust, Fredo. How can you trust unless you allow someone to let you down, until you give someone the power to disappoint you? And you love them anyway. You honor her by telling her the truth. You give her the power to walk away, truly leave you, if she can't handle your truth. And in giving her that power, you demonstrate your love."

"So what you're saying is that what's keeping me up at night is that I am holding back."

"Perhaps that's part of it, Fredo. Only you will know, and you can't really know until you try it. Ask yourself this: wouldn't she love you enough even if she knew you couldn't father a child? Really?"

Fredo searched his hands laced together in his lap like he was in Sunday School as a boy. "I just don't want to take that risk, but no, I think she'd love me still."

"Love is risk. You risk it all when you fall in love. You allow yourself to be irreparably changed by the experience, right? You aren't forced to love. You *allow* yourself to love, *and be loved*. It's a gift to her, but it's an even greater gift to yourself."

The conversation with Dr. Brownlee made a severe impact on Fredo. He did feel calm and for the next several nights, while he thought about how he'd talk to Mia about his situation, he was even able to sleep without interruption.

Fredo took special care in their lovemaking. The morning and evening sessions with Mia were long and slow, heartfelt and tender like he'd never experienced before. Brownlee was right, more love was the cure for everything that ailed him.

Finally, with their impending deployment coming up in two months, he decided it was time to let her know his secret. As he locked the Center up and said good night to Julio, he decided to stop by and buy Mia some flowers, perhaps take her out to dinner if she wanted.

He called ahead to their favorite Thai restaurant and made a reservation. He picked up red long-stemmed roses at the florist for her. He bought her the perfume she loved and one of her favorite scented candles. He'd light it, and in the glow of the flame, he'd worship her flawless body with all he had. He'd give her everything, even the truth.

Mia was wearing a flowered silk bathrobe tightly tied at her slim waist. Fredo presented her with the roses and she inhaled their scent, closing her eyes and letting the aroma completely overtake her. He didn't think anyone could look so orgasmic as she did when she got flowers, and wished he made enough to give them to her every day.

She placed the long stems in water and then returned to focus on him. Her long curly hair hung softly around her shoulders and upper back and the familiar flower scent of her shampoo made his heart sing. She cooed as he took her into his arms, sliding under the cool silk to find her hot flesh beneath the robe, parting the sash, peeling the front open so he could gaze on her beautiful breasts.

Her eyes sparkled. Mia licked her lips, generously layered with cherry lip polish. Her eyes were made up alluringly. She'd spent time getting ready for him to come home, and it thrilled him.

"I was going to ask you to go out to dinner," he said as he kissed her neck, his hand finding its way between her legs. In the warm lips of her folds he found her nub and pinched it. She moaned and wrapped her thigh over his hip.

"Fuck me, Fredo."

"What about dinner?"

She flashed that wicked wild-child smile he loved and knew so well. "This," she said as she stepped back and dropped the robe to her feet, "is all you need tonight. I'm only hungry for you."

Fredo decided one more night of secrets wouldn't hurt. Tomorrow, he'd tell her the truth. But tonight, he didn't want to bask in anything but the love of this woman and the miracle that was their life together.

She pulled his hand, walking backward, naked, giving him a granite boner, almost making movement painful. Her head turned from one side to the other, as she showed her nakedness to him unashamed, her eyes calling to him.

"Where's Ricardo?" He realized Ricardo wasn't around.

"He's with Coop and Libby and the kids. All night. I told Libby it was a special night."

"A special night?"

She nodded. "Come here, Fredo." She continued to lead him backwards to their bedroom.

The bedspread was covered in rose petals. She had candles lit at the head of the bed, and the light Spanish guitar music he loved was playing softly. A chilled bottle of champagne was in a bucket at the foot of the bed.

"You did make special plans. I must have known somehow, sweet Mia."

She nodded. "Come here, Fredo. Have some champagne and then you make love to me all night long. Can you do that?"

Of course he could. Of that he was totally confident. He expected she'd say something about making babies, but was so grateful she said nothing.

The cork was popped, the glasses poured. He drizzled some down her front and lapped the sweet mixture from her chest, sucking her pert nipples. She took a tiny sip, then placed her glass on the bedside table.

"What's the special occasion?" he asked.

"Us." She undressed him, her fingers delicately cupping him, tracing long hot lines down his chest, down one thigh.

"I like us," he said, having difficulty breathing as she took him into her mouth. In a few swift strokes he was long and hard and aching to be inside her.

"Fredo, my love. I have wonderful news." She got to her feet, placing his palms on her breasts then bringing one down to her belly slowly. "You have done it. Inside this belly grows your child, Fredo. You have given me a baby. Our baby, my love."

CHAPTER 5

Fredo stared blindly at the sunlight streaming through the front window at Gunny's gym. He'd agreed to meet Coop later on for their regular PT workout, but he got impatient waiting the whole hour for his best friend, so he sat in his truck until Timmons opened the storefront.

Now he was seated on the padded bench, a twenty pound barbell in his left paw, resting between his curl reps.

The sun felt good splashing on his knees, warming his calves and upper thighs. Later in the day, they'd lower the blinds, but it was not necessary yet. He watched a young couple jog past the window, their lithe and upright bodies in perfect tandem with each other. Her blonde ponytail whisked back and forth, sweeping the top of her warm-up collar. His torso was fit, with a slim waist, and muscled arms, a square jaw covering up all emotion as he kept perfect step with her. They wore matching sunglasses.

Fredo's youth and early courtship and married life had nothing in common with this couple. Mia had spent their first few encounters nearly spitting on him as he longed for her day and night, certain that one day he could satisfy her. And, until last night, he thought he'd done a pretty good job of it, with one exception. Now there was a second exception looming as big as one of those cruise ships that docked at San Diego harbor.

She'd danced around the room, holding her belly, ecstatic that she'd finally gotten the news. He now realized, as he continued with his left arm curls, that it was perhaps the most important thing in her life. It suddenly all made sense. She'd been strangely quiet on the subject of getting pregnant the past couple of days.

When she'd told him, he nearly dropped his champagne glass on the bedroom carpet. His guts dropped to his knees. In that hollow space between his ribs he inhaled, sadness deflated his heart, now knowing she was unfaithful to him. This bitter fact cut him deeper than anything else he'd ever experienced. His once perfect love was now tarnished. What was he to do now?

Just to be sure, he'd even had the test re-done a week after his first results. The technician had given him the old thumbs up with the bitter comment, "So, my man, you got no worries. You can love all those ladies and never have to worry about a damned thing, if you take the normal precautions, of course."

The pimple-faced kid sporting peach-fuzz cheeks slipped off his latex gloves one finger at a time, a ritual he probably exercised a hundred times a day. The little specimen glass plate, containing the evidence of Fredo's failure as a true man, was tossed unceremoniously into the trash after the gloves.

That's where Fredo's happy spirit lay too. In the trash.

He wasn't sure he was good company, so told Mia he had to be gone for a few days of training, which was a complete fabrication just to give himself some space. He wasn't sure where he was going to go. Maybe he'd go down to the Center and work quietly. Maybe he'd go down to the Diocese office and beg for more donations by phone, since all their lists were there.

He didn't want to look up any of the married Team guys, and the single ones he found nothing in common with. He was going to let this one good and fester. He wasn't sure he'd ever recover from the effects of her betrayal. His shock was so great he couldn't even talk to her, couldn't look at her. He certainly wasn't going to reveal his paternity issue. He was sleepwalking, pretending, doing all the things he told the doc he wouldn't do. He just didn't know what else he could do.

He considered going up to Sonoma County for a couple of days, but that would raise too many eyebrows. Word would get out to the Team, and then the wives would find out, and soon Mia would get that "concerned" call from someone and he'd have to explain himself.

It was the first time in all his years of loving Mia that he really didn't want to go home. What made it so much worse was the fact that she was so excited and happy, flitting around the house, scantily clad, and not looking pregnant at all. He'd even had difficulty staying hard last night when she crouched over him, rode him in that beautiful way she had with him, trying to shower her love all over him. Every time he snuck a peek at her, his eyes watered. His heart felt like it had a fishhook in it, maybe two, pulling the two halves apart.

If she noticed anything, she didn't say so. She told Ricardo the news first thing that morning. The boy's big eyes were glued to Fredo's face as if getting direction on how to act. Mia was all over him, kneeling down, tying his shoes and combing his dark stubborn hair. Her motherly fussing annoyed Ricardo, especially when she covered his face with kisses, which she was famous for.

"It will be like your friends, like Ali and Griffin. Like Gillian and Will," she explained.

Ricardo had spent considerable time around other Team families, but Fredo could see he still didn't have the concept of a little brother or sister. Thinking about it now brought Fredo even more pain.

He discovered he'd lapsed into daydreams in the warm sunlight when he heard the little bell over the doorway at the gym. Without looking up, he knew it was Coop, because the shadow that fell over him also covered most of the corner of the place.

"Impressed am I," Coop said in his Yoda impersonation.

Fredo continued pumping, and then handed the barbell to his buddy. "Just trying to keep up."

"So you still having trouble sleeping?" Coop set down his bag, removed his warmup top and sat next to Fredo. The care and concern, even tenderness Coop showed him was normally something he could joke about, but today, Fredo was numb. He needed a whole day, maybe a whole week, to figure out how he really felt. Until then, he was a lethal combination of emotions on an inverted plane, where joy caused him pain and anger settled him down.

He'd have to be careful. They'd been trained to recognize these signs. It was a form of PTSD when a Team guy couldn't deal with his family in an appropriate way. There wasn't anything appropriate about being depressed that Mia was pregnant.

He wasn't worried he'd do anything dangerous, but he just couldn't process the fact that Mia had gotten pregnant. And the child was not, could never be, his.

Coop wisely stood up when he saw Fredo wasn't interested in talking.

"You guys coming to the barbeque Saturday?" Coop was stretching his long arms overhead and rolling his head from side to side. He lunged into thigh stretches before he sat facing the machine and began the overhead pull downs.

"I'm going to miss it. Collins has me going up to Sonoma County for a couple of days. I'm supposed to talk to the detectives who worked the Zapparelli Winery explosion."

"Really? Why didn't I hear that?"

Fredo had no problem lying to him. He needed to get away from all of them. Mia would be telling everyone today. He didn't want to be there when everyone started toasting him, patting him on the back and looking right into his eyes to see the joy was missing there. There was no escape from this community. There was no way these men he had fought with and nearly died with would miss what was going on with him. And Cooper would guess it in a heartbeat and would go digging with a dull spoon until his chest was a bloody mess.

"Mia and Ricardo going?"

Fredo shrugged and pretended to wipe down his neck but the sweat had long dried in the sun. He wished he was alone. He needed to be alone.

"So, asshole. You tell her yet?" Coop said in his casual drawl, turning around on the machine seat to face him.

Those were the words that launched Fredo over the edge like jumping from the Golden Gate Bridge. On his feet, he grabbed Cooper's tee shirt, pulling the giant's torso and face within inches of his own. Cooper's eyes opened in shock and Fredo was grateful for the hesitation that shock created. It gave him enough time to push off the giant and get more than swinging or grabbing distance away.

"Fuck sake, Fredo. What the hell's gotten into you?"

"Don't talk to me about that shit."

"That's fucked up, man." As Cooper stared up at something behind the display, Timmons came over with his spray bottle and a towel, discreetly listening for something he should not know about.

Fredo and Cooper were always joking with each other, but never angry. And Fredo had nearly given his best friend a punch that would have been hard to cover up. But instead, Fredo forced his arms down to his sides, flexing and unflexing his hands, grinding his teeth and trying to find something he could kick, hit or throw. He picked up the barbell, and Coop was immediately on him.

Timmons ran up behind and had the barbell removed from his grasp in two seconds. The spray bottle was at his feet, contents leaking out onto the rubber mats.

Fredo's two friends held him until he released his jaw, took a couple of deep breaths and dropped his shoulders. "I'm good," he whispered, nodding.

Carefully, Coop removed his hold on Fredo's arm and shoulder, his other arm coming from around Fredo's waist, taking a step that allowed a foot gap between their bodies.

With some of his tension waning, Fredo rolled his neck and shoulders and adjusted his balance. They stood before him, not saying a word, doing him the honor of coming clean on his own. But Fredo didn't want to tell the whole world. He didn't even want to tell Coop what was really eating him. He eyed Timmons in a stare-down. Their former handler lowered his gaze and went back to work spraying cleaner on the equipment and quietly moved away.

So that left Coop, his hands on his hips.

"I gotta keep it tight, Coop. I'm not telling anyone about my issue. But Mia came home last night and told me she's pregnant. And Coop, there is no fuckin' way it's mine."

"Maybe things reversed."

"Impossible, Coop. I retested. They told me no fuckin' way."

"So how's she acting?"

"She's on cloud nine. She's beautiful. My God, Coop, my wife's the most beautiful fuckin' thing in the whole world, and some other guy knocked her up."

"That can't be."

"Remember what I said? I got re-tested. They said no way."

"So get re-tested again."

"No."

"Why the fuck not?"

Fredo held up his thumb and index finger, measuring something smaller than a molecule. "I got a tiny grain of hope that it's mine. Some million to one thing I'm holding on to. I'm gonna pretend she's pregnant with my fuckin' dented headed sperm."

"But don't you want to know?"

"No. I'm gonna cling to that belief. If I go get tested and they tell me I'm still sterile, then I'll know she did it—"

Fredo whipped around, showing Coop his back as he ground his teeth, picked up his towel and threw it at the front of the gym. Once sure that he wouldn't break out into a little boy cry, he resumed his stance in front of his best friend.

"I'm gonna work hard on it until I believe that fairy tale. I'm gonna pretend I fathered that kid, because that's the right thing to do. But I gotta get adjusted to the idea. She's being the best actress in the world, trying to make me feel like a million bucks. I have to match that act, and right now, I can't do it. I need time. I need a couple of days to clear my head. I need to figure out who she screwed first. And then, Coop, swear to God, I'm gonna kill him."

"You want company? I mean with the couple of days to go clear your head. Not sure I wanna go kill someone."

"I'm horrible company. Horrible."

"But you want my horrible company or not, asshole?"

"Sure. Why not? How could things get any worse?"

Fredo knew his words wounded Coop, but he could also tell by the way the guy squinted at him that he was fully in control, that he understood Fredo's pain and the need for just brotherhood stuff. Besides that, Coop's armor was strong. He'd be prepared for whatever shit Fredo would throw at him.

Coop started out raspy, choosing his words carefully. "Well, on that getting worse shit? She could be pregnant by a zombie and that kid she births could eat Ricardo. Now that would be some serious shit—"

Fredo reached for the towel, but he couldn't get it in time, so he stood right in front of Coop and shouted, "Shut The Fuck Up!!" The visions of all those toddlers in his dream were too zombie-like for his own tastes.

The room went deathly silent. Timmons didn't make a sound. Fredo's outburst was so loud, an older lady jogging down the Strand jumped and then walked in front of Gunny's Gym window. Cooper revealed a perfectly formed shit-eating grin.

"Okay." Coop began, glancing sideways. "I'm going to go home and pretend you didn't say that. I'm going to tell Libby I'll be with you and I'll tell her, what? We're up in Healdsburg?" he finished as he rolled his shoulders and extended his palms.

Fredo nodded.

"Okay, man. I gotta go check out my tourist wardrobe. I gotta fuckin' dress up like a fuckin' yuppy. We're gonna go wine tasting!"

CHAPTER 6

Fredo and Coop stopped by the Center before heading up the freeway for the ten-hour trip to Sonoma County. Reconstruction had been going well. Like before, when the gang who used to tag the buildings set fire to one of the classrooms, the community rallied together and several local contractors and business owners jumped in to donate money and services. They wouldn't have enough to finish everything, but Fredo was confident they'd get there with fundraising activities. The publicity of the fire and the devastatingly poor community surrounding the Center made for great news, which brought in donors from all over the world.

"This place is going to be better than before, Fredo." With his hips slanted, hands resting gently over his khakis where a belt would have been, Coop shook his head in amazement.

Fredo was grateful he'd have something like this to occupy his time away from Mia when he got back from the trip. Every day he used to thank his maker for sending Mia into his life, and now every day that thought sent an arrow through his chest.

But he knew it wasn't healthy to walk around in such fear and dread. So this would give him a legitimate excuse to feel happy until the rest of it could be resolved. But right now his stomach felt like it hadn't digested Thanksgiving Dinner—from last year.

"What's that?" Coop pointed to the rounded framed wall of the new mini-auditorium. The kids were going to have a state-of-the-art sound and recording studio, all donated by a country band from Nashville who heard about the Center. One of the returning SEALs, who was now making documentaries, had been hired to teach filmmaking and drama to the local children. Phones were ringing off the hook from parents of kids from wealthier districts of San Diego County who wanted to attend. Best thing about the whole project, there would be no debt, which meant they could afford to pay some decent salaries.

"We can use this building partially for Amornpan's dancing classes," Fredo remarked. He was in awe at how fast everything was progressing.

"Need to get Jameson in here to give some concerts then."

"Not sure we can convince him, but he did say he'd give guitar lessons. He's great with kids."

Julio showed up just as Fredo and Coop were headed to Coop's Hummer.

"Hey there, ghost," Fredo said to the youth.

"Nothing for me down here. I've offered to help them, but these contractors aren't interested."

"You should just concentrate on your school. When the holidays come around next summer, Julio, you could do so much around here."

"Whatever. Just tryin' to help." Julio shrugged.

Fredo knew he was irritated. Consistency was non-existent in the kid's life, and Fredo felt bad for him. But there wasn't anything more he could do. He saw the kid had something on his mind.

"Listen, Julio. You know not everyone understands you guys. We got white guys down here, in construction, and they're, well they're sort of afraid. They don't trust you yet. In time, maybe they will. You gotta start out slow, give them a chance."

"You didn't."

"Well, that's because where I grew up makes this place look like a country club, Julio. Give people time. Most everyone wants to be decent. Just be cool, and eventually it will work out, man."

The kid rolled his shoulders in a half shrug. "I gotta tell you some things."

"Shoot."

"You talk to the police?" Julio had that sideways glance that told Fredo he was more interested in his answer than he wanted to let on. The gang kids all had that casual air the belied something deeper and usually sinister. Julio had fallen into a sullen manner of some kind and appeared to have a blackening mood. He even started to walk like some of the other kids. That gait their fathers and brothers taught them, the prison walk. That worried Fredo, so he'd have to be careful.

"Not anymore. Not much anyway. Corcoran as much as told me if we didn't hear anything in a week or two, nothing would probably ever be done. We can't expect miracles here."

"They aren't doin' *anything*," said the boy.

"Well, they're busy all over the City. I'm sure they feel understaffed, from what I hear from some of my friends on the force."

"We're not important to them." Julio's eyes were downcast. Fredo was right to be concerned and wished he didn't see the new change in him.

"Don't say that, Julio. You must respect those guys. They have a tough job. And those contractors? They just don't know you."

"No one has seen anyone in uniform since the blast. It's like they're staying away."

"Why? You didn't really expect they'd find the kids, did you?"

Now Julio seemed reluctant to open up. Fredo glanced up at Coop, who was slow to catch on, but he jumped like he'd been hit with lightning when he realized it was his cue to exit the stage.

"Oh, I forgot to get that card I came down here for, Fredo. If you'll excuse me?" Coop smiled a little wider for Fredo's benefit.

While watching Coop jog toward the crew of framers, Julio was fussing with his toe in the dirt. He wasn't meeting him eye-to-eye. The walk, his stance, everything he saw in Julio was more like the gang kids.

"You okay, Julio? Everything okay at home?"

The boy stiffened, bracing against something. Fredo began to smell fear. Maybe that's what had been bottled up and was causing him pain. He wasn't yet a man, and no doubt he was feeling the burden of trying to protect his sister and mother. It was an impossible task, especially for someone so young. It broke Fredo's heart that there wasn't a clear way to get him out of the neighborhood. Fredo wished he could save them all.

"Everything's fucked, man." Julio still didn't look at him.

"You gotta look me straight in the eye when you say that." Fredo made it a whisper so no one would have a chance of hearing it.

Julio nodded and gave him a quick, angled stare, but then diverted his eyes and went back internal. Fredo was going to say something, but stopped when Julio began to talk, finally.

"Remember when I told you those guys were hanging around Lupe? You know, that night?"

"Sure do."

"I thought they was just punks. New punks come in from LA or somewhere. But they bought the Christian CME church two blocks over on Clovis."

"Wait a minute. You mean those young assholes bought the church? Where the hell did they get money for that? And besides, that thing needs to be torn down."

"And that's what they're gonna do."

"So you're thinking they're selling drugs and with the drug money they bought that church? What would they want with that old thing?

Julio shrugged, shaking his head, *No.*

"Buy a fuckin' church for a hangout? That takes some *cojones!*"

"No, Fredo. They aren't punks or even young kids."

Fredo knew he wasn't going to like what the kid had to say next. "But you said—"

"I was wrong, Fredo. They're building like an enterprise. An office of sorts. These guys are really organized. Organized crime."

"Fuckin' A, they are not." Fredo's stomach lurched.

"They're goin' around the neighborhood, telling everyone they are here to take over from Caesar and Sonny and the others. Like it's their turf now. And these guys, they don't mess around."

"So why would they blow up the school? That's a hell of a way to win over converts."

"See, that's the thing, Fredo. They're asking our help to find the guys who did this. They said it wasn't them. They're here to stay, Fredo. Or die going to war. We're fuckin' stuck right in the middle."

A half-hour after the Hummer threaded through the grapevine from Los Angeles, Coop pulled off the freeway to get gas and some sandwiches.

Fredo left for the men's room while Coop gassed the Hummer. After re-parking the beast, they entered the coffee shop where Fredo ordered a chicken salad and bought Coop an egg sandwich. The tall Nebraska SEAL had iced tea while Fredo ordered his usual cappuccino.

Clutching the salad in his right hand, Fredo followed Coop to a table in the corner and sat across from him. He'd have to go back for the coffee later when his name was called.

Coop made lots of noise unwrapping the cellophane from his sandwich.

Fredo knew his buddy was trying to needle him into talking. They'd not said a word for three hours while on the road.

"Not sure it's possible to make any more noise with that wrapper than you are right now, Coop. You win the prize." Fredo knew he'd get a wisecracking remark in return.

"Good. Sure as hell gives me something to listen to since you're as tight-lipped as a virgin on her wedding night."

That wasn't so bad. Fredo knew Coop was being careful. He looked around and didn't see anyone paying particular attention to either of them.

"Look, you gotta tell me what Julio thought was so important you had to do it in private," Coop whispered. "I know something's wrong when you don't give me shit about my driving or my choice in music."

"Quad large cappuccino for Fred?" The barista yelled out.

"Fuck," Fredo whispered under his breath and left to retrieve his drink. He knew Coop was right.

"Thank you, Fred," the cheerful barista said.

Fredo restrained himself easily, not for the name mishap, but for the kid's cheerfulness. He didn't think anyone could be that happy giving out a cappuccino, not with what else was going on in the world.

He'd not been able to put into words all the dark worry he'd been harboring. As he returned, he scanned the room again for someone who might be too interested and found nothing of importance, so he turned his attention back to Cooper.

"I don't think the cops are gonna find these guys, and if they do, there won't be anything they can do." He dug into his salad without waiting for Coop's reaction. He was famished and knew that in another hour he'd be starved for ice cream, chips and cookies. That was a sure sign he was worried, but it helped him cope.

"And why is that?"

"Cause they're not who we think they are. They're building a fuckin' criminal enterprise," Fredo said to the top of Coop's head. Cooper had leaned into his sandwich to take another enormous bite, his mouth wide open, anticipating the food. That last comment got him sitting straight up pulling back from the sandwich as if it were made of poison.

"You gotta be kidding me."

"Wish I was. First, they do this little war against the project that threatened their takeover. Then they show us their balls by buying the old Missionary church a couple of blocks away. You ever hear of gangs buying old buildings to make money off of or run their enterprise from? They're here to stay."

"Is this a done deal or what?"

Fredo knew he had to get confirmation. "It's just what Julio told me. I've been thinking about this the whole start of this trip. Something wrong with it. Smells funny."

"They do this right under the radar. No one would object there. They do their form of community outreach and we do ours." Coop's head was moving from side to side. "Except their final solution and ours are two totally different goals."

"Yup." Fredo crumpled up his napkin into the empty cardboard bowl and threw his fork into the middle of it. He sat back to stretch and then placed his forearms back on the table and leaned in. "We keep the older kids busy learning how to use computers, how to paint and work a stage performance—"

The two SEALs stared at one another across the table as the full import hit both of them at the same time.

Coop finished Fredo's thought. "While they steal their sisters and the little kids, sell them for slaves, put drugs in their veins, and tell everyone to have a nice day."

"But Coop, the one thing that doesn't make sense is why the hell they'd blow up the school, or go around asking about it. Why would they bring that much scrutiny onto themselves?"

"You're right. Doesn't make any sense at all."

By the time the two SEALs made their final stop, they were only an hour from Sonoma County. The late fall day was clear. The bright blue sky was dotted with "clotted sheep" clouds, as Fredo liked to call them. Near San Francisco's Golden Gate Park, they stopped for a water for Coop and another coffee for Fredo.

Fredo's phone rang.

"This is Detective Clark Riverton, returning your call, Mr. Chavez. What can I do for you?" The crusty detective had been a friend to the SEALs over the years and was a close friend of the good doc, Coop's father-in-law.

"Thanks for calling, Detective Riverton." Fredo raised his unibrow to Coop, who nodded understanding. "We got some information about the St. Rose School fire—"

"You mean bombing, son. It's been officially ruled a bombing," corrected Riverton.

"Good. We agree. I'm with Coop, and we're up in Northern California for a couple of days."

"Greetings to Coop. Now, what can I do you for? I've got a meeting to get to."

"I'm in contact with one of the local kids from the neighborhood, Julio Hernandez."

"I'm familiar with the family. I've not had the pleasure, but I've met his sister."

"Yes. He's a good kid. Helps me with the project. He's my eyes and ears in the community. And I trust him."

"Go on, Mr. Chavez."

"He mentioned to me there has been little police visibility as far as questioning the neighbors who might have seen something about the bombing. And he also said something else. He told me a group has been hanging around. They're probably from Central America, but they're a real tough bunch. Not locals at all. And, they have money."

"I'm afraid it happens all the time. They know how to blend in well, especially if they have ill intent. We can't tell who's new and who grew up there. So go on. Where is this leading me, because I gotta go."

"They've bought property just a block or so away. An old CME church. And they're developing plans to turn it into a clubhouse, like our Center."

"So maybe you guys work together? That what you're sayin?"

"No. No way. I don't trust them, sir. But you gotta know Julio says they've been asking who blew up our building. It's like they want to be the only game in town. They've been offering their services, to help."

Riverton paused, and Fredo could almost hear the squeaky wheels turning in the detective's head. After a long minute, he exhaled and said something to someone else nearby, with his hand muffling the phone. He returned to the conversation without apologizing.

"And you definitely see them as not connected to the bombing?"

"Julio's sure they didn't do it."

After a brief pause, Riverton asked, "Can you get the kid to come into my office? Probably safer for him if we do it that way. I can interview him in safety without worrying about eyes on us. Maybe he can help us find these guys, ask them a few questions."

"I'll try to get word to him, no promises."

"Good. Anything else?"

"They're telling the folks they're going to help them."

"That sounds like what a couple of groups up North did. Some of them turned out to be legit, though, Mr. Chavez. Actually did some good work. So what's your point?"

"They're trying to buy favors. Coming in like they're new best friends."

"Just like the old gangs did in New York way back when. Good thing you guys got there first."

"So, Riverton, you gotta admit, that school might have been a target not only for what it was, but for who's behind it."

"You run afoul of any locals?"

"Well, Caesar, Sonny. Just the usual gangs who prey off the local population. Maybe they don't like that we're trying to free them. In other words, maybe because people know SEAL Team 3 has taken it on as one of their pet projects, it put a target on the place."

"I'd say it's more because you've left a vacuum and are filling it with good deeds. Well, I appreciate the good intel. I'll check with the force and see what's going on. The Feds are working on it now, so I don't think you'll see many beat cops want to get involved. And they probably can't even if they wanted to. Cops get killed over stuff like this."

"I was thinkin' the same way, sir. So can you find out about the investigation? I'm a concerned citizen and I don't want to mess with the Feds." Just like there was a degree of jealousy the SEALs had to endure with regular Navy guys, not those who tried out for the Teams, but regular Navy assholes, there was some professional lack of respect and trust between the SEALs and several Federal agencies. A long-standing source of this was the Federal Government's wanting to meddle in some of the secret tactics the SEALs used. The community worried some of their ranks could be called to task for how they operated overseas.

"Let me see. Not sure I'll get much. But I'd need to share this. I'll only release the information if I have to."

"Don't go giving out Julio's name."

"I'll protect your little guy. But you get him in here for an interview. That's what's going to put the wheels in motion, my friend."

Fredo heard background talking.

"Sorry, I gotta go. Give him my cell, would you?"

CHAPTER 7

When the two SEALs crossed the Golden Gate, the bright red of the girders contrasted well with the perfect blue of the sky and the grey waters. Fredo had always loved this view of the City on a nearly clear day. The white buildings of the city's skyline, along with the red and the blue, always gave him a patriotic boost. It was a welcome feeling. He was doing good. He was helping people live their ordinary lives, which included sailing, shopping, and walking the bridge. People from all over the world took the trek as if it were a right of passage.

"You know how they got the bridge built, Fredo?"

"Something about getting tourists up north? Devon or someone was talking about it," answered Fredo. He was grateful Coop was allowing the conversation to drift from all the problems brewing.

"Some engineer wanted to bring traffic up to the redwoods and the Russian River resort areas. In those days, people had to travel all around the bay and come up the other side or by ferry, and some came by steamer to Petaluma, all the way to downtown via the Petaluma River."

"There used to be a ferry to Treasure Island, too," said Fredo.

"Yup. Ferries all over the place. Before cars were used. Now we go zipping around when it took people a whole day to travel up north. How things have changed."

"And stayed the same. I'll bet the Gold Rush spurred a lot of that."

"Fortunes lost, fortunes gambled away, and fortunes won. San Francisco has a sordid history. Would be interesting to go spend a few days sometime and look over the maritime museums here. They dig up ships all the time when they build new buildings in the City. Lots of history. Half the financial district was part of the bay at one time."

Fredo examined the green hills and turnoff to the art community at Sausalito. "That guy was right. Damned pretty up here. You come up, and you want to stay."

Coop chuckled. "I'd say it's snagged some of our buds."

"Wasn't the guy who designed the bridge from Sonoma County?" Fredo asked.

"That he was," said Coop. "You see those pictures of the cars crossing the bridge? He's the guy in the top hat in the middle. He did a favor for the whole North Bay."

"But they got a lot more cars."

"And a lot more revenue. I think he went into banking, was a friend of the Stanfords. It was his theory more business could be done if they didn't have to ride the ferry from San Francisco."

"Smart man. I guess it worked."

"Danny was telling me there is oral history among the Natives in this area about the land being connected, and then during one long migration they came and found a bay there. Scientists think it was caused by an earthquake."

"I'll bet that was a shock," said Fredo.

They took the turnoff north of Healdsburg, traveling the winding road which cut through green and golden hills of lush grapevines. They'd decided this time to stay at Zak and Amy's Frog Haven winery, the new project the SEALs were involved in. Nick and Devon were adjusting to life with their toddler and were in the midst of finishing up crush. Coop suggested they do a little sweat equity for the couple. Fredo knew it would be good for him to put all his concerns out of his mind with the manual labor working in the vineyard would provide.

As they neared the turnoff for Frog Haven Winery, Coop cleared his throat and asked the question Fredo knew was on the tip of his tongue the whole drive up.

"So, when are you going to tell her?"

"Not today."

"You're playing with fire, Fredo. But then, I already told you it was a dumb idea."

"Worse if I don't know what to say and how to say it."

Coop was going to interrupt, but Fredo cut him off. "Look." He placed his hand gently on the giant's forearm, firmly. "I know you're doing what you think is best for me, and thank God I got a friend like you, Coop. But you're gonna have to trust me."

Coop once again tried to say something.

"No, Coop. Hear me out. Why ask the question before I'm one hundred percent sure I can live with the answer? I owe her that much. I don't want to ask her until I'm certain I can behave like a gentleman with whatever her answer is."

"But maybe it's not going to be that bad, Fredo. Would you give her some credit? She wouldn't do that to you, man."

"Our hearts want to believe what our hearts believe, Coop. I gotta be okay if that's not the truth."

"I just think you're putting your mind in a double bend when you might not have to."

Fredo peered into Coop's unblinking, bright blue eyes. "Might. You said might. We plan for every eventuality. I never thought this would happen, and then it did. I gotta plan for all the possible outcomes. *All* the possible outcomes. And then make myself adjust to what that is."

"Look at the odds, Fredo."

"I'm not a betting man, Coop. I'm not talking about odds. I'm talking about certainty. Things already are uncertain. I'm eliminating one unknown by being prepared for it."

He knew Coop could understand in time. Coop shook his head, looking up and smiling at their one-eyed former teammate, Zak, dressing more like a pirate every day. Zak had accepted his station in life. Fredo wondered if he ever could accept the fact that Mia had been—might still be—unfaithful to him.

While Coop went inside with Zak, Fredo held his hand up as he dialed Mia.

"*Mi amore.* You are safe?" she said in her sexy Puerto Rican accent.

"Yes, Mia. Coop and I just arrived at the winery. You should see how beautiful it is up here." He intended on keeping his conversation to the weather and the scenery, topics he thought would be safe.

"Ah, well, we'll take a nice romantic vacation up there someday after the little one is born. How was the trip?"

"Uneventful and long."

"Poor Fredo. I wish I could give you one of my most famous naked back rubs."

Fredo found himself fantasizing about some of the things they'd done, covered in massage oil. Her fingers were adept at finding just the right spots that kicked his libido into overdrive. His dark mood was slipping away. That was making him hard, much to his surprise. Everything about Mia sent him wonderful places.

"How are you feeling, Mia?" His voice was raspy.

"I'm missing you too much. But my belly feels soft and warm. Your little one grows stronger by the hour."

That brought on visions of his dream.

"Good. I miss you too." His words stuck in his throat. His eyes filled with tears. The emotional reaction was unexpected. He'd run away from this delicate, lovely creature, and he was convinced, despite his worries and suspicions, that she loved him with all her heart. He wanted to ask her, *Mia, why did you do this?* But he couldn't bring himself to. Not yet.

"Missing me is good, *mi amore*. It will make when we are together again that much nicer...you'll see. I promise."

No doubt she'd make it an occasion of a lifetime. He closed his eyes and willed his negativity to subside. Inhaling, he worked on his concentration, asking for clarity in the fog of emotions.

"Fredo, is there something wrong?"

His eyes popped open as his spine stiffened. He clutched the cell phone so hard he thought it might break. Again, he closed his eyes, inhaled one long breath, and answered her, "I'm fine. Just missing you is all."

"Three days. You'll be back in three days, right?"

"Yes, Mia. Two days here and one day driving back."

"I can hardly wait. I want to show you some little clothes I picked out today. And Shannon is helping me pick out some colors for the nursery. Luci and the kids came over today. You should see how well little Ali fits in. He and Ricardo are like brothers already. He loves Legos. Oh, Fredo, my love, it's going to be a wonderful year."

"Mia, I want you to go careful on the buying things. We must save now."

"Yes, but I just wanted these little things to look at. It makes me so happy, *mi amore*."

"Let's just be careful for a little while. Promise me, okay? We don't have enough to waste it. Especially now."

"Yes, my love."

She nearly wouldn't let him get off the phone. This was a routine of theirs, seeing who could hold on the longest, stringing the kisses and the good-byes to minutes, sometimes many minutes. Today he was pretending to participate. And with each good-bye he felt more and more guilty. She was going to find out and had already suspected something was up with him. Time was running out and soon he'd have to face the truth about his suspicions.

Amy had a light supper ready for them. Coop had already showered so Fredo followed, setting out his things in the spare bedroom he was sharing with Coop, then he joined everyone at the dinner table.

The conversation was light-hearted and soon Fredo allowed himself to relax. He made a comment about Zak's choice of costume. "You're really taking on this pirate role big time, Zak." Silence descended out while everyone waited for him to continue. "I mean that in a good way. You could use it in your marketing."

Amy took Zak's hand. "We're all proud of how he's doing. He's found his calling. I can't wait for the tasting room to be built. This guy would be able to sell sand to Arabs."

"It's a role I'm practicing for. I think it fits, since I have to wear the patch." He smiled then leaned down and kissed Amy's hand. "Truth is, I'm seeing more and more light in this eye every day. The images are still blurry though."

"That can happen, Zak. But best not to get your hopes up. It does mean you're getting blood supply to that eye, though, and we like that." Coop's medic training rivaled what some physicians saw in Emergency Rooms every day.

"You ever thought about what you'd do after the Teams, Coop? I think you'd make one hell of a doctor," Zak answered.

Coop chuckled, nearly spitting out his green beans. "Libby would like that, especially if I became a plastic surgeon." The handsome SEAL smiled to his group of diners. "I just work it one day at a time. But Libby's dad said if it wasn't for some investment in some crazy winery, he might have the money to send me to medical school."

That drew a round of laughter.

"Zapparelli wants to come over later, if you guys are up to it. He's become a good friend," said Zak.

Fredo recalled the movie director-turned-winemaker coming over to cook pasta at Nick and Devon's barely a month after terrorists had blown up his own winery. He'd been wrong about the gruff movie director. He was a hard-working guy who sized up people about as well as the Team guys did.

"Why not? He going to help us tomorrow?" Fredo asked.

Zak nearly spit out his beer. "Hardly! Fredo, he likes to be in charge."

"He really has helped us quite a bit. Especially with some of the contract deals we've been negotiating," added Amy. "Not everyone gets along with him, but they sure do respect him."

"How's the rebuild going over at his place?" Coop asked.

"Place looks like an anthill. He's going to get a brand new winery out of it." Zak took another sip of his beer. Fredo looked at the bottle carefully, squinting.

"You serve me this stuff, and look what you've got. That's your beer, Zak, right?"

"It's our test run of Frog Piss. Didn't want to poison you. Not all the way happy with it yet. But hell, if you want one, you can have it."

"Holy crap, Zak. You've been holding out on us," barked Coop.

Zak brought out two green bottles with tan and green labels, the *coat of arms* being a bone frog with Trident spears. "This is pretty young still. It will get more mellow and more carbonated, and then it will be really good." He handed a bottle to both of them, but Coop passed his back.

"Coop, I didn't think you'd pass up drinkin' in your old married age," Zak teased.

"Nope. I'm the designated driver. If this one wants to go wine tasting, I drive. He's not allowed.

"Nothing wrong with my driving." Fredo allowed himself to get slightly offended.

"Just ask the others on the road, Fredo. This leaves more for you, my friend." He handed the bottle to Fredo and then nudged it with his long fingers.

"To Frog Piss," said Zak. Everyone toasted, Amy and Coop with their ice water glasses held high.

Fredo examined the label, "Because drinking pond scum is better than water." He chuckled. "That's your motto?"

"Yessir. We got another one for the stout." Zak jumped up and retrieved an envelope out of a desk drawer in the pantry, tossing it across the table to Fredo and Coop.

Fredo opened the flap and pulled out a shiny black label with the white Punisher skull in the middle, glaring with red eyes. Beneath that was the name of the brew, *Punish Yourself Beer.* Fredo held it up. "Even better. This one's a moneymaker."

"We've toyed around with lots of labels. Really having quite a good time. We've had contests on Facebook," added Amy.

"I didn't know your hops could grow that fast," said Fredo, taking another sip and then making a face. "Wow, that's kinda bitter."

"No, we won't be ready with our own hops until next year. These we bought," said Zak.

"Wait until you see the vines," Amy started. "The rows are like walking in a giant cathedral. They go up nearly thirty feet tall. Hops grow like weeds around here."

"So can you sell this crop, or are you looking to go into beer production?" asked Fredo.

"I guess a little bit of both. But we wouldn't make much on the hops." Zak looked at Amy. "She's working with Zapparelli to help get the necessary permits. Luckily, we already had the zoning for the tasting room. But you have to get permits and inspections for every operation, from crush, to barreling, to brewing beer. But the hardest permit to get, and the reason this property was such a good deal, was because they already had the permit for the tasting room. They don't just dish those out like candy. It's controlled. And all the equipment and operation is heavily regulated and inspected."

"I think Zak's a frustrated chemist," Amy said, blushing. "He loves to tinker with the equipment."

All three SEALs laughed. "Oh, we know all about that," said Coop, giving her red face a wink. "Fine tuning is our specialty."

"Hola!" said a booming voice from the front room. Into the doorway marched Mr. Marco Zapparelli himself, carrying two bottles of wine. "Gifts for the lady of the house," he said, leaning down to give Amy a kiss on both cheeks. He presented her with the wine, which had a plain label, something scrawled in felt-tipped pen. Zapparelli appeared to have gained considerable weight.

"Thank you, Marco." Amy looked at the labels. "You're experimenting again. Not sure I can read your writing."

"One is my blended Cab. Most of the fruit is from here, but I added about a fifteen-percent mixture from my Napa vineyard. This one," he held up the second bottle, "is a blended

Cab and Cabernets Franc. See which one you like best. We had some fun in the lab today."

Zapparelli grabbed a couple of jelly jars they used as wine glasses then returned to the table, pulling up a chair between Amy and Zak. Coop declined a glass, so the four of them tasted the two wines carefully. Zapparelli discussed the virtues of both blends and pointed out the wine's character. Fredo could see they were getting a world-class education from the famous director. They'd given him a small glass to sample. He hated to tell them that both wines tasted the same to him. But then, he only used red wine to make Sangria at home. This was probably not the time to mention such things.

"So…you come up here to work in the vineyard, yes?"

Coop and Fredo nodded, along with Zak.

"Just a little change of pace. We had a couple of days, decided to come up and visit, see how they're doing," Coop lied.

"These kids have a good nose for the business. That, and they have a first-rate vineyard manager. I'm sad to say we had a falling out some years ago, so we can't work together, but he's too good to let go. They'll win some awards if they are able to keep him."

"Amy tells us you are rebuilding. When do you open again?" Fredo asked.

"Officially? We are fast-tracked for fourteen months from now, but it's an ordeal." He shook his head, staring down at the table.

Fredo could see worry lines cross the director's forehead. He decided to wait to see if there was something Zapparelli wanted to offer, so he wouldn't have to pry. It didn't take long.

"The crime scene was horrific. I'm just now putting the images of those kids—" He looked off to the side, leaning into his palm, elbow braced on the table. "Horrible. Just horrible."

Fredo could only imagine. He'd seen similar things, and he was prepared in advance and trained to deal with it. But seeing innocent loss of life was never easy and always took a chunk out of a man's stamina. *When confronted with hell everyone deals with it differently,* he thought. Zapparelli was a civilian and certainly not prepared for what he had to endure.

"No one should have had to witness that carnage. No one. It will take time, and I warn you, some of it never goes away," whispered Cooper.

Zapparelli nodded, then focused back on Fredo's face, breaking a broad smile. "Of course, nothing interferes with the harvest. Luckily, the fruit processing and fermentation tanks and bottling areas were untouched. But the restaurant, the bar and tasting room—unrecognizable. Gone."

"And your movie collection." Fredo hoped it would jar him loose of the horrors he could see residing in the man's head.

Zapparelli shrugged with a kind smile. "For what they were insured for, I'm good with it. I also have a whole warehouse of old movie sets and props. Now I'm glad I was such a packrat. My wife had been getting after me to auction them off or donate them to a museum or my alma mater, UCLA. I will, after we make our final selections."

"Anyone from the Feds get in touch with you about the terrorist group?" Fredo wanted to know.

"I've given up calling for updates. I think everyone feels it was a cell sent to do this. Or perhaps they just stumbled upon the children's program."

"They gave you a letter first, didn't they? A warning?"

"My Head of Security got a call from someone and then a call from the Healdsburg police. No one believed it was going to happen." He held his jelly glass up. "To your Elvis SEAL, who also was a mighty fine shot. Wouldn't be here today enjoying this fine evening without that guy."

Coop and Fredo answered with their own glasses, "To Jameson."

CHAPTER 8

Zak and Amy retired for the night. Coop talked to his kids via Facetime. Fredo could hear Gillian's voice carry, echoing through the kitchen and all the way out to the patio. Coop was patient with her and it was fairly plain to see she adored him and vied for all his attention, giving her little brother as little airtime as possible.

Zapparelli smiled. "Nice, isn't it. Hearing them. Life goes on."

Fredo nodded. He was glad the man lived next door and had driven a Jeep the back way since Zapparelli had consumed quite a bit of wine. He was waxing eloquent sitting in the warm night air under the stars and a nearly full moon. The romance and feel of this place was soothing, full of magic. The grapes were bursting or fermenting in their stainless steel coffins. Coyotes were howling as if time stood still. It had been like this for generations here in the Dry Creek Valley.

Coop was now whispering into the phone, chuckling to the sounds of his wife enticing him to just pick up everything and drive straight home.

Zapparelli watched this too, appreciative. "How long's he been married?"

Fredo had to think. He leaned back in the rocking chair, peering at the stars, as if they held the answer. "I'm thinking maybe four years. Kyle was the first to get married, and then Coop met Libby soon after."

"You guys always been close?"

"Right from the first day at BUD/S."

"What's BUD/S?"

"Basic Underwater Demolition/SEAL."

"No shit?"

"The Navy isn't known for their creativity, sir. It is what it is. But I can't complain. It's been a good life. And Coop's been the best friend a guy could have."

"How come he doesn't drink?"

"He had an accident when he was younger and blames himself for the death of someone dear to him."

"I can't add the number of cars I've totaled. Haven't killed anybody, though."

"There's still time," Fredo winked, and both men chuckled.

"They're hell up here. Got a Federal prosecutor just to convict DUIs. That's her full time job, and she's busted most of my winery owner friends too."

"Well, it is a serious issue. We laugh at your wrecked cars, but the truth is we don't want people drinking and driving. Such a tragedy. Coop will never get over it."

"I get a cab or a driver now," said Zapparelli.

"Smart."

Coop's whispers ceased, and they figured he'd gone to bed.

"You miss not being in LA?" Fredo asked the director.

"Not on a night like tonight. There isn't any place in the whole world as beautiful as this. Just look at what we have here, Fredo. Do you know how many people the whole world over would give everything they had for just one night here, under the moon and stars?"

Fredo agreed. "What got you started in the wine business?"

"My great-grandfather's family all were winemakers. But in Sicily, that's what you do. Either olives or wine. They used to make it in glass milk bottles. My grandmother kept a barrel in the bathtub at her apartment in San Francisco. She never stopped making wine, even in her nineties."

"So I guess it's in your blood."

"Just a tad. When I got out of high school, funny how I didn't appreciate that at all. Film school was way sexier. Girls wanted to marry a director or a famous actor. That was way more to my liking."

Another coyote howled in the distance, setting off a chain of dog barks.

"So what really brings you up here, Fredo?"

Zapparelli swiveled in his chair, adjusting his legs to allow him to turn in Fredo's direction.

Fredo felt the pressure of the director's perusal. "Just needed to clear my head. Not sure if you know it, but our Team sponsors a teen center in San Diego. We've taken over an old Catholic school. We got, or had, after-school programs, you know—computer classes, an auditorium and even working on a radio station and public access TV station. We ran into problems with some locals at first. But now we have something bigger going on."

"So you come up here? Geez, I thought it was because of woman trouble."

Zapparelli was far from dumb. He'd gotten part of it right. Fredo weighed whether or not he should tell him, and decided not to reveal everything. "My wife just found out she's pregnant. All of us involved here are supposed to do some labor, pitch in, as part of the sweat equity. I figured I'd get it out of the way early on, because I'm not going to want to leave her side when she gets further along."

The lie made him feel terrible. If Zapparelli noticed, he didn't mention it. He was lost in a fog of a memory somewhere, and Fredo knew well enough to not touch it, or ask any further.

Fredo thought he'd ask him a safe question. "Got any kids, Marco?"

"My wife was pregnant once, but there was a complication. We were only able to save my wife's life. But as a result she cannot have children. So we adopted four. And then my brother passed away and we took in three of his, so we're just one big Italian family. But children of my own flesh? Nope."

"And how did you feel about that?"

"They're mine, just as if they got my juice, if you know what I mean. I'd die for those kids and my grandkids."

"Well, that was pretty much me. We just found out about the pregnancy, and I admit I'm having to adjust to it. Mia had a child with another dude."

"Another SEAL?"

"Nope. Far from it. He was supposed to be in for fifteen years for murder. Real nice dude. Just the kind of guy you want being the father to the little boy you're raising."

"At least he's behind bars."

"Well, that's the other thing. He's getting out soon. Just after Christmas, I guess."

"Ah, man. Sorry. He'd be making a mistake tangling with one of you SEALs. Doesn't he know that?"

"Marco, I think he flushed his smarts right out with all the drugs he took. He's a little short in that department."

"Garry Marshall used to say, 'One taco short on the combination plate of life.'"

It tickled Fredo. "I like that, man. I might use it."

"Garry's gone now. Use it all you want."

"So your wife and kids live over here?"

"Napa. But she spends a lot of time in the City, and she travels with some friends of hers. She's always going on these cooking tours. Doesn't really have much interest in the wine business. The kids are all out of the house. And you know what? None of them came back either. Imagine that?"

"Well, that means either they had a horrible time, or you did a good job launching them." Fredo had to ask the director one additional question, hoping he wouldn't take offense. "So, you have any contact with the biological parents of your kids?"

"My sister isn't around for her three. They consider me their dad, anyway. We've had some contact with two of the kids' parents. We let them go find them when they could, but not when they were little."

"How'd that go?"

"Two of my kids didn't want to look. Can't say as I blame them." Zapparelli finished off his glass and set it down on the concrete patio. "You got some reason for asking?"

"Nope."

It was Fredo's second lie of the evening.

"What else?" Zapparelli asked.

"I don't get your meaning."

"You drove all the way up here, and you're not going to bed early like Coop. What's got you bothered?"

"I was asking you about the winery attack because our school has been attacked by a group too. We're thinking it was some new players, gangbangers in town, but we don't know for sure. Just seems to be happening more and more, you know?"

Zapparelli nodded to the distance.

"I thought I'd ask you a few questions about anything strange that you noticed before the attack. Did you have any inkling things weren't going according to plan?"

"Did you?" Zapparelli asked.

"Not a thing. No warning."

"See, I think it was different for us. I'd seen a guy hanging around the shop and the tower bar where the blasts went off. But we get strange people all the time. We're a tourist destination. If it wasn't for your friend, Zak, there would have been even more loss of life. I would have been one of the casualties if it wasn't for—you said—Jameson?"

"Yessir. Jameson Daniels. Helluva nice guy. You see him, please don't call him Elvis."

"He shouldn't be in show business if he's that thin-skinned."

"Well, let's just say he was a favorite with the BUD/S instructors too. He still hates to be called Elvis."

"Ah." Zapparelli stood to stretch his legs. "I'm not going to be able to stay up much longer, but let me think about all this and maybe we can talk about it tomorrow. Okay, son?"

"Sounds good to me."

Fredo woke up to the smell of bacon and coffee and the television blaring, which never happened at his house. Then he realized where he was: Frog Haven Winery with Coop, Amy and Zak.

He threw on a T-shirt, found his flip flops, and re-tied his flag pajama bottoms.

The kitchen was buzzing with activity. Coop and Zak were setting the table while Amy was cooking. But their eyes were consumed with side glances to the TV.

"What's up?"

"Hey, Fredo, got some black coffee for you. And breakfast's coming up. Hope you're hungry," said Amy.

"Starving."

"How's your head?"

Fredo rolled his neck and shoulders, shedding the stiffness that came with the long trip. "No headache. That's amazing."

"Yeah, they've been experimenting with their wines, doing an organic fermentation and it's supposed to cut down on the morning after a bit. Really pretty amazing. Been reading up on it."

"That's cool," he said, wandering over to the stove and stealing a piece of bacon with his name on it. "What're they watching?"

"Something going on overseas. I guess they know guys in the fight."

Fredo saw pictures on the big screen, unmistakably Syria or Iraq. He knew their sister Team, 5, was over there and some of them had deployed to train local militia.

"What's on?" Fredo shouted to Coop and Zak.

"Not sure, but looks like a botched rescue attempt," said Zak.

"And it could be propaganda. They're getting really good at that," added Coop.

"Who was being rescued?"

"One of our embassy staffers. Being held for ransom," said Coop.

All SEAL Teams had been briefed about newsfeeds deliberately given to the world press to distribute, showing American Special Forces blunders and mission scrubs. They'd all been warned that this was perhaps the best way to clip the wings of the Spec Ops effectiveness, to show the Americans as either a ruthless bunch of killers or merely incompetent stooges. It was a blatant effort to turn the US population against the Spec Ops community, and it came at a time when the SOF commands were being more effective than ever before.

But of course they all knew the truth was never seen on American television.

Coop pointed to the screen. "There. See that? That clip came from their attack in Mosul eighteen months ago. What kind of idiots do they think we are?"

Pictures of children, injured or dead, covered the screen. The broadcast had numerous disclosures as to the graphic nature of the story.

"Fuckin' FBN. They'll put anything up that makes us look like idiots," said Zak.

Fredo completely agreed. Bringing his coffee over to where Coop and Zak had landed, the three of them watched as a white-turbaned mullah came on screen. His name was written in Arabic. An interpreter spoke into the broadcast.

'This message is addressed to the American people, who we recognize as good and decent. You have allowed your government to lie to you about their mission here in Iraq and in Syria, which used to be peaceful countries where Christians and other faiths worshiped in peace and freedom. Now you can see—' The screen showed the body-lined streets of a bombed-out city impossible to identify. *'Women and children are among the dead. Innocents paying the price for your aggression. We aim to even the score. Our children suffer. So let the children of the American people suffer.'*

The room was silent. Fredo hadn't been able to make out the name of the robed leader. He'd heard threats like this from prisoners undergoing interrogation, but never broadcast on a US television station.

"They're upping the ante." Coop muttered, crouching over his cup of tea as if huddled at a camp overseas, "It's a very definite threat. We've been seeing this, haven't we?"

The two Teammates and Zak shared glances. The large showy winery attack definitely had the militants' thumbprint on it. Fredo didn't think the Center bombing was the same MO. There were probably hundreds more they never heard of.

Fredo had a new mission: Get the Feds working on the Center bombing without delay. He'd also need Julio's help in obtaining more information about the group or persons he thought was responsible. It didn't matter who they were. They'd pay. Fredo would see to it they'd get them.

He needed to do this to keep Julio and his family safe. He also needed to protect his own little growing family. Suddenly, the issues of paternity weren't as important as they'd seemed before. Not when taking into account that the war he'd fought overseas was creeping closer and closer and could threaten everyone he loved at home.

CHAPTER 9

The work day was going fast. Zak and Coop worked on one of the destemming machines, which had jammed and been shut down. That left lugs of fresh-picked grapes stacking up in the shade of the processing shed. Fredo was driving the Kubota out to the fields to collect these lugs and then transport them back to be washed and prepared for the mashing.

He delivered Zak's message to the English-speaking crew foreman to give everyone an early lunch break since the process had been halted temporarily. Zak and Amy had employed a dozen workers on contract through the vineyard manager for the next four days or as long as the weather held. So far, they'd been lucky. But skies could be unpredictable in the early fall. Rain was always a possibility.

Fredo had help loading up the lugs, then drove them back to the shed, noticing Coop had crawled on top of the machine, like he was working on a truck motor. The stainless steel hatch door had been raised, giving him access to the spiraling blades which were now idle.

Fredo stacked the lugs near the stainless steel sink that housed the water sprayer. A short, rotund woman, wearing a straw cowboy hat tipped at an angle over a red bandana, hoisted one lug into the large sink and hosed them down with a commercial sprayer. She stacked four washed lugs near the crusher and then left.

Amy exited the house, bringing several sandwiches, some apple slices and a handful of carrot sticks on a large platter, holding it up to Fredo.

"Let me go wash," said Fredo, who used the lavender soap scrub at the stainless steel washing tank.

"Isn't that dangerous, climbing up on the machine like that?" Amy asked when Fredo rejoined her.

"Nah," Fredo said, "Only if he sticks his fingers in there and the machine kicks on, or if he steps in it barefoot when the power's on." He took a bite out of his egg salad sandwich. "Wow. These are good."

Amy smiled and took the platter to her husband.

"Not right now, Amy. We need to get this thing up and running."

"What's the problem?" she asked, standing on tiptoes to see down into the machine. Fredo stood next to her, watching the two men work, while holding the sandwich in his left hand.

Coop was balancing himself on his knees, using a wide plastic spatula to dig out some stubborn stems. Eventually, he put his hands down into the mashers, but before he got inside, he barked a command, "You sure it's off? Blood and bone don't do anything for the wine."

"Good point," said Zak, who rolled aside the large stainless steel tub the mashed fruit was depositing in. "Okay, now good to go!" he shouted up to Coop.

"I want to know the fucker's off first. Would you double check?"

Zak grinned. "I knew what you wanted, and yes, it's off. Power's off at the breaker for the whole barn, Coop. Not taking any chances."

"I thank you, and my fingers thank you!" Coop held up eight fingers and two thumbs, all covered in deep red grape juice.

Coop leaned toward the innards of the machine, reached into the blades and retrieved a long thick grape stem that had wrapped itself around the blades.

"Whoever put this batch in here must have been blind." He held the dripping vein of green up in the air as if it was a foul-smelling alien of some kind.

"I know who did it. That's the second time today I'll have warned him. Too many times. Excuse me." Zak removed his work gloves and stuffed them in the back pocket of his blue overalls, leaving the area.

Coop hopped off the destemmer, put a green bucket down on the floor, and flipped the breaker switch. Then he turned on the red button to start the blades, watching the mash exit the machine into the waste bucket until nothing was left.

Then he moved the stainless steel mash tank back into place. He took fresh grapes from one of the washed lugs, and laid it into the V of the processing tray, allowing the spiral blades to roll over them, squeezing the fruit into one side and the green stems and seeds into another. A couple of leaves surfaced as he added more fruit and he quickly removed them. He followed the stream of purple liquid gold as it continued to fill the tank and nodded his approval.

"Time for a sandwich," he grinned as he listened to the purr of the machine and satisfied himself it was fully operational.

Fredo chuckled. "I gotta hand it to you, Coop. I've never seen anyone who could fix things like you can."

The giant shrugged. "I grew up with tractors. They're way more complicated than this stuff," he said, nodding to the whirring stainless steel machine spewing purple liquid like an alien.

Zapparelli arrived just after they'd finished their sandwiches. The sun was beginning to get hot and even the three-sided shed was beginning to feel humid. Two workers wheeled the filled tank toward new fermentation tanks stored in an adjacent building.

"Smells divine," Zapparelli sang.

"Well, at least the equipment is working. Up to you guys to do something magic with it," Coop said to Zak.

"That's what it's about. A little alchemy, science, luck and magic!" His eyes flared behind the black-rimmed glasses he was so known for. Fredo could nearly see flames coming out his ears, he was so excited.

Amy asked the vintner if he could step to the kitchen to review some contracts and he dutifully followed behind, waving, with a silly grin affixed to his face.

Fredo knew the crew would have more grapes picked so he ambled over to the Kubota. "I'm headed up," he said to Zak.

The afternoon sun was beginning to cool as a stiff breeze floated over the tops of the vines. He watched the rounded backs of the strong vineyard workers, clipping clusters of fruit with sharp curved short-handled knives. Happy banter and light mariachi music floated overhead, a perfect backdrop to his day surrounded with lush green foliage. He understood their Spanish and commented back when one of the women told her girlfriend she liked the shape of Fredo's ass.

"I know Gustavo is your boyfriend. Should I tell him?" he answered in Spanish. The four women nearby tittered and placed aprons across their faces, hiding their embarrassment. One of them swatted the perpetrator with her hat.

Fredo loaded up another cart of lugs, noting how silent the field had suddenly gotten, and drove them back to the wash.

The next trip over, Zapparelli joined him on the front seat of the Kubota. The big man bounced, and Fredo nearly got him tossed when they hit a protruding capped water pipe on the left side sending the front seat about a foot into the air suddenly.

Zapparelli hung onto the frame housing the canopy top with his stubby hands and fingers. "You're a regular cowboy," he said with his affable grin, the light reflecting off the glass in his huge horn-rimmed frames.

Fredo thought about the little ATVs the Russians had littered all over Afghanistan, some pieced together creatively with duct tape and wire with modified scooter, outboard, or lawnmower motors. There was also the two-man American

Jeeps made in Turkey that were used by their Special Forces. In those days he barreled through neighborhoods where almost everyone wanted to put a bullet in him, learning to avoid everything from dogs, children, goats and donkey carts to militia aiming at them during firefights.

Going a little faster than he should with the world-famous director at his side giggling and shouting commands and observations while hanging on for dear life, Fredo ground the gears, pivoting to stay in control, and created a dust cloud worthy of any Greek god coming to earth. By the time they reached the row where the workers had brought the lugs, Zapparelli had begun to sing opera.

"Seriously, Marco. You're going to scare the natives," he barked above the high-pitched squeal of the engine.

"Let them enjoy a little culture."

"They got culture. Just look at all this? Who's the dummy now? Get to work out here on the valley floor, nice warm day like today. This is heaven, man."

"That it is, and that's exactly why they need opera!" Zapparelli launched into another refrain. Fredo appreciated how hard his new friend played as well as worked. Seemingly carefree, life on life's terms was a good way to describe the flamboyant director.

Fredo knew that in time he could come to accept Mia's infidelity. He needed to hear her say that whatever happened it wouldn't be repeated. He'd even agree if she told him it was a relationship that had gone on for some time, just as long as she told him it was over. That she was sorry. Then, with the pregnancy and even the fact that she was carrying another man's baby, just as Marco accepted the fate of his paternity,

Fredo would forgive Mia. Marco celebrated what was real, right in front of him, not what he didn't have. He'd been honest and faced it, and then moved on. Zapparelli was more of a role model than Fredo had thought he ever could be.

He still wondered if recollection of the afternoon the terrorists had nearly killed the director would continue to haunt Zapparelli.

Of course it will.

Fredo also knew the man was strong. Forged from warrior stock back over a hundred years in Italy, born of a fighting man—that Fredo could understand. The blood of a warrior in anyone's veins made them a whole person. Not a perfect person, but a whole one, as if some guiding hand was protecting him and all others like him. That hand kept him alive and gave him the courage to face the demons and visions of pure evil that inserted themselves into his life. It wasn't what happened to a man, it was what that man did with the evil that showed his metal.

The world isn't a warm bubble of happy days.

But accepting near-death? Seeing others die while you lived? Those were special places in Hell, and only the strong received redemption from it. Those were the ones who could go on and keep fighting.

Keep loving.

Keep being human.

Maybe, Fredo thought, Coop was right. The biggest act of love he could show Mia was to either accept what was there right in front of him, to love Mia and the child, no matter what, or to confront her and accept whatever truth she gave him back. And to trust that the woman he was sure loved him with her whole being, would *never* stop loving him.

No matter what his sperm looked like.

CHAPTER 10

Coop pummeled Fredo with questions about the terrorist attack on Zapparelli Winery and what information he'd gotten from the director. They'd just crossed the San Diego County line, heading home at last.

Fredo recounted some of what Zapparelli told him.

"Apparently, the group was traveling north and stopped in town. They found one of the posters for the children's library event in the shooter's car. That's what drew them to the place."

"Sick bastards," mumbled Coop.

"They've been telling us. Looking for targets all over the US. It's coming, Coop. You know it is."

"What, the zombie apocalypse?"

"Don't fuck with me. You know what I'm sayin'."

"Hold on there, yes, I was just making fun, and of course you had to take it personal. In case you didn't know, zombies aren't real."

"I'm serious, Coop. I know you are more concerned about it than you let on. You don't have me fooled. Just wish there was some way we could get these guys."

It was one thing to have bad guys overseas, disrupting their own countries or exporting to nearby terrorist-friendly states. But in the US? The probability was increasing with every passing day.

"So are the Feds on it at all? Marco say if they had any leads about a cell or some coordinated attack?"

"I don't think so. Not sure they're giving him anything, Coop."

"He got a name, someone heading the investigation?"

"Nada. I'm thinking Riverton is our best bet. Of course, I asked Zapparelli about the bombs, if there was any information on how they were constructed, etc. He didn't have a clue, man. He's been spending most of his time dealing with families of the victims."

Coop silently nodded. "It's like what you said earlier, not sure the attack on the Center feels the same, man. If they'd wanted to inflict a lot of pain, they'd have done it in the middle of the day when all the kids were there."

Coop's point was well taken.

"A good idea to check it out, but don't hold your breath, Fredo. Whoever it was, they don't want it built, so when we get ready for the grand re-opening, that's when we need to worry again. Only this time, I think we'll be ready for them."

"You got some super-surveillance contraptions buzzing around in your brain, Coop?"

"No *End of Days* thing. I just want to catch them in the act, and then turn them over to the cops. I don't want to do anything that would hurt the kids. But we'll catch them eventually. Of that I'm sure."

They pulled up in front of the house. Fredo sucked in air like his life depended on it. He felt a paw squeeze his left shoulder.

"Tell her, man. Make sure you take that burden off you. If it's her story, she has to unburden herself. But you don't take that on for her. You can't save her from everything. And you're tough, Fredo. You're the toughest motherfucker I've ever seen on or off the battlefield."

Fredo didn't know why, but he thought of something funny.

"Until this thing about the baby, you know what was the toughest challenge I had?"

"What?"

"Getting my pants on with a stiffy. Damnedest thing, I've been fuckin' hard ever since she touched me that first time on the cruise. That first time I knew she wanted *me* for *me*."

"See? Normally, I'd give you a ration of shit for that one. But that's good. Focus on that."

Fredo glanced down at his lap and grinned as his boner came back to life.

"Some men fuck better scared, so think about that and not what you might find out, either now or later. Doesn't matter. She loves you. You know—hell, the whole platoon knows—she loves you. Whatever happened, I'm sure there was a good reason. And you know what I think about the testing. Just get yourself goddamned tested, asshole. You're like those new recruits who cry when they get their first Wompa Shot."

"Okay, I'm ready." Fredo grabbed his duty bag and got out of the Hummer. He leaned back into the window to accept Coop's final words of advice.

"Suck it up, Buttercup."

Why couldn't it have been something manly?

"Fredo, you don't do this, and I'm gonna get Danny and Kyle and T.J. and Jones, and we're gonna hold you down and tweeze that fuckin' unibrow. Who knows, under all that hair, you might be a handsome man!"

He swore but was much more pleased with this "normal" sendoff. He started laughing to himself and then remembered one more thing and ran back to the window. "There were two things I struggled with. You won't believe what the second one was."

"You wear pink women's underwear and were hiding it from your wife."

"In your dreams."

"Not *my* dreams, asshole."

"I actually learned to get used to tofu and stir-fry vegetables. I actually got to like the taste of some green in my diet. Can you believe that?"

Coop shook his head and started the vehicle, shouting back, "Go fuck your wife, Fredo, and quit pulling my leg." He drove off with a low rumble, screeched his tires at the corner, and was gone. Just before he disappeared, he held up his middle finger.

Fredo knew he'd remember this day. This would be the day he'd come to grips with being a father, a real father. Well, he was a real father to Ricardo. But Ricardo was part of Mia and came with Mia, and so he was easy to love. This new little one he was going to pretend was part of his own flesh, and it didn't matter what she'd tell him or what any doctors had to say about it. He would make it so through sheer force of mental energy.

The sky was blue, the morning warm. They'd not spent the night in Sonoma County but had left after dinner and driven all night. They both gladly gave up sleep to get home to their wives. The trip had been good for him. Now he was thrilled to be home at last.

Birds chirped. The steps to their Spanish stucco bungalow were freshly swept. It looked like she was taking after her mom, Felicia, because new red, white and blue flowers of different varieties were planted along the rose-colored walkway. His heartbeat echoed throughout his chest cavity and made the soft tissues under his chin vibrate with every stroke. He hadn't called her ahead of time because he wanted to be the surprise.

Peering through the small iron-grated window, he didn't see anyone inside, but heard salsa music. It was a common routine for her. Maybe if he got lucky she'd do one of those little numbers in front of him, lifting her shirt for a quick peek at her large brown areolas. Or she'd bend over and show him that exquisite ass of hers. His fingers tingled with the anticipation of what that smooth flesh would feel like as they stroked and explored her lovely body. She was perfect in every way, inside and out.

But there was no dancing this morning. He heard a voice in the backyard and noticed the curtains at the sliding glass door from the bedroom were flying in the breeze. That meant the door was open, which probably meant she was in the backyard. He pressed his finger on the front door latch and found it to be locked.

He never carried keys, always leaving his extra set at home, for some reason. Just could never remember them. So he made his way along the side of the house, opening the wooden gate carefully so he could surprise her.

She was on her knees, using the seat cushion for protection, planting some yellow flowers. She had gardening gloves on. She owned only one pair of shorts, and they were very short white cotton that hitched up, showing more than they should have, her ass making the perfect heart shape. He focused on that as his blood began to boil.

Sitting next to her, also kneeling, was the muscled body of some other guy. Some guy who didn't look anything like Fredo. He hadn't had acne in high school, so his back and shoulders weren't scarred. No ugly pinup tats or iron crosses or barbed wire or Gaelic sayings. He was smooth and he was huge, probably bigger than Coop, more like T.J. or Rory. His short black hair and neat moustache made him look like he was military. And then he watched as the man reached in front of her to grab a plastic container with little plants. *In front of her!*

She reared back, nearly to her heels to avoid the brush of his arm against her breasts, but Fredo knew he must have touched her, because she swayed to her left at the waist and put distance between their upper torsos.

Fredo heard an apology, as the man put his hand on her shoulder, the other on his chest as if professing love for her, despite the apology he was spouting. She smiled and coyly lowered her shoulder to allow his hand to slide off.

But in her side profile, he could see she was blushing. Uncomfortable with his attention? Or uncomfortable with her own feelings?

Fredo dropped his duty bag with a loud thud, thankful he'd brought his long gun. It was just a fleeting thought. A quick determination that whoever this person was, he was the enemy. Maybe this was the man she was having the affair with. This could be the man he had to kill.

Mia and the other man—a *handsome* man with dark features and latte complexion like a cover model, shirtless, with arms the size of his own or perhaps larger—stood and abruptly turned. The look on Mia's face wasn't one of excitement.

She was in panic.

CHAPTER 11

Mia ran to Fredo, her mouth in anguish, as tears flowed down her cheeks. He knew her insides were in pain, but not nearly as much as his.

"Ah, Fredo, *mi amore*," she moaned, her arms outstretched, fingers splayed. Her cheeks were puckered up, her eyes mere slits as she raised her eyebrows and squinted. He caught her by the forearm, holding her a distance away from him without looking at her. He was looking at *him*.

The guy walked backward a step, wiping his hands on the back pockets of his jeans. He leaned over, retrieving his shirt and slipped it over his head quickly. Fredo thought he looked even bigger with the shirt on. Mia was struggling, but he held her wrist almost to the point of causing pain. He couldn't look at her yet until he decided what he was going to do with the guy, because it had nothing to do with her. It was between him and the guy.

"Who is he?" Fredo asked her while he kept his eyes on the stranger, without loosening his grip.

"This is Joel. He's a friend of the landscaper, one of his crew. He just stayed to help me get these flowers in."

"Um hum," Fredo said, visibly scanning him from foot to the top of his head and then back down again, like he was a big green lizard standing on two feet. He didn't like anything he saw, even though he'd calculated exactly where he could kick the man and disable him for more than a few minutes, which would give him time to do whatever else he needed to do with him.

"Sh—she's right," the dude said in clipped English. Although he didn't have an accent, he sounded foreign. "Carlos is her landscaper—"

"*My* landscaper because I own this house with her. This is the house me and my wife occupy, so if there is a landscaper who works here, he works for me, which means you work for me too, if you work for her. Get my drift?"

The man was beginning to shake. He swallowed hard, tried to hook Mia's glance, but she was only looking at her husband. She stopped struggling, but Fredo didn't let go or look at her still. She remained silent, perfectly still.

"That means if you fucked her, you fucked me and that really pisses me off. I don't like to get butt-fucked."

"Fredo!" She wrenched herself loose, or rather Fredo allowed her to disentangle. He waited to see if she'd go over to him to protect him. That would speak volumes. But Fredo wasn't ready to look at her. She retreated to the side, halfway between both men, and looked down. He heard her cry. That wasn't going to work.

"Mia," he said as an order. "Not now. Now you're gonna tell me exactly who this guy is who dares to sit next to my wife and feel her up in front of her husband."

"He didn't do that!"

That made Fredo turn and face her. The dude started to dart away, and Fredo put a hand out. "Stop! I'm not done with you."

He focused back on Mia. Lowering his voice, like he was speaking to a child, he asked her, "Mia, now tell me why this man is here."

"I wanted to surprise you with the pretty backyard. We worked all day here. Mom took Ricardo so I could work with these guys. They did the house across the street, remember? You said they did a good job, so I hired them to do—"

"With what? How did you pay them?"

"I haven't yet. But I was going to write a check. I just wanted to get it all done so you would come home and see how pretty everything was. Why does that matter?"

Her tears were still silently falling down her cheeks. He changed his gaze back to the man who flexed and unflexed his hands.

"Sir, I am an honorable man." There was that funny feeling again. Fredo didn't trust him, feeling he wasn't who he said he was.

"Where are you from?"

"I'm from here. Why do you ask?"

"Because you're home alone with my wife."

"I work for the landscape service."

"This right?" Fredo asked his wife.

"Yes, my love. It's what I've been trying to tell you. The only day he's been here is today. I am so sorry, Fredo. You are completely correct. It was stupid of me to have him here at my home without you being present." She halved the distance between the two of them as she inhaled and lightly growled her answer, her voice cracking. He could feel the warmth of her delicate breath on his face, making the hair on his neck and upper chest stand at attention. Her fingers on his forearm did him in. "Honest, Fredo. Please, I do not deserve this, but please forgive me my love."

The words had the desired effect. He felt himself melting from the inside out. He wet his lips and then turned to see her pretty face, not more than a foot away from him.

"Please," she repeated. Her lips were full and red, her watery eyes were pleading with him to soften still. He could smell her hairspray and the muskiness of her female sweat mixed with the body crème she rubbed on her chest and neck each morning. She barely moved, but somehow came up alongside him, just slightly pressing her breasts into his upper arm and her mound into his thigh. It was just enough to let him know she was surrendering to him, but not enough to be obvious to their guest.

One look at him, and Fredo was angry again. "I wanna see some I.D."

The man reached for his rear pocket and extracted a thin wallet with nothing in it but some cash and a school I.D. Remarkable was the fact that he had two twenty dollar bills, and no credit cards, insurance cards or even discount drug cards. And no driver's license.

"So you are—" Fredo squinted at the crude typewriter spelling of the name. It was a temporary Student Body Card from San Diego State University, "—Joel Hernandez?"

"Yes, sir."

"Fredo! Give him back his wallet! This is silly."

"Sorry." Fredo gave the wallet back to the young man.

"No, no, sir. I don't mind." Now he was looking all Joe-College. "You can ask me all the questions you desire. Please. It was my intrusion on your space. I am very sorry."

Fredo still didn't trust him, because his English sounded non-native, but without an accent. Fredo would have punched him in the gut if he so much as looked at Mia, but the guy never snuck a look to check her out, just kept his focus on Fredo or his hands as he placed his wallet back.

"So you were born here, then?"

"You would be correct, sir. Sacramento. My mother was pregnant with me when we arrived twenty-two years ago, as refugees. I am born here, so I am a United States citizen."

"What are you studying at San Diego State?"

"Well, currently I'm enrolled in Nursery Science. I hope some day to build many fields of olive trees. Perhaps grapes."

Fredo didn't think the man posed a threat, and he believed his wife that they were but strangers, but he had to take precautions. Something still nagged at him. "Joel, why don't you have a driver's license?"

"Because I do not drive. I just haven't had time. And my family cannot afford a car for me. Neither can I. I walk or take the bus."

Fredo let it pass. "Joel, you are never to return to this house to work, is that understood?"

"Yes, sir. I am so sorry, sir."

"Even when I'm, home. You're not welcome here. She got it wrong. No one comes here when I'm gone, or when I'm here, you got it?"

"Yessir."

"You may go. But the next time I find you here in my backyard, you're going home in a body bag. Do I make myself perfectly clear?"

"Indeed, sir. Yes, you do."

"That's all. Get your stuff and get out."

"Thank you, sir. Welcome home."

Fredo had started toward Mia, to take her in his arms, but hearing the *welcome home* made him stop short. Alert and fully focused on Joel, if that was his real name, he asked "Home? Who told you I was away?"

"I did," said Mia. "I wanted everything finished by the time you came home. I thought you'd call me, Fredo." Her eyes were honest.

Fredo lingered on how beautiful she looked, now fully under her power. And he'd been a dumb fuck not to think about what she said when he was away. He had to have that talk again. The wives and girlfriends had to be forewarned. "You can go, but you heard what I said."

"Yes, sir. I will not come back. Ever. No worries about that, sir."

Joel stepped up to walk through the bedroom open slider and Fredo stopped him, pointing to the wooden gate at the side of the garage. "That way, kid."

"Of course," said Joel. In seconds he'd grabbed his jacket and a square purse he slung over his chest, and was gone.

Fredo nearly called him back to search the purse, but decided against it.

They heard the gate click. His fingers laced between Mia's and he led her to the side yard to make sure the gate was indeed closed and properly latched.

"So he walks home?" Fredo asked as they entered the house.

"Yes, he walks. I see him all the time. Sometimes he rides a girl's bicycle. But mostly I see him walking or waiting for the bus."

"No more, Mia. No one comes into our house when I'm gone. Only police or rescue crews. I will never send a repairman or someone to fix something when I'm not home to fully check them out. We can't be too careful. You will never have anyone I do not know here when you are alone, understood?"

"I understand. Oh, Fredo, I am so sorry." She threw her arms around his neck, nuzzled her forehead under his chin, pressing herself against his chest and moaning as he could not stop one of his hands rubbing over her butt cheek, then sliding under the fabric to lightly rub and then squeeze her flesh. His worries faded as his desire for her kindled.

"Are you angry with me?" he whispered to her ear. He knew he sounded needy. His voice was all gravel and lust. Her body softened and began to tremble.

"Not now. And you are very right. I was so stupid, Fredo." She kept her fingers entwined at the back of his neck as she pressed their thighs together and she arched back to look at him. Her breathing had picked up tempo. Her face was becoming hungry. She licked her lips, focused on his. He leaned forward, nibbling her gently on the lips, feeling her nipples knot, her scent filling his nostrils. He kissed under her ear and she moaned again, rolling her head to the side and touching his chin with her shoulder.

He pulled her shirt forward with a finger to the neckline to peek at her beautiful breasts all trussed and in need of release underneath, and then slid the shirt over her head. Fredo used his thumb and first two fingers to undo the front clasp of her bra. The material broke away, exposing her lovely flesh. His mouth watered to suckle, to taste her, to smell the dark crevices of her body and make her flesh burn with passion.

She drew one hand down, cupping one breast and offering herself to him. He was mesmerized at the sight of that flesh in her hands, bent and took her nipple deep inside his mouth and sucked until he knew she would feel it all the way to her core. With her other fingers, she smoothed his ridged forehead, lacing them through his scalp above his right ear.

"Yes, my love."

"I need you, Mia," he said between kisses. "You are mine and always will be, sweet Mia. I need to know I own your whole body."

"Of course, Fredo." She held his face between her palms. "Why would you ever doubt that? You are the only man who has my heart. You stoke the fires inside me. You bring me your love, and now you bring me your seed."

He wanted to look down, perhaps take another long pull at her nipple, but she held his face firm.

"Your seed, Fredo. You, a little piece of you grows inside me. Do you understand how that makes me feel? I am a vessel of your love, Fredo."

He really wanted to believe it, and even told himself she'd been faithful. But he put it out of his mind as an irrelevant fact. Right now he was going to forget the reality of the past, and focus, like Zapparelli, on the future they had together. Whatever was done could be forgiven in the lush jungle of her arms. Every kiss would make him more and more certain he was created to love Mia, and she was his and always would be. There would be time enough for the truth. Tonight it was about the pink baby fantasy of their love, and the miracle it gave them both.

CHAPTER 12

She was fully naked, her fingers lost between her legs as she watched him undress. She bent her knees and showed him her pinkness, rubbing a finger up and down her slit, circling her nub and taking short pants at the pleasure it brought her. He liked that she wanted to arouse herself in front of him. Her uninhibited way with her body as she let him examine her, and the way she freely gave herself to him made him feel more of a man. She was not a girl. She loved with the passion and intensity of a full grown woman, every bit the woman to his manhood.

He stood at the foot of the bed, his cock fully erect, filling in girth and length as he watched her pleasure herself, squeeze her breast with her other hand and then place her fingers in her mouth to taste her own arousal. That's what spurred him forward. Before she had a chance to lick and swallow that away, he needed to taste her hotness on her lips, feed from her, savor the magic that was her juice.

He climbed on top, positioned her arms over her head and secured her wrists with his fingers. Stretched and arching to meet him, her thighs found his hips as she lifted herself up into him, enabling him to seat himself at her opening. He let the head of his shaft lick the tender moist folds and lazily encircle her bud, inching dangerously close to the entrance. Her breathing became labored. Her eyes were opening and closing dreamily, her focus somewhere else, yet accepting him fully and attempting to climb his hips higher, begging for penetration.

He leaned forward, kissing her hard, tasting the sweetness of her sex. He sucked her lips, pulling them inside, exploring her tongue and mouth with his, inhaling and feeding off her. Their hot connection made him growl. She was made for him, created just for the love he had to share with her. Her lower back was arched like a bow, and he pressed his chest against her, feeling her lovely breasts and then pushing himself inside her opening slowly.

He watched her eyes as he entered her. He loved seeing the surprise there first, then the little wrinkle between her brows as she pulled him in, as her expression moved from need to satisfaction and back to more need. Satisfying her need was what spurred him on as nothing in the world could do.

He let go of her wrists and bent his knees farther, pulling her lower torso up onto his groin and, holding her hips, he ground into her, angling his body in a salsa of fluid stokes that quickly brought her to the brink of orgasm. Her hands flew along the coverlet, clutching sheets and pillows wherever she could find purchase.

He stopped temporarily, gave her a chance to catch her breath. Smiling down on her lovely body, now beginning to glisten with sweat, he waited for her to open her eyes and come back to him as he slowed his movements. Their connection brought a smile to him, and matched hers.

As she became more present, he pumped her again, holding her gaze as her breasts vibrated with his thrusts, watching her melt and bite her lip as her body began to burn. Each thrust penetrated deeper. He felt himself get huge, swelling and filling to stretch her delicate channel. Her internal muscles began to milk him. Sweat broke out on her upper lip and forehead as she shuddered beneath him, arched and writhed beneath, joined and pinned together. She took in one big breath, then held it as her muscles seized him. Slowly, she released, loosely letting out air, only to inhale again, to pull him back inside, squeezing him up and into her inner depths.

He felt her vibrations begin to ripple all over her body as her beautiful orgasm took her away, and he was right there alongside her. Beautiful Mia, the woman who belonged to him, the mother of his children, the only place in the world where he felt safe.

He spent everything he had, holding himself against the smooth ridge of her cervix, friction tugging at her nub and making it stiffen into a little peak. So as the last of him came, he held her close, kissing her ear. Whispering his love poems in Spanish, little things he thought about when he was away from her.

Being home was better than he'd expected. Gone was any feeling of worry about the upcoming pregnancy. Whatever lay in the future, it wasn't nearly as important as the way their bodies fit together at this moment in time. The perfect living puzzle of parts that mated in every sense of the word, both physical and spiritual.

The world was perfect in her arms. Somehow it would all work out.

"Should we get Ricardo?" he asked.

"You want to, my lover?" Two hours had passed and they'd been watching TV in bed, naked, hungry, but readying themselves for a third lovemaking round. Her fingers were tenderly stroking his shaft up and down, squeezing his balls and watching him enjoy it, hardness taking shape in her delicate palm. She always enjoyed teasing him with that coy smile, making him want to get harder still.

"You arranged for him to stay there perhaps overnight with Felicia and Gus?"

She nodded, dipping her head low to lick a thin trail up the underside of his dick and then finally twirl her tongue around his head. He loved seeing her smile at him with her mouth full. With her expert tongue massaging his shaft and her sucking motions, he was worked up to tank full and ready to ride her all night long if she wanted.

"Let's keep our tonight just the two of us," he said. Fredo was going to say something else about maybe in the morning they could talk, but he couldn't focus. She had him deep down her throat. He doubted he would be able to repeat all of the six proper names his mother had given him. They deserved this night together, and then tomorrow they'd solve whatever was left to work out.

Somehow, they'd do that.

He was to the point of coming in her mouth, and she let him know that's what she wanted, not pausing for permission to swallow his seed. He focused just enough to hold her arms and draw her up and over him, her thighs hugging his. She rose above him, her breasts hanging in front of him to enjoy. She slipped her legs beneath him, angled and then found his cock, setting herself back down with him fully inside her.

"This is what you want, my Fredo?"

"Yes." He had nowhere else in the world he wanted to be.

"And you like this?" she said as she held her breasts together.

"Yes," he said as he watched her massage herself, then pull her brown nipples forward into knots of tasty pleasure.

"And you love this?" She asked as she undulated on top of him, her muscles pulling him up and to his hilt, rocking her hips back and forth so he could feel everything inside her, while squeezing and letting loose with her thighs.

"Ah, Mia. You are too much for me."

"I like you deep, Fredo." Her stern gaze told him how much she needed him. She lifted her hair atop her head, one hand still squeezing her breasts, pinching them together as she began to bounce on top of him, then slowed to travel up and down his shaft, shuddering with every stroke down against him, her opening devouring him completely.

His hands smoothed over the warm flesh of her butt cheeks, then fingers trailed across her thigh to the place between her legs. His thumb found her nub, and he encircled it, halfway sitting up to apply more pressure. She gasped and began bouncing against his thumb, matching his every ministration with her own.

She rocked forward placing her forearms at the sides of his head, as he arched up into her, letting her feel the length of his stroke and the size of his cock. In long smooth strokes he let her build her passion. Her eyes closed, her lips in that perfect "O" of surrender. He stroked deep and held her hips in place. The little spasms inside set him off and he came, releasing everything he had.

She exhaled, releasing him and then drawing him in again as he finished.

"Mia, the baby?"

"Will be fine. I hope it's a little girl, Fredo. I want your daughter. She'll have a unibrow like Frida." She looked back down at him as her head angled, teasing him.

He chuckled. He could see it all now. One thing that hadn't been in his dream: all the toddlers didn't have unibrows.

They showered, which turned into another wonderful sexual encounter. He had missed the closeness to her he normally felt, the familiarity of her scent, the delicate way she did things, loved him back. He couldn't get enough of her.

He was planning to have that talk later on, the talk he'd practiced in his mind for days. Then he was going to discuss what he could about the mission to North Africa and the Canaries. He thought perhaps it was time, with everything going on all over the world, that the women be reminded of the dangers that lurked just outside the perimeter of their seemingly normal worlds.

He took her for dinner to the Rusty Scupper, where he'd hoped he could have a nice, leisurely conversation, but several other SEAL families were there. Danny, Luci and their two children, Griffin and the little Iraqi boy Danny had brought back, Ali, sat down next to them. Fredo and Danny pulled their tables together.

"How was your trip up north?" Danny asked.

"Good. Coop was in a good mood," Fredo answered. He neglected to tell Danny the reason for the trip was his own nasty mood. He watched as the two children wiggled their way out of their seats and Luci got up to chase them. He noticed she was pregnant again, a small bulging belly barely visible.

"You Dine motherfucker. Got her knocked up again?"

"I can't help it, man," Danny said. "We were going to wait, but it just happened. So happy this time I get to be here for her during part of it at least." Danny watched Luci bend over, and he shook his head.

"See that?" Fredo smirked. He covered Mia's ears. "You gotta stop looking at that or seriously, you'll have ten kids."

"You know it." Danny grinned and took another sip of beer. Mia took Fredo's hands and placed them on her chest and wiggled her eyebrows at Danny, who nearly spit out his beer.

"You guys kill me. Luci would never do that," the Navajo SEAL said.

"Maybe she should?" Mia answered, winking back at him.

Danny shook his head and took a long pull on his beer.

Fredo removed his hands, respectfully, and threw his arm around her shoulder. "We've been just getting reacquainted."

"That's the best part." He turned to watch Luci chasing little Griffin while Ali ran behind.

"It's been a wonderful few hours, and I've got plans," Mia answered, giving Fredo a kiss.

Danny didn't stare too much, which Fredo appreciated, but the admiration in his eyes was something he could handle. "We got it bad, Fredo. We're staked, drawn out, and tied to it. Just like they used to do with errant husbands. They'd take them, stake them to the desert floor and make all the old and uglies in the tribe ride his cock as punishment."

"Holy crap. That almost sounds like some of the stuff we've seen overseas."

"Not quite, but I guess the thought of having to screw old dried up hags was so awful, if they strayed, it was usually outside the res where they wouldn't get caught. But the hags loved it."

"You guys are savages." Fredo shook his head.

"I think that's terrible," added Mia.

"Absolutely, and proud of it." Danny said with a wink.

A loud wail began, unmistakably belonging to Griffin.

Luci returned to the table, holding the crying Griffin. She threw the blue sling shot down on the table. "I said he couldn't bring it to dinner, Danny. You have to stop him from doing that."

"Ali?" Danny saw him hiding behind Luci's back, his head hung in shame.

Luci's lips kissed a tiny cut on Griffin's forehead. Some red sticky substance adhered stubbornly all around the cut. Luci took a napkin, dabbed it in their icewater, and rubbed away the gunk.

"Is that what I think it is?" Mia said. Luci nodded.

Danny was still trying to catch Ali, reaching behind Luci's back. Finally he got an arm and quickly hoisted the boy to his lap.

"Ali, never. You're supposed to be nice to your little brother."

Ali collapsed crying into Danny's chest.

Fredo didn't know what had just occurred. He examined the slingshot, picking it up delicately. "This the one you made for him over there?"

Danny nodded, holding Ali to his chest and rocking slightly.

"What'd he do?"

Griffin leaned forward and shouted in his three year old voice, "Ali, you dirty rotten axel!"

"Griffin!" Luci scolded. "You stop that right now."

Fredo burst out laughing and then covered his mouth. It wasn't lost on Griffin, who grinned.

"Sorry. I'm so sorry, guys." Fredo continued, "I can't believe I just witnessed that."

"Well," started Mia, "at least he hit Griffin with a jelly container and not a spoon or fork. Looks to me like Griffin was lucky."

"Glad he didn't bring his marbles," whispered Danny. "You should see what a shot he is. And one of those could take out an eye."

Griffin wanted to go sit on Fredo's lap, so Luci let him. His dark Dine eyes with his straight eyelashes looked admiringly up to Fredo. No one would ever mistake his lineage. With the precious cargo in his lap, Fredo put his hand on Mia's shoulder. "Should we tell them our news?"

Mia leaned into Fredo, then scooted her butt next to him on the bench seat.

"Yes, we're pregnant. I go next week to the doctor to find out exactly when, but we're definitely pregnant."

Luci ran around the table to give Mia a hug. "I'm ecstatic for you guys. How exciting. Little Ricardo will have a brother or sister. Isn't that great, Ali?"

"No girls. He should have a brother. Girls are not good."

The hush that fell over the table was heavy as all of the adults knew that though they'd gotten Ali at four years of age, certain patterns had been imprinted on him, even by a loving father who sacrificed his life for his boy. The message about women's roles in Iraqi society had already found its way into the boy's thinking.

"No, Ali," Danny said gently. "Girls are good. Girls are just like us, except better." He smiled to the ladies. "You'll see. In time, Ali, you'll see."

CHAPTER 13

Sayid was furious with himself for not having had patience. He knew it was wrong to be alone with the wife of the warrior SEAL, but he couldn't help himself. She was friendly, wore those impossible white shorts, was so utterly immodest, unlike the women he'd been introduced to from his home country. He couldn't stay away. He couldn't stop staring at her chest. He couldn't help fantasizing about what it would feel like to take her. Even with his limited knowledge of women, he knew it would be thrilling.

The United States had been the only country he'd known, but as he dug into the roots of his faith, he requested and received the gift of a trip back to Syria where his parents had emigrated from. That's when he saw how they had become infected with the pox that was Western Civilization and in particular, the evil empire of the United States. How they had been seduced by secular things: money, power, ownership of things they had no business owning, and lack of will to raise their children in the Way of the Prophet. It was there he was introduced to proper women who would make proper wives when the time came.

He found Western women attractive, and it was explained that his body had been created that way to ensure there would be children. But that was a base and bodily function of his human birth, and not a higher calling. The way this woman flaunted her body around—tempting him, making him hard, and having the nerve to walk so close, speak so softly, and show her parts—made it difficult to stay away. He found her mesmerizing. But now he'd spoiled the element of surprise. And he should not have attempted to be around her until he was sure the warrior wouldn't come home.

He'd been back to Syria once in high school with the uncle of his father as his companion. The man was a power broker and paraded him in front of wealthy families who wanted daughters married to an American citizen and would pay large sums of money to him for arranging such a marriage.

But then he stumbled upon teachings at another worship center. It didn't take long before he understood his father's uncle had been seduced by the great Satan and could not be trusted.

His relative was furious when he refused to accept one of the several marriage proposals and wanted to return home to California. There, he followed his teacher through the internet, and his real studies began. They finally arranged another trip, carefully crafted as to be hidden from his family and friends.

He traveled through Turkey, telling his parents and school that it was a cultural visit to Italy since he had been interested in Italian architecture and gardens. He'd even been given passage on a large cruise ship during the summer, working as a cook's helper to the cousin of his father. That's when he decided to abandon ship and take the call when it was given, traveling the path to find the camps who would train him. He met with the teacher he'd studied under online in the US, and the whole world opened before him.

They arranged a sexual encounter with a Christian prisoner who had been recruited to be a bride to a fighter and then had changed her mind. She was paying for her treason, for her coldness of heart. She didn't deserve and would never receive mercy, but instead would live to receive the consequences of her defiance until it was beaten, *fucked* out of her. His teacher told him what that word was and how to use it.

His teacher showed him how to penetrate and to force himself on this woman. He watched as it was demonstrated. He felt the woman's fear, felt it all the way to his heart through her blue eyes that stared at him in shock, and it spurred him on. He found that he could rape when it was his turn. His teacher was pleased he didn't shrivel and was immune to the woman's screams.

He returned home this time a different person. The quiet transformation was boiling deep inside him, and everything about living in California only added to his fervor. His parents didn't suspect this change at all.

Being a devout student, he did what he was ordered to, and enrolled in college, near the forces stationed at Coronado, where some of the elite teams were sent. He watched them on the beach, studying how they trained, how they ran. He was told he'd be allowed to kill one some day. He watched the way women looked at them, the way they got drunk and abused themselves with women who shunned him. With hatred, he followed them sometimes, learning how to do so undetected. He practiced and studied little teachings on all the arts he'd need as a future warrior for The Path. The internet was his guide.

Sayid became obsessed with making bombs. Instructions and resources were sent his way. The craft was so easy, and he took to it quickly. He became noticed.

He knew when they selected the right bride for him, she would come as a chaste woman, and she would not scream or squirm beneath him. No man would have touched her, lifted her clothes and taken her virginity. She would belong to him and him alone.

She would not have to be bound, unless he wished it so. It was explained she would arouse in him the world of the virgins. And if it was necessary, he would martyr himself, even martyr his seed if it was required. All was possible through The Path. He would face death and would not flinch, would not shrivel in the face of his responsibility.

For The Path was a whole system: political and spiritual, mated into one, a way for the whole world to live without a single exception. Allowing exceptions and caving into the debauched Western way of life was saying no to The Path, was watering down the teachings he'd been given, and those he knew in his heart of hearts were the one true way. Anyone who would try to alter that, including even his parents and his Westernized cousins who made fun of him and tried to stand in his way, would feel the power of the sword. He would not allow any of them to deter him.

He'd been warned that he should not change his appearance, grow a beard or pray in public. He should be chaste, attend worship, follow the teachings and in his heart, magnify the word for the day all Heaven came to earth. That would be a glorious day. The sick Westerners and their fat and flabby existence would be eliminated or would suffer until they would submit.

Cut by cut, he would help with the millions others of his kind, and they would cut at the legs of the giant Satan until he was injured and then tripped. And once he was down and afraid and had lost the will to fight back, he would be misled and shown mercy before his wives and daughters were taken from him and used as vessels for The Path. Before his eyes, he would see the folly of his ways. He would wish for death, and death would be delivered to this soulless creature.

It would be a triumph, bathed in blood.

"You will look like a Western youth," his new teacher commanded online. "Understand that there will be some days, maybe even weeks, when you doubt me or what I have said. You will learn to purge that from you. For while you are having doubts, the great Satan parades the streets of the world, his belly bloated and his wealth corrupting the faithful, making it difficult to be a believer. But you will not fail me. You will survive and hate that Satan and all his drunk followers even more as you notice what he has done to your women and children, your parents and your family. We are your new family, a family you may have to die for."

So today had been a misstep, but it revealed to him that he was vulnerable to the charms of such a woman. He had to remember and be careful. He could not be found out. He would hide in the plain sight of people around him who suspected nothing. He had to work on his impatience while waiting for the call to action. He'd prepared the path, passed the test by showing he could blow up the school and remain undetected to live for another mission.

The teacher had been very pleased. The riches of Heaven awaited him. He was trained, unsuspected and committed to a cause he was willing to die for. He was ready.

So, finally, Amid Khan was coming to see him in three days. Sayid thought about him on the walk home, and what an honor it would be to meet the teacher. Word was he was a harsh man who had been tortured at the hands of the American Special Forces, and he had a special lust for killing them overseas. Khan messaged him that Sayid was given the opportunity to be one of the architects of something glorious being planned in the United States. The fact that he was visiting in person, since travel exposed him to certain risks, meant that perhaps Sayid had been chosen for a special mission, and it might be happening soon.

It was a great honor to know that they believed in him so much, that this most holy man would risk his life to communicate with him in person. He could hardly wait.

CHAPTER 14

Fredo's plans to discuss the event at the house earlier were beginning to weigh on him. As was the promise he'd made to Coop. On the drive back to their place he asked her permission.

"I need to discuss some things with you at home, if you're okay with this."

Her beautiful face reflected colored traffic lights and streetlamps as they drove the freeway then wound their way back to the start of their neighborhood.

"So serious," she whispered. "You have a surprise for me, yes?" She was toying with him.

"Always, my love. I hope I always surprise you in many ways, for years and years to come. But this is something different. I need to explain something to you."

"You and Coop up to something, Fredo?"

"No, nothing like that." He smiled and tried to sound relaxed, but it was clear she wasn't quite in the serious mood she'd have to be. Then, upon weighing it further, he decided the light-hearted approach might be the best after all. "Just some things I need to speak with you about. About us and about some things about the Teams. It involves me, and so it involves you."

She turned back to face front, her profile that of a goddess. How had he been so lucky?

She stared down at her hands, folded in her lap. "Is this going to ruin my perfect day?" She remained focused on her hands, waiting for his answer.

"No." He lied because he wasn't sure. But he had to lie. Would she not like the news he was going to tell her?

"Good. As long as it doesn't stop me from wanting to wake up in your arms in the morning, I'm good with it."

He admired her courage and wondered if he had the same.

After he parked the car, he held her hand and brought her to the living room, where he took a seat beside her on the couch. "Do you want something?'

Her large brown eyes looked up at him long and did not smile. "Will I need something?"

He wanted to change his mind, but he'd put it off long enough. He took her hands in his, and then brought them to his mouth and kissed them. She followed every movement, waiting. He sensed she was holding her breath or taking small breaths.

"Mia, sweetheart," he said as he replaced her hands, but remained entangled in her fingers. "We've been warned again that there are imminent threats to our local population, especially to the SEAL community."

"I always understand this to be the case, Fredo." She was rubbing his fingers with her own. "You don't have to remind me, but I like that you want to protect me, lover. That's very sweet."

Fredo's stomach clenched. She wasn't being serious enough, embracing what he was trying to tell her.

"Sweetheart, it's more than that. We have specific threats against the community, but not just us, our families. We wouldn't care one whit about us. It's our families that hurt the most. Like police are targeted—"

"I know, such a disgusting way—"

"Those folks are just crazies, trying to deliver a hateful message, hitting the core of our society: our families, our innocents. Only cowards do that. Cowards that won't win in the end."

She nodded.

"What I'm talking about are zealots who hate us. Hate everything we stand for. And they're all around. You might not recognize them. Heck, I might not recognize them, but we can't take chances and let people like that into our homes, into our lives. We don't want them to know anything about us."

She began to tear up. "I'm so sorry, Fredo. I was not thinking."

"I understand. Believe me, I wish I didn't have to have this talk with you. But we all are. We all are telling our kids and wives that there are going to be some big things coming up. The chatter is there, and we believe it will happen on our own soil. We're good once the action starts."

"So, Fredo, the Center? You think that is involved somehow?"

"The Center, well, we're not sure. We thought it was some gang element, but now, we just don't know. Now the winery up in Sonoma County? Yes. It has to be, Mia. That's partly why I'm telling you this. They're after kids, innocents, wives and girl-friends. Parents. That's what drew them to the winery event. Lots of kids. Although the police haven't found any definite suspects, we believe they are working on it. But after these guys are gone, there will be more. That's what I'm saying, Mia."

"Oh God, Fredo. When?"

"Well, that's just it. We never know, do we? We aren't good with the waiting. In fact, it's the hardest thing we have to do, knowing people are watching and planning things—"

Mia had inhaled at that last comment, closing her eyes and holding her breath.

"Mia," Fredo reached forward, touching her chin and lift-ing it so he could look into her eyes. "It serves no good pur-pose to not be vigilant, ready. To be mentally prepared. You have to watch everything. Study everything. Remember to be careful. Stay amongst the other Team families. Do not reveal anything outside the family, only to first responders, police and fire. But that's it."

She nodded her head and tried to smile, but tears were streaming down her cheeks. He wished he didn't have to deliver the rest of his message. He leaned forward again and kissed her gently on the lips and then stood.

"And there's one more thing. I've struggled with this for days and days, well over a month now."

Mia's expression was one of resignation. He paced back and forth, inhaling, drawing strength from what was real. He wasn't telling stories. He was going to tell her the facts and let it be whatever it was for her. He was willing to face whatever he would find out in her reaction.

"What is it, Fredo?"

He stopped, faced her. With his hands at his sides but fisted, he just began. This would be the point of no return for Fredo. "Mia, I'm sterile."

She didn't move except flutter her eyelids several times. He watched as his question sunk in. "Excuse me? How can you say that, Fredo?"

"I've been to the doctors. Twice. I've seen what my sperm look like, and they come out dead. Blanks."

"Impossible." She leaned back into the couch, crossing her arms. "There must be some explanation," she mumbled, her eyes downcast.

The house was still. His own heart was beating in his chest while he waited for the full import of this to sink in. Waiting for her to give the explanation that was necessary now. It hadn't been necessary before, but it sure was now.

You tell me, Mia. Tell me the explanation. He hoped it was something like, *I went to a sperm bank.* That he could forgive.

"Mia, just tell me. Is there someone else?"

"No!"

"Then, what's the explanation? *Was* there someone else? Just be honest with me. There has to be an explanation, honey." He was beginning to lose his footing.

"How could you ask me that?"

"Because I love you anyway, Mia. I forgive you. But don't lie to me. Tell me the truth."

Her face formed a cruel smile. She adjusted her neck as if she'd been hit, then started to shake her head from side to side. Looking up at him, he could see the hurt and pain in her soul.

"So that's what's burdened you? All this time we've been dancing together, and all this time you've been wondering about me? You've made love to me still with this burden? What, did you think that just by doing this it would all go away?"

He didn't know what to say. "Maybe. I didn't know what to think. Please tell me."

She slowly stood. "So you think I've been screwing around on you? You don't think this is your child?"

He didn't want to answer her. But he did so anyway. "How could it be? I can't be a father. I've seen the proof."

She picked up the cushion from the couch, threw it at him, and screamed, "Bastard!"

"Mia. Wait. Stop this."

"No, you stop this. How dare you ask me that question? So now I see why you are concerned about men hanging around the house. You are afraid I would go back to my old ways? Is this true? You think I'm a slut. You go away for a couple of days, and I've got myself a little love interest, is that right?"

"Initially, yes, I thought this could be so."

"All the *I love you's to the end of time* are just hollow words, Fredo? You struggled with not being able to tell me this?"

"I did. I admit that." There was only one way through it. He had to stick to reality as he knew it. "I'm not proud. But how could you get pregnant when I can't father children?

Tell me that? And that leaves one additional question I need answered. I deserve an answer. Who got you pregnant, since I cannot?"

"You actually think I'm sleeping around, Fredo?" Her eyes were hard.

"What else am I supposed to think? Did you go get a sperm donor? Or, did someone—?"

"You think I would fuck someone else when you're gone? You really think I'm capable of doing that? How could you, Fredo?"

He was cautious and became uncertain. What had he done?

"I don't have any other explanation. Like I said, I've been tested twice. I cannot have children. So tell me, how did you get pregnant?"

He began to wonder if he'd made a huge mistake, and he partly blamed his best friend, Coop. He started hating Coop, and then stopped himself.

Get a grip, asshole. Keep it together.

"Mia, just be honest with me. I deserve the truth. I need to know."

But he was thinking the fantasy was better than the truth of it all. Yes, he found enough in her and her past to doubt her. It was a fact. And now he'd told her as much. And maybe he'd ruined their marriage, irreparably damaged her love for him.

The truth wasn't setting him free. It was an undelivered promise.

"Get out. I'm not going to dignify that question with an answer." She delivered the ultimatum with cool detachment.

"Mia," he began, "Wait. Let's talk about this. I mean you no disrespect, but try to see it from my perspective. You have to understand how I feel about all this, where I am coming from."

"I do? Really? No, Fredo. I don't." Her calm collection cut him to the core. "I don't have to accept anything you tell me now. You just told me you think I've been lying to you about the pregnancy. You think I've slept with another man. Maybe lots of men, right? Well, I have, but in my past."

"See, honey, that's what I—"

"Get out. Get out now. I want you to leave me alone."

"But I love you. I don't want to leave."

She walked past him and headed toward the hallway to the back bedroom, looking at him like road kill. He *felt* like road kill. She stopped at the doorway.

"Yes. You love me. But you do not trust me. I never would have thought in a million years this would be coming from you. Get your things and get out of the house tonight. I don't want to see your face."

CHAPTER 15

He knew that pleading wouldn't work with Mia. Before they'd gotten together, when he'd been her devoted admirer, she had shunned him, treated him with disdain. He never gave up then. He knew then that somehow, it would all turn out. Coop had warned him. Armando, her brother, had suggested he perhaps give up on the unrequited love for the beautiful Mia. But Fredo knew he could fill her heart with joy and make her life bloom as no other could.

His instincts had been correct, he thought as he put things together in a large bag. She had softened her heart, seen him for the first time on that cruise ship, and opened herself to a life with him. He'd been ready to protect her, to die for her if need be. He was the most grateful man on the planet.

So he'd waited until that glorious day when she'd fallen in love with him. He could be patient then because he knew once she fell in love with him, there would never be a separation.

That was before he would have to endure the loss of the love he once had tasted. After he saw how perfect they were for one another. Trying to live without it now was impossible. He'd rather die.

It was a fleeting thought, but a dangerous one.

He finished with the clothes, then checked to make sure he had all his guns and ammo. He wasn't going to leave anything behind in the house, just out of an abundance of caution, even though he knew he didn't have to worry. It was just habit. The guns would stay with him.

She balanced against the wall in the corner of their living room, her arms crossed, tears making her eyes puffy, streaming down her face. He was near the front door ready to exit for what he hoped would be a short departure. He wanted desperately for her to change her mind. And he knew he couldn't force her in any way. He couldn't beg. If she was going to let him back into her life she would have to do it on her own terms. He also worried her upset would affect the baby.

He decided to try one more time.

"Mia, please don't do this. I love you. I will always love you," he whispered to her, dropping his bags, taking one tentative step to her direction. "Let me explain. This should not be happening."

"Stop. No farther, Fredo." She angled her head and stared at his feet, not wanting to look at his eyes.

"I am the same person I was when I came home, the same person I was way back then onboard the ship. The same person who held you in my arms and carried you out of the burning house where you were held hostage. There will never be another woman for me, Mia. And now you are to be the mother of my child."

She drilled him with a look he never thought her capable of.

"Words, Fredo. Now you say I am the mother of your child, yet you doubt the very foundation of our relationship, my integrity." She melted to the floor, sobbing, her face buried in her arms.

He ran to her. "Mia," he whispered. He threw his arms around her shaking body and was grateful she did not resist. He smoothed her hair back from her forehead, allowed her head to rest against his chest, hoping she could feel his heart limping in pain but beating still ardently for her. "I will never stop loving you, Mia. I never have and I never will. You must believe me." He kissed the top of her head.

He waited, though he wanted to pick her up, bring her over to the couch where she would be comfortable and warm. But he continued to stroke her hair, pulling long curls back behind her ears, whispering what he felt, how he loved her as she sobbed. He hoped she could hear it through her heaving chest.

He'd stay there all night if she allowed him to. He'd stay squatting in the corner with her, letting her cry and hoping by God she would come to her senses. He wondered why he'd decided to even bring up the subject of paternity tonight. Wasn't it better to just keep it a secret? Look what he'd done. He'd made a mistake. It was a terrible mistake with consequences he would bear the rest of his life.

But he couldn't bring her back. That would have to be done on her own terms, in her own way. He could come this far, but he knew, even if he were capable of changing her mind, that the right course was to let her do it on her own. She had to want to come back. To forgive him. He decided to test it.

"Forgive me, dear Mia. I have made a terrible error in judgment. I was confused. I was anxious. I didn't make the right choice. I never doubted your love. But I had to tell you the truth, finally. I don't know where this leaves us, but I love you just as I've always loved you. I don't care how all this happened. Just know that I love you. I am your husband, Mia. Nothing else matters. Believe me when I say that. Nothing else matters."

She stirred, and he thought she was going to rebuff him. She angled her head up, her face so close to his. The pain in her eyes sending a spear right through his chest. Her eyes scanned his face back and forth, tears still erupting and coursing down her cheeks. Her inhale was ragged. She opened her mouth to speak, but she said nothing, just continued to look at him, as if trying to figure out what to do.

"Mia," and now he felt his own tears streaming down his cheeks, "I will never leave you. I have only room for you in my heart. I have loved you forever, it seems. Please, please forgive me. It was a terrible mistake. I have no right to it, but I beg forgiveness."

"I—" she started.

Fredo's cell phone rang with the distinctive tone only Kyle's contact would bring him. He wished he could throw the phone against the wall.

He stood, lifting her up and setting her back on the couch and covering her up with the throw Felicia had knitted for them. She took comfort in it and buried her head in her knees again, sobbing.

Fredo answered the phone. "Kyle?"

"Fredo, you gotta get your butt to the airport. We're moving out as soon as we can assemble the team. Secretary Harrison has been murdered and all hell has broken loose. The President himself has ordered us to go over and rescue the rest of the Embassy staff and to retrieve his body and bring him home."

"Kyle—"

He looked across the room to Mia, who brought her head up, wiped her face and nodded. "Go."

"Fredo? Something wrong?" Kyle asked.

Yes, everything was wrong. The timing sucked big time. Everything he valued was on the line, and he had no time to work it out. He was kicking himself all over the house for having waited so long.

"I'm on my way."

He ended the call and came back to Mia's side, sitting close to her but not wrapped around her.

"We're all leaving. Again, I must ask for your forgiveness. I can't say no. It is what I do, and you know this, Mia. But please tell me you'll think about this and know that I love you. We will talk when I get back."

Her glow was gone. She looked tired, on overload. He worried about her condition. Daring to touch her face, just her cheek, just a gesture to show her how he cared for her, his thumb brushed the tears from her cheek. He came in slow and kissed her on the mouth. But his kiss was not returned.

"It's okay. I'm leaving now, but I'm coming back." He tilted her chin up. She didn't look at him. "Mia," he leaned to the side to catch her gaze and their eyes met. "Know that every fiber of my being belongs to you, my love. I cannot, and will not, even if you ask me, give up on us, give up on you. I made a mistake. That's all it was. A horrible mistake. I will never do such a thing again. Please trust me. Can you do that?"

He knew he was on thin ice, and he desperately wanted an affirmation she was going to be here for him when he returned.

And then it occurred to him he was being selfish. This was the point where he had to trust *her*, not the other way around. She was the wife of a SEAL, and as such, she had to do her part of the healing. He'd told her the truth. And this time, that was a mistake. He had to trust that she'd believe him. If she couldn't, then she couldn't. But, regardless of what effect it had on her, on their love and their family, he was a SEAL first and foremost, and he had to rush to do his job, perhaps never to be able to return to her. He'd have to leave without the reassurance he selfishly desired.

One last time, he placed his palm at the top of her head, smoothing down the beautiful curls of her jet black hair. It might be the last time he ever touched her, he thought.

He decided to take it as it was, because now he had to reel himself in and prepare for something altogether different. He had to descend to the gates of Hell itself and possibly death. And he had to walk there willingly with his wits about him, or he'd get someone else killed as well as himself.

He stood. Approaching his bags, he knew it would be easier if he looked back to see if she even followed his movement to the door. It might give him some degree of hope, some indication she'd remain by his side.

But he overruled that decision, picked up both his bundles which always contained his tactical gear, and opened the door. But he couldn't leave like this. He glanced over his shoulder. That's when he saw her running to him. He dropped the bags and allowed her body to slam into his. Her kiss was urgent, the gallow's kiss he'd heard about so many times. That one last time to touch the heart and soul of the most important person in his life. It stung, but he held her for as long as he dared, kissed her hard, and then pulled away.

"Come back to me, Fredo." Her fierce stare was intended to show him her strength and to give some to him as well. But he saw she was petrified, just barely able to scrape up enough to show him what she had.

"I promise."

"I don't understand how all this could happen, but you have to be the father. I swear to you it is so."

"I believe you. We'll sort it out later. Nothing in this world will keep me from coming home. Nothing."

CHAPTER 16

The large transport took off abruptly, its frame and insides groaning like a huge dinosaur with wings. The evening was fully upon them without a hint of light on the horizon. The red glow of the beast's interior was a familiar sight.

He'd changed clothes into his lightweight tactical gear when he arrived at their hangar. It wasn't like a boy's club for him, nor was it for Kyle, Armando, Coop and several of the other guys. T.J. was in a rotten mood, so when a couple of newbies began fist-bumping he gave them a scowl like they were children. What they were going into wasn't going to be any picnic. Yes, Fredo understood how exciting it was to go on your first mission, but it didn't mean he or any of the older Team guys wanted to see it.

As he followed behind the newbies getting ready to board, hanging back with Coop and Kyle, Armando sidled up to him.

"Nice job, Frodo. Knocked my sister up good and proper." The handsome SEAL showed him a bunch of white teeth Fredo wanted to punch out of his mouth.

He wondered how he'd gotten the news and then remembered they'd told Danny and Luci last night at dinner. No, *tonight* at dinner! And he hadn't even had the chance to say good-bye to little Ricardo who would wonder why he wasn't around.

"Hey, you in shock about the new little one, bro?" Armando seemed to notice Fredo wasn't all smiles.

Armando of course had no clue what had transpired. Fredo didn't want to be the one to tell him. He just didn't have the energy. He noticed Coop grab Armani's arm and pull him aside. He was grateful someone was going to explain it to his brother-in-law, but it still sucked someone else was carrying his bags. He should have had the *cojones* to do it himself. But he remained feeling numb, hating to leave Mia in that tangled state. Worried about her, the baby, and just about everything else. He knew he had to adjust his thinking so he could focus on the mission or he'd never make it back home.

Danny caught up to Fredo. "Sorry. I shouldn't have told them."

Fredo stopped and T.J. ran into him from behind.

"Them?" Fredo felt he could punch Danny too.

Danny was fidgeting, searching from side to side. "We ran into T.J. and Shannon, Armani, Jones, and Carter." He rolled his eyes. "At the ice cream shop."

Fredo just continued walking. T.J. passed him but bumped into his left side on purpose and nearly knocked him off his feet.

Love you too, asshole.

"Surprised you didn't get a fuckin' bullhorn out and stand in front of Joe's to shout out to traffic going up and down the Strand."

Danny shrugged "Sorry, man." He stayed in step with Fredo.

But it was the wakeup call he needed. Time to remember where he was at all times, to know who was behind, who was leading. When to speak. When to act. Watch everything. He knew if someone had tossed a grenade into the belly of the plane, it would take him more than a couple of seconds to fall on it like he'd been trained, and that would cost everyone their lives.

But knowing he was dangerously distracted was the first step. He had to face that fear, step on it like he did the sand spider over in Iraq.

"Naw, Danny. No apology needed. My wife would be on the horn to everyone. I was actually surprised she'd held off." He rolled his shoulder just before he took the climb to the plane's innards.

"Probably wanted you to be there."

Yea, Mia would be like that. Would want to share the news with him by her side. Because she had no idea what he was going to say, talk to her about. She must have felt like a yo-yo for all he'd put her through.

Fuck!

He sat down, stowed his bags with all the others, and strapped in. To his right was Coop. To his left was his brother-in-law, Armando. Directly across from him was Kyle, and he was watching. The giggle boys at the end stopped their punching and hitting when the plane abruptly roared into the sky. They all got looks from the older guys and quickly shut up.

Fredo leaned back, closed his eyes, and tried to will himself to dream. If he could just get some rest, get into some fuckin' dream about normal life before the emotional events of today, he might gain the additional strength he'd need. This would be the last time he'd be able to check out. And that's all he wanted to do right now. Coop knew to leave Fredo well enough alone because he told the Nebraska farmboy what had happened. And Coop had the smarts not to tell Fredo he'd predicted what would happen.

Motherfucker's right like ninety percent of the time.

He hated that about his buddy.

And Armando? Well, he'd had his share of turmoil in his life. But all that was past him. They were brothers on the Team and brothers by marriage on the outside too, which was common on all SEAL Teams. Always would be, too. These bonds sometimes lasted beyond the marriages that initiated them. Fredo knew Armani wouldn't blame him too much for upsetting his sister, because his efforts were legendary in winning Mia's heart.

Now he was going to have to do it again. He left with the expectation she wouldn't leave him, but he had to make sure their relationship healed solid. And damn, wasn't this emergency deployment sucky with the timing?

Before he began to feel the effects of his willpower shutting down everything so he could quickly catch some Zs, he opened his eyes a slit—just enough to see Kyle staring back at him, expressionless.

Fuck! Now I'm on his radar. He re-closed his eyes, settled and told himself the truth: it was Kyle's job. He needed to know if someone wasn't whole. He hoped to God he could wrap himself around that place he went to when he went to war.

The tires touching tarmac jolted Fredo awake. Everyone was unstrapping and rolling out in single file. He did the same.

It was early morning in Virginia. The air was brisk with the early fall chill, unlike San Diego. With the sun barely coming up, he longed for a cup of coffee to warm him up. Maybe some soup for breakfast.

He didn't engage in banter, and everyone but Coop left him alone. They sat on the metal bench, their nostrils filled with jet fuel fumes and the sounds of take-off and landing. It wasn't exactly a nice waiting room, but Fredo was grateful the noise and smells made it so normal chit-chat and conversation were not possible. He wanted to call Mia, but wasn't sure it was smart, and didn't want to cry in front of his buds. Asking Coop might subject him to hearing something he might not like or would set him off. His emotional volatility was off the charts, and he didn't like being dangerous.

Coop wandered off to a mini-store built just inside the hangar. The place had a microwave and smelled like decent coffee. Without asking, his friend came back with a bean and cheese burrito and a cup of coffee.

He looked at the burrito, the cheese melted on the inside of the plastic wrapper which had been cut off at one end, and he nearly threw up. He grabbed the coffee instead. "Give it to one of the froglets."

What a change from his first few deployments. Fredo'd packed so many energy bars that he nearly had enough to feed the whole squad. But it helped him make friends of the older guys who weren't exactly affectionate to newbies. As he watched Coop offer the burrito to the first youngster, he remembered what it was like being in their shoes. Scared to death, trying to act like you knew what you were doing, but afraid you'd pee your pants or do something to injure another Team guy or get someone killed.

Now? Now he wasn't worried about it. If he got killed, it wouldn't be their fault, but he wasn't going to tell them. It would be his fault for not paying attention. And they'd learn that, too. Forget about looking good or cool. Just do what you'd been trained to, trust the training and don't worry about anything else. He also knew that being nervous was just part of it, and if at any time he wasn't nervous, he'd probably come home in a body bag.

The coffee was bitter, but thank God it was strong. He burned his tongue on the liquid, and he actually liked the feeling.

Coop sat down, sprawled his legs with knees spread, and leaned back against the corrugated metal wall, and pretending to be sleeping.

Fredo decided to act human. "Any idea how long we wait?" he asked Coop.

Coop had picked up some bubble gum and blew himself a bubble that popped all over his mouth and nose. He looked like a kid of eight. He gave Fredo a crossed-eyes look and a goofy grin. Leaning over, he whispered to Fredo, "Word has it the pilot is about to get his rocks off with one of the pretty nurses back behind the fuel truck over there. She's got a thing for the smell of tires and a place she can scream and not have to reveal her secret."

"What secret?" Fredo knew it was a mistake the instant it left his mouth.

"*She's* got three titties." Coop blew another bubble and wiggled his eyebrows, showing with his hands where they all sat, in a row across his chest.

Fredo wanted to pour his coffee on Coop's knee, but that would just be mean. All his friend had wanted to do was cheer him up. Fredo mocked checking out the fuel truck to the left. "Yea? I think I can see him on his knees. Oh man, I wish he'd hurry and quit eating her out and get to business. My fuckin' butt is getting cold, and I'm looking forward to a little vibration to satisfy myself some too."

Coop chuckled. "Now that was funny."

Yea. I'm a real hoot.

A couple of the froglets saw them checking out the fuel truck and started leaning forward, whispering to themselves and then winking back at Coop and Fredo. In spite of himself, Fredo chuckled.

"Were we ever like that, do you suppose?" Coop asked.

"I don't think so. I don't remember being that clueless. But remember old Tank and Gruber? Those guys wouldn't let up on you and all your health food crap. And they were going to drown you in beer by the end of that tour, remember?"

"God, I miss those guys. They were real men."

"Yup. They made it home so they could move to Florida and walk around in aloha shirts and flip-flops."

"And scaring tourists with all the stories at the UDT Museum. They deserved it, man," answered Coop. "They both got pretty young wives."

"That's right. I heard they take turns parachuting into the parades and festivals they have there sometimes. I loved those guys."

"Gruber's working on wife number four, I hear," said Coop.

"Fuck that."

"Knockers the size of Texas, too."

"No shit?" Fredo clutched at his chest, angling as if he had boobs the shape of the state of Texas and shook his head, rejecting the logistics. "I'd go for cantaloupes."

And that was that. The conversation had to end, because one of them had finally referred to Fredo's present situation, which brought back all the dark feelings. It just had to stop before it got worse.

"You should call her. I know you want to."

"Not sure I'm ready."

"Then get ready. Were you ready for sex your first time?"

Fredo chuckled. "I have no fuckin' idea. I don't even remember it, I was so drunk."

"Well, I sure do. It was the highlight of my summer. A real Mrs. Robinson event. She did more things to me than I ever thought possible, and it wasn't for a couple of years until I found anyone else who could do those things."

"Like what?"

"She sucked my balls, man. I could never get any of my girlfriends in high school to do that."

Fredo looked at him cross-eyed. "You should'a had them waxed, man. You're one hairy motherfucker. I'll bet you were about to ask some jock on your football team to do it."

"Soccer. Lots of horny motherfuckers like you on the soccer team. They'd have done it, too, but then I found that little minister's daughter and oh man! The girl could suck. She loved to suck, and I loved watching her suck."

Fredo was feeling better. The normal smack talk was what he needed. He was beginning to feel his edge coming back. That part of him that was unstoppable. The part that made him look like a dog who would rip your head off if you weren't careful.

"So, speaking of sucking and shit, call her."

Fredo did empty the contents of his coffee cup into Coop's lap.

Coop didn't even react. "You want me to dial the number or can you figure it out yourself?"

CHAPTER 17

The phone rang three times and then started to go to voice mail. Fredo watched several new men darken the open hangar door, looking like Naval Intelligence or CIA interrogators. While he'd been distracted watching them, his phone buzzed.

"Fredo. It's me." Her voice was hoarse, and she sounded tired.

"Sorry to call you so early, but I had to hear your voice one more time. We take off in a few, and I'll be black for twenty-four to forty-eight hours. How are you feeling?"

"Thank you. I couldn't sleep last night. I brought Ricardo home and he is a comfort, but also a handful."

"Don't do too much, Mia. Can you get some help? Have someone else come over? Maybe Luci or Shannon?"

"They have children of their own, Fredo. Their men are deployed just like you are. I can't put any more burden on them. I will ask my mother."

"Both your parents should come over. Please do that, okay Mia?"

The pause was awkward. "How are you?" she finally blurted out.

"I got some rest on the plane. Now that I've heard your voice, I will be better, my love."

He heard her explode. Her sobs were difficult to hear. "I am so ashamed, *mi amore*. I ruined our perfect day. I was so selfish."

"No, you didn't. I did." He cleared his throat and had his back to the bulk of the team, who were gathering by the front of the hangar. "Mia, so good to hear you. I will carry it with me until I come home. Please get some rest. And have Felicia and Gus come and take care of you. You have to do what's right for the baby. Promise me you will."

"I promise. And you have to promise to come home, Fredo."

"Already asked and promised."

The signoff was harder than he thought.

A Lt. Commander and several other top aides were discussing something in private with Kyle.

His LPO motioned to the group to form a gathering away from the open doorway of the hangar. Someone slid the door shut, which kept a lot of the noise from interfering with what Kyle wanted to say. The base at Oceana was hopping, busier than Fredo had ever seen it. Jets were landing and taking off like World War III was in the works. It made him shiver. They normally weren't part of such heavy operations.

Lt. Commander Kastian was introduced and began. "Listen up, because I only have a few minutes. You're heading to the

Canaries again, which is why your group is tasked with this mission. Some of you on Kyle's team have been there before, as you will recall, last year."

The audience began buzzing.

"They have transport waiting for you outside to deliver you to Morocco. We're going to send you in two private charter jets from there. Like before, you're going to travel as business leaders, on a fact-finding mission to explore trade with the islands. You are not to identify yourselves as military, understood?"

Kyle interrupted Kastian. "Once we get to Morocco, you'll have support from Uncle Sam, although no one is officially on this mission. Here we have two special State Department security units from Washington, Emergency Extraction Teams or EETs, as well as some high level SDSTs coming with. Coop and T.J. and the other medics work with the SDST, especially if we take on casualties."

Fredo watched Coop and T.J. look among the group of black-suited professionals, as if they could make out who had medical training. They'd never done a joint mission with this security grouping.

"We've also got a couple gents from a few teams here at Little Creek. I'm going to let you get acquainted on the ride over. We'll be greeted by diplomatic personnel in Morocco once we land and pick up a couple of new additions from Tenerife. Oh, and we're coming in through some storms off the coast of Africa, so hang onto your butts and get some sleep early." Kyle stepped back behind the Commander.

Lt. Commander Kastian added, "The one thing we know is that Secretary Harrison is deceased, and that's been confirmed through DNA. The extraction of that information came at a heavy price. The rest of his security team is being held hostage or dead. We have no one on the inside who knows we're on our way, and we believe they want to remove the hostages to somewhere on the mainland, possibly Morocco."

Kyle stepped next to the Lt. Commander. "If they successfully get them transported, we'll have approximately eight US personnel, including the body of the Secretary of State, and the Secretary of State's private records, computer, and cell phone, all headed into the hands of local rebels on the Canaries, trying to sell to the highest bidder, who will be someone from Morocco."

Fredo knew what kind of an explosive situation this was going to be. He hoped they had some decent intel. He raised his hand, and Kyle called on him.

"Sir, do we know the current location of the hostages and the body of Secretary Harrison? And what about the fate of Pat Lyman? Is he among the hostages or the dead?"

"You mean the Secretary's security detail?" Kyle asked. He turned to Lt. Commander Kastian.

"We believe Lyman is alive," said Kastian soberly.

"And the location?" asked Coop.

"Villa Las Palomas. I believe you know it, Coop."

It was the location Zak had nearly been killed, the house the Secretary had rented before in his brief meeting with Yousef Amir, the Secretary's friend from Stanford soccer days.

Amir was now the Prime Minister of Morocco. No one knew, Kyle said, whether he was friend, or whether he had ordered the hit on Harrison. The news started a grumble among the audience.

This was even more fucked up than the previous mission they'd been on. But the Secretary had been a patriot and had believed in what he was doing, believed he could negotiate a successful settlement and help create an in with a possible new government forming in Morocco. Now that Amir was part of that new government and the Secretary was dead, so much was left unknown. It was never good to go into a situation this way and wasn't normally how it was done. But this was a full-scale emergency and their insertion was ordered by the President himself.

Lyman, a former member of Kyle's SEAL Team 3, became the new mission. Getting him home safely became the new agenda. And of course, not taking on any Task Force casualties in the meantime.

"When you step out of that plane in Morocco and rendezvous with the chartered jets, you'll be dressed as tourists. Remember, you are business tourists, looking to make investments in Tenerife or the Canaries in general. The local news doesn't know about the Secretary, and we want it kept that way, so no speaking about it. Do not trust the locals at all. No talking about any of this amongst yourselves until we're secure. Understood?"

The crowd of nearly two dozen men nodded.

The door was opened, bringing in much-needed air into the stuffy hangar. The men lined up and boarded the huge transport plane.

Fredo and Coop stayed together. Before Fredo could begin the climb up the gangway, Coop grabbed him.

"Remember, Fredo. This is what you were made for. It's showtime."

"Roger that. I'm ready. And I'm keeping my promises. *All* my promises."

The hot Moroccan desert breeze hit them like a furnace blast, even though it was still pitch black and wouldn't lighten up for another three hours. So scorchingly hot it nearly took Fredo's breath away. He was grateful he had an aloha shirt that wasn't decorated with women in grass skirts, as it would draw too much attention and be seen as inappropriate. Several of the other Team guys wore logoed golf shirts. But the aloha shirt would identify him as an American, and that was part of the plan.

Again, they were directed to wait inside a hangar away from the prying eyes of others who might sport night vision equipment. Chairs were provided in front of a small cluster of officials preparing to address them.

An attractive career diplomat, Allison Nouri, Assistant Deputy Consular General to Morocco, spoke first, making the introductions. "Welcome to Morocco, gentlemen. While we expect that we won't be hosting you this particular trip, we trust that you will have success while on your mission to the Canary Islands. We are deeply saddened by the events that have taken place regarding Ambassador Harrison, whom I was lucky to call a friend."

She bit her lip and smiled down at a gentleman in black sitting in the front row. "I have a prior engagement and was not planning on being here today, but couldn't miss this opportunity to welcome you and to let you know the entire embassy staff welcomes you. If there is anything I or my staff can do for any one of you gentlemen, please don't hesitate to let us know. The United States is grateful for your service."

She smiled again and extended her palm toward the front row. "This is Fernando Cabrera, and he's our liaison on the islands. Anything happens and you're alone or offsite or need backup, please call him first before anyone else. While we are cordial with the local police, please do not attempt to engage their support. Mr. Cabrera?"

She stepped back, gave Cabrera an efficient bow, and abruptly shook several hands before exiting out of the rear of the building. They heard a car motor roar to life.

Cabrera took his time to stepping up to the front. He walked with a very slight limp and also appeared to have an artificial foot below the ankle. Fredo thought Cabrara looked more like an ex-military type, perhaps a freedom fighter or mercenary of some sort in his past. He left his sunglasses on. His square jaw, thin moustache, and fit physique gave him an intimidating look.

"Mrs. Nouri was not expecting this little meeting today, so I apologize for her early departure. I am a US citizen, but have lived in the Canaries my whole life. I will be your eyes and ears while here, and I also interface with the local police. As Mrs. Nouri said, you are not to engage local law enforcement at any time."

He inhaled briskly and straightened his stance, scanning the room slowly, as if checking out every man seated or standing before him. "Now the rules. The local police, called Policia Local, appear harmless and for the most part, they are. You will find them most cooperative and friendly, as long as you don't challenge their authority. They find stray dogs, write tickets for drunken behavior in public, and make sure the trash is picked up and that traffic laws are obeyed. They also are here to ensure that all tourists are treated fairly and that there are no complaints from any of the big cruise ships that dock our shores. They make sure shopkeepers don't over-charge or give incorrect change."

"The second and third groups of officials are called the Guardia Civil and the Nacional de Policia. They deal with everything from low-level crime to prostitution, human traf-ficking and the drug smuggling trades. Don't even talk to them. Easy to identify those two because they'll be dressed in all black." He stood back, hands on his chest, to demonstrate the point.

"And they wear the same glasses and gloves," Cabrera demonstrated by tapping a finger of his black gloved hand to the side of his face. He smiled, and bowed. Fredo instantly didn't trust him, and he guessed most of the Team made the same assessment.

"I believe we have a Mr. Lansdowne?" Cabrera searched the crowd, and Kyle stood and took his place beside the man.

"I've been here several times, mostly as a tourist but once most recently on our mission. When it comes to the local police, claim complete language stupidity and do not stare back at them. These are not nice guys and they're armed to the teeth and possibly—"

Cabrera interrupted Kyle. "Corrupt? Was he going to say corrupt?" He grinned, showing a glint of gold teeth in his mouth that reminded Fredo of Jaws from the 007movies. "Officially, we do not have corruption. If it exists, and I'm not saying it does, it is unofficial and small. A man does what he needs to do to provide for his family." Cabrera was cool, but his upper torso was toned and hard as any of the SEALs. Fredo wondered if he was some kind of hired gun for the State Department or CIA spooks.

"Wonder who he really works for," Danny whispered to Fredo. Fredo put his finger to his lips and frowned.

"Keep your eyes and ears open," Kyle continued. "I've got a map of the compound. It has thirty-five rooms, is relatively remote, and at the top of Las Palomas with a view of nearly the whole island. But only one way up the hill and one way down, by car. We do not have authorization for nor have we attempted to use any choppers."

Outside the open hangar door a sleek Gulfstream with an Avjet logo taxied next to a larger one already on the ground.

"Best of luck, gentlemen," Cabrera said.

Everyone rose. The two teams boarded both luxury jets, Coop, Kyle, Armando and Fredo staying together in the larger of the two. Cabrera boarded the other Gulfstream along with several members of his staff and a couple of Team Guys Fredo recognized from SEAL Team 8.

After the initial quick tour of the boardroom, the rear bedroom, a full library, and galley kitchen, Kyle, Coop, Fredo and Armando took over the small cluster of seats at the rear near the back bedroom. Everyone else paired up and sat in clusters on the opposite side of the galley behind the crew quarters. The jet came with two male stewards. Everyone adjusted their seats and prepared for the roughly three hour flight to Gran Canaria.

CHAPTER 18

After they landed, Cabrera whisked the teams into black Suburbans and they were transported to a luxury hotel complex at the base of Las Palomas. The two presidential suites were adjoining, taking up the entire top floor of the hotel, with good visibility to the villa at the peak of the mountain. Kyle and several others searched the area with high powered scopes from their long guns and found no sign of activity. But going down the hillside, little houses and more modest villas dotted the countryside, any one of them within a few hundred yards of the grand estate.

"Do they have the road blocked off?" Kyle asked Cabrera.

"You see up there, the home with the turquoise roof?"

Kyle nodded.

"I have a man there. This is the house of my uncle who is vacationing in the US as we speak. If we can somehow get to that house, we will have an excellent vantage point. Angel, my niece, is available by phone. There are no roadblocks as of yet and no sign of any activity."

"How far up is that?" Coop asked.

Cabrera thought about it for a second. "I think it's about three miles, maybe four from here."

"That's within range," said Coop, picking up a black hard case. He opened it and held inside the grey foam padding was a tiny four-propeller drone with controller box. "This thing," he held it up like holding onto a live a crab, "I can control with the unit here for up to six miles. If I can get it in the air, I can calibrate and take pictures to send to my computer here."

"When did you get this?" Fredo asked.

"I made it." Coop beamed to the flock who admiringly drew around him.

"No shit," said Kyle. "Thank God we didn't go commercial. They'd have taken this thing away before we got out of the states."

Cabrera peered over the top. "How quiet is it?"

"Oh, she purrs all right. Just like a kitten. Very quiet. Brushless motor. With just a tad of a buzz, which you might expect."

He showed the little camera installed with a remote lens.

"Should we give it a try?" Kyle asked Cabrera. "Any local laws against it?"

Cabrera's smile lit up. "I don't think anyone knows about these. Otherwise, all the local boys would be using them to spy on the rich ladies in the villas at the top who like to sunbathe naked."

"And just how do you know?" asked T.J.

Cabrera removed his glasses, his grin wide and his teeth blindingly white. "But I've already told you. My uncle lives up there. There are advantages of living on top because you get the best view."

Several of the men chuckled.

Coop was putting together the machine, clicking the wings and rotors in place and connecting the batteries.

"We got a balcony up here we can test this a little?" he asked.

"What's wrong with the roof?" asked Fredo.

Coop handed him the laptop. Holding the drone, and with the controller unit under his arm, he followed the stairs one of the men found that led to the top of the building. Broken bottles littered the area along with an iron bedframe and a stained mattress left out in the elements for what appeared to be several years. Two plastic lawn chairs looked like recent additions to the litter.

Coop gingerly set the drone down and took back the computer, logging in to the drone seeker software. A tiny beeping sound indicated the connection was made. He clicked the camera link and promptly viewed the crowd's shoes and lower legs.

He gingerly handed the computer to Fredo. "Keep it steady and don't move around."

"Roger that."

Coop brought a plastic chair over and sat, placing the controller on his thighs. He adjusted the speed of the rotors, and the drone rose nearly twenty feet up and then with a push of a button, came back down, landing softly.

"It has an automatic homing device on it and landing sensors. Pretty cool, huh?"

"Big improvement to the one we bought in Cupertino."

"I still have that one, but this one can run for nearly an hour and go wider in range. You'll see."

He maneuvered the machine up and down several times, testing every control and adjusting the magnification on the lens. He glanced over to make sure the picture on his computer was of sufficient quality.

"Now all we have to hope for is consistent internet."

Kyle piped up. "It won't operate without internet?"

"Oh, it will, but we won't see a picture. But even without internet, the camera records everything. We'd just have to manually download it. The beauty of this thing is that with internet we can see it real time and therefore direct it to fly in certain areas."

"So let 'er rip," said T.J.

With a steady hand, Coop directed the drone to rise one more time, and avoiding the heavy grid pattern of wiring that extended above the rooftops and occasional radio and TV antennae, sent the drone up the hill toward Las Palomas. Kyle and Cabrera followed it with small Swiss-made binoculars.

On the computer screen, Fredo noticed the camera and sound were turned off. "You want this on, yes?"

"Yes. Yes. Yes. Turn it on."

After the white bird was out of sight, the men circled around Fredo and the computer screen. He brought the other chair so it would be more steady, and he sat. The bird flew over rooftops, flew over backyards, the sounds of chickens and dogs barking, occasionally a dog barking at the drone itself. Coop watched the screen and tested his skills following a couple cars up the steep road towards the top and then moved on when the car found a garage or driveway to turn into. He kept it at sufficient height that, except for the occasional dog, no one noticed it moving above them.

At last the drone arrived at the villa. On first glance, it appeared not much was disturbed until they saw a body floating in the pool, a stream of blood leaching into the otherwise blue water.

"So that's today. The body wouldn't leak more than about twelve hours in water like that. That's new."

"Can you get down closer?" asked Kyle.

Coop kept the machine double the roof height and searched the sky to find the angle of the sun. "Don't want to cause a shadow someone would recognize."

Before he lowered it any farther, he did a quick surveillance of all the windows and doors, looking for anything they could see from the outside. One sliding glass door was broken, shards of the pane spilling out onto the patio in the direction of the pool.

Cabrera turned his head and squinted. "Can you get that car there? That little dark one?"

Coop pulled back and then swung in lower, away from any visible window in the house. He clicked pictures of it. "We can enlarge this later and see if we can find a plate."

"Look at that," he said, pointing to the roof of the car. That's when the red strobe light became visible.

Fredo was stunned. "So it looks like the locals are investigating."

"Search to the right, over there in the bushes," ordered Cabrera.

With magnification, Fredo saw the legs of a body lying on its side. "Okay, we got two dead. But I'm not sure we've counted the police in the hostages, so that means we got the Secretary, one other dead guy, and an additional police officer."

Voices could be heard coming from inside the house. Behind a set of closed white drapes, a red explosion formed as something slammed against the glass on the inside. Several in the group began to swear.

"Do one more loop quickly, and then bring her home," said Kyle. "If we have any hope of rescuing anyone up there, we gotta go." While Coop recorded the entire perimeter of the house and grounds, Kyle stood and walked over to Cabrera. Placing his hands on the man's shoulders, he began, "Fernando?"

"No, Lansdowne."

"We gotta get up there and now. It would be a whole lot faster if we had a bird."

"No. The population here demands there be no helicopters. Crime is a problem. We'd have them up here all the time. The answer is no, my friend. Sorry."

The drone returned to the exact same spot where it took off. Coop quickly removed the batteries and stowed the parts and controller in a smaller, more portable pack.

"Okay, then we get up as far as we can in the Suburbans, but we pack light, gents." With another look to Cabrera, he decided, "I gotta go with my guys, Fernando. They go first, the first two vans. Then you guys come up behind. If we bring four vehicles, everyone in the world will know."

"Agreed. And we'll stagger the drop-off. There is a small park just down the hill where the trucks turn around. They won't be able to see it from the villa. But they'll hear it."

"You gotta leave someone back here to be our scout. Pick one of your guys," said Kyle. Cabrera made the choice and left him a radio with binoculars.

Everyone scrambled off the rooftop, leaving the Cabrera's man to stay behind and spot from the position at the hotel.

The men loaded their weapons and packed everything they could carry, and Kyle's squad put on their Kevlar. Fredo only had three mics, so he gave one to Kyle. He kept one and gave the other to Armani, who was the first sniper. Danny would hang with him to be his second. T.J. checked his medic kit, making sure nothing was loose and that he had swabs, saline solution and duct tape for emergency patches. Then he absorbed some of the contents of Coop's kit so Coop could insert the drone and controller.

Kyle's twelve piled in the first two Suburbans, and they raced out of the town center, briefly got caught in traffic, and then found a route that lead to the La Palma Park road up to the top. Within minutes, they found the park entrance, which had been cabled closed. Danny cut it loose with bolt cutters, and they stowed the vans in the back corner of the lot under dense foliage.

The beautiful blue of the bay below, dotted with three huge cruise ships in port as well as the glistening ocean beyond, painted a picture of a peaceful little island perfect for a sunny exotic vacation. Away from the bustling city center with its collection of bicycles, scooters, small cars and tourist busses, it probably resembled the island a hundred years ago, the only exception being the maze of electrical wires and cisterns atop roofs.

Kyle laid out instructions on where everyone was to go. Armando and Danny were to get high and be able to pick off anyone trying to escape. The rest of the squad had their designated assignments.

While they waited for word everyone else was in place, Fredo glanced down at the blue water, aware that some of the most deadly places looked like paradise.

The spotter confirmed no further movement at the villa. Kyle got word they were all in place.

It was time to do what they did best.

Piece of cake.

CHAPTER 19

Sayid Qabbani prepared himself for meeting his spiritual father, his teacher. He was searching for someone to cook for the leader so that when the man came to his tiny apartment, Sayid could honor him with a good home-cooked meal prepared by loving hands of a true believer. He was unsuccessful so decided to consult his regular teacher at the local Center.

Malmoud Suleimani was not pleased Sayid had qualified for a visit from the infamous holy man. His distrust of Kahn surprised Sayid.

"We are Americans, Sayid. You have been born and raised here. We take on traditions in this country that perhaps wouldn't be as accepted in the country of your parents' birth now, but were very much in favor for hundreds of years before the craziness. Peoples of different faiths even worshiped at the same temples, even though they no longer do today."

Sayid was having a hard time listening to the man.

"Being tolerant enables us to live in peace among the Christians and Jews and people of other faiths here. We are an experiment in tolerance, brought here to spread peace and understanding. This is the way I choose to see it. We have been brought here by the Prophet so we can be examples of the true teachings. It used to be so in Syria. All religions lived together relatively peacefully. That was before all the madness. If it can work here, perhaps it can be reintroduced back to Syria."

Sayid would have agreed with his teacher a few years ago, but the more studying he'd done over the internet and the two trips he'd taken, the more he understood that tolerance was the *weaker* side of devotion. Allowing the margins of one's faith to slip away or shift slightly made for sloppy habits. Sloppy habits created a lazy mind. A lazy mind soon disengaged the heart, leaving no devotion to the Prophet or his teachings.

"You are wrong, Teacher. We must prepare the way. There is work to do to hold the standard, to conquer new lands in order to establish the kingdom. And I agree, if we can do it without war, all the better. But I'm not afraid to fight."

"But the Americans have the right to their country, their beliefs. We came as guests, generously accepted as a refugee peoples your parents benefitted from. We must honor their hospitality."

"No, I disagree. How can you say that?"

"Because it is the wise and the true way. These people are our hosts, not our enemy."

"But, Teacher, they are non-believers! Of course they are the enemy. You doubt what is written in the book? *All* shall come under the shield of the Prophet. If they do not honor Him, they are not afforded protection."

"I do not understand my faith the same way, Sayid. I do not teach this. Where have you learned such nonsense?"

That's when Sayid decided he could not trust the teacher. He had perhaps said too much. If he consulted anyone, it would be the great holy man himself. The internet cautioned against those who only gave lip service to their faith and were not willing to die for it.

He ended their conversation quickly and decided he'd never have further contact with Suleimani.

Later in the day, he received a text message to telephone the great Amid Khan as soon as was possible. Could the visit be cancelled? He hoped not.

They gave each other blessings from the Prophet. Sayid was nervous, but the holy man had a gentle, uncritical voice. He was older than he expected.

"You sound like a strong young man, Sayid. Your test was quite impressive and left your mark on the San Diego Christian complex. Much will be asked of you in the coming weeks. Are you ready?"

"Yes, Teacher."

"Good. I have need of a place to stay for a few days. Can you provide me with this?"

"Yes. I would be most honored. You said you would be coming Saturday? Is that still the date?"

"No, Sayid. I will need to come tomorrow and to stay a week. Do you live with a woman?"

"No, Teacher. I am alone, single."

"Ah, perfect."

"But, Teacher, I have a simple apartment. Nothing close to what you have been used to."

The teacher clucked his tongue in a high-pitched laugh he'd heard some of the older women do. "You have no idea what I've lived through or been used to. You would not say such things."

"Sir?"

"All will be revealed soon. I will text you before I arrive in San Diego. You can pick me up? You have a car?"

"No, Teacher. I own no such thing."

"Then you will borrow one."

"But I do not drive."

There was a pause. "Is there anyone you trust who could drive you?"

He thought about his boss, Carlos. "There is Carlos, the man I work for, but no one who practices our faith. There are public busses."

"Not acceptable. Very well. You will text me your address, and I will find passage to your home. I will arrive tomorrow with a car. And I think the first thing we will do is teach you to drive."

"Teacher?"

"Yes, my son."

"I work tomorrow. I thought perhaps you were coming on Saturday. I do not work Saturday."

The long pause on the other end of the line worried Sayid. At last he heard a great sigh of resignation. "Then you will quit."

The line went dead.

CHAPTER 20

Fredo and Coop came upon the body in the parking lot near the police car. Coop verified the man was dead. He'd had his throat slit. They carefully checked the foliage near the body for signs anyone had been lying in wait and found no such evidence. They had good visibility on the front entrance.

Fredo rummaged carefully through his bag of tricks. He was to place an explosive charge on the front door which was made of solid mahogany roughly two inches thick. He remembered these well and noted that if need be they'd make good cover, unlike the crumbling and often-patched plaster walls. He listened to Kyle's message, coming from the rear of the structure.

"Body is not Lyman and appears to be a local uniform. Someone is on the phone inside."

He relayed Kyle's message, coming from the rear of the structure, to Coop and the two others who had come with them. One by one, they hugged the front of the house, looking for some access to view the inside, but drapes were pulled everywhere. It was not ideal to go in blind, but the element of surprise might be enough to protect them.

Fredo attached a breach device at the front door activated by a remote detonator. He gingerly protected the trigger, tucking it inside his vest pocket.

"Blow and go set," he whispered.

"On my count of three."

"Roger that."

"At your ten o'clock," messaged Armando. Fredo stood away from the house and peered up and to his left, spotting Armando flattened on a rooftop, the barrel of his rifle peering from behind a cistern. He couldn't see Danny, but knew he was there somewhere. From this vantage, Armando would have unobstructed sight to both the front and back entrances.

All of a sudden, a skirmish broke out inside, and they could hear sounds of someone being beaten. Fredo could make out just enough in Spanish to determine that one of the hostages was a woman, probably part of the housekeeping or cooking crew. Although she was apparently not the one being beaten, her terrified screams pierced the quiet mountaintop. A large crane was startled from a nearby tree and flew off gracefully. A dog began to bark.

A conversation was being conducted by telephone. The speaker was relatively calm, but firm, speaking in an Arabic dialect Fredo couldn't make out. Coop scanned the driveway and foliage up the hill. Fredo continued to listen to the speaker's demands and then heard the crack of something being struck against flesh. A man's voice responded in pain, but barely able to speak, more like a groan. He knew they were running out of time.

"I count three voices. One woman, Spanish, one Arabic male, and another male, injured."

"Copy that. I got three, no four males."

Fredo had an idea. "Can I hot the car?"

"Go ahead."

Slowly, Fredo pulled out the detonator and handed it to Coop, who held it gingerly in the palm of his great hand, nodding. Then Fredo ran back to the police car and opened the passenger door, careful not to make a sound. He packed the center console with a wad of C4, stuck a detonator cap in the middle of it, and closed the lid. He unwrapped and pressed another strip of the explosive underneath the dash where it couldn't be seen. Closing the passenger door, he ran back to join the rest of his team.

"This is taking too long," Coop whispered. "Ask him what the holdup is."

"Car is hot."

"Stand by." About thirty seconds later he heard Kyle's voice and counted to the rest with his fingers. "On my mark, three, two, one, go!"

Coop pressed the detonator, and simultaneously, they heard breaking glass as the front door flew off its hinges, sending long, sharp splinters of wood everywhere. Inside the house, they heard automatic gunfire.

Coop and two others dove through smoke and debris at the front while Fredo waited outside to pick up anyone who managed to escape. He heard a second woman screaming on the other side of the house as a barrage of automatic gunfire sprayed the interior.

The firefight was over in a matter of seconds, which was how it usually went when they were on a mission. Fredo remained alert, sensing something was about to shift. These were the dangerous times for a SEAL if they dropped their guard too soon.

He was not surprised when, all of a sudden, three men in dark clothing bolted through the gaping front door opening, headed for the little police car in front. Fredo hung back in the encroaching jungle at the side but maintained a view of the car and the men running toward it.

"Three going for it," he whispered.

"Send them home."

As soon as the passenger door closed, Fredo detonated the C4, and the car erupted in a ball of fire, sending pieces of metal flying, including a flaming trunk lid that landed at Fredo's feet.

He started to hear the "clear" shouts by several of the men inside. A contingent with Cabrera approached the corner and split into two as Cabrera and three others entered the front and a handful of men went around the back.

The all clear sign was given, and Fredo relaxed for the first time in twelve hours, nearly peeing his pants. Squinting up to the rooftop, he caught sight of Danny climbing down the side of the structure while Armando was on his knees, protected by the cistern, scanning the countryside with his scope, looking for escapees. When they made eye contact he gave Armando the thumbs up, which was returned.

They heard sirens snaking their way up the winding road toward their location.

When Fredo walked inside the house, the carnage was everywhere. There were at least six dead terrorists. One woman in a white apron had been shot through the stomach and was crumpled up near the shattered window, blood spattered all over the drapes blowing in the breeze. Fredo recognized one of the security team who had worked with Lyman last year, shot but alive. Lyman was on the floor, his face a bloody mess and unrecognizable from beatings, but breathing. He found a cook huddled in one of the cabinets in the galley kitchen, unharmed.

In the back bedroom, the room where Zak had been shot nearly a year ago, lay the body of the Secretary of State, Porter Harrison. His face had sunken, his eyes, still open, were glassed over and bore an expression of surprise. Fredo felt sorry for the man who had tried to negotiate the cesspool that was politics in this part of the world and had lost.

Coop and T.J. prepared DNA samples of all the victims including the Secretary, as was required.

Cabrera was now in charge, and Fredo had a renewed respect for the man, who seemed to be familiar with the newly arrived units from the Guarda Civil. He did a good job running interference, keeping the police away from any of their squad. His men answered questions politely and explained in sketchy detail how the gunfight happened.

Kyle was on the phone reporting back to San Diego and making arrangements for the body of the Secretary as well as his security detail to be returned to the States. The two survivors would be airlifted to a Naval ship arriving from the coast of Morocco.

Fredo wanted to call Mia, but he thought the sounds of sirens and all the rescue equipment might scare her. He decided to find a more private spot back at their room, over a beer and after a nice cool shower.

"And that's how it's done," Coop said as they high-fived. They both slung their duty bags over their shoulders and with the rest of the Team headed back to the Suburbans waiting for them at the park entrance.

It had been a stellar morning. Still plenty of time for lunch and maybe a beer or two if they didn't have to go patrol or do some intel. No one in the world would understand what his days were like, or what kind of a man he'd become. There wasn't any way to explain what it felt like to kill, to not have the slightest doubt he was doing something good and honorable, and that he got to do it with his best friends, men who would die for him anytime. There was no way to explain that and never would be.

He looked at Coop's tall gangly frame walking down the hill, a shitload of firepower in one bag and enough medical supplies to treat the entire squad in his other. He could drop and take a man's leg off with a pocket knife in a minute, tie off the veins and get him on his way, albeit with help. He could rescue a child and shield that child with his body gladly, maybe at the cost of his own life. In a million years, he'd never expected to have a friend who looked or acted like Coop, who came from the other side of the tracks and with whom he had both nothing and everything in common at the same time.

It was what they shared as brothers, this high intensity mission not many could execute. He felt like the luckiest man in the whole world.

CHAPTER 21

It was just past daybreak in San Diego when Fredo was able to get a call to Mia.

"So is everything okay, *mi amore*?"

Fredo actually cracked a grin. If he told her the truth, she'd never believe it. He wanted to say something deep and meaningful, but the truth was, he was going to get shit-faced if Kyle said they were done and headed home. He couldn't tell her that either. He couldn't tell her he'd just blown up three guys in a car and enjoyed watching as all their body parts went flying over the grounds, that a cook was hiding in the kitchen, or that the Secretary of State was dead, because the news hadn't picked that up yet. He could make some stupid shit up, which wouldn't be fair. So he didn't have anything to say, and yet he had everything to say.

"I'm good."

"So, no bad guys, no big fights?"

He grinned again. It would be so much fun to mess with her. He'd wait and do it when he got home, and then he'd spend the entire evening making it up to her. Now, that gave him an idea.

"I got a stiffy."

"Really?"

"You think I'd lie about that? I never lie about stuff like that. I'm wishing you were here, Mia. Honest I am."

"If only." Then she laughed that little laugh he loved. "You're pulling my leg."

He grinned again, and yup, got even harder. "Oh man, that is such a lovely thought. I'd could just pull that lovely leg of yours right out from under the comforter, pull your naked body all over me, and I'd let you do whatever you wanted to do to me. Honest, Mia."

She obviously liked that. It made him happy to distract her.

"So, you *are* coming home soon, then?"

"We're on call. Nothing going on this afternoon, but you never know." If she asked him again, he'd have to get a little firm with her. She knew she wasn't supposed to ask. "How are you feeling?"

"Lonely."

Fredo sat down in the cushioned wicker chair out on the veranda, overlooking the blue waters offshore. A loud horn blasted from one of the cruise ships leaving port.

"What was that?"

"I farted."

She laughed. "So you're at the dock, then. Watching the ships? You having an umbrella drink?"

"Something like that," he lied, but oh, how he wished. He wished she was there with him. That they were eating oysters and shrimp and drinking Tequila and waiting for Round No. 2 or Round No. 3. She'd be completely naked, of course.

"Actually, I'm drawing on a beer." At least that was accurate. "So how's Ricardo?"

"Oh, you want to talk to him? He's right here." Fredo heard Mia waking the toddler up. "It's your dad, Ricardo. Want to talk to him?"

Fredo could hear the little one enthusiastically grab the phone.

"Papa! When are you coming home? I want to go to the park and play some baseball."

"I will be home soon. You taking good care of Mama?"

"Si, Papa. Hey, Papa? We're having a baby. Did you know?"

"Of course I know. I'm excited. How about you?"

"Yes. A brother. Not a sister. Girls are no good."

Fredo knew that probably came from Ali, from the conversation the other night. "Listen, Ricardo. I need you to be extra careful and look after Mama. You are the man of the house now."

"I will. Papa, when are you coming home?"

"Soon, Ricardo. Very soon, I hope. Not long at all."

"Here's Mama."

Fredo heard him wiggle his way out of Mia's bed. She was in the habit of letting him sleep with her when Fredo was gone.

"I'm so sorry, Fredo. I think he has to pee. I'm bringing the phone. I have to ask you something."

Fredo heard the echoes in the bathroom, Ricardo's objection to having to sit on the potty seat, and the sound when Mia dropped the phone on the floor once. Then he heard Ricardo peeing. He didn't mind hearing all the normal things about being home he was missing, all the little things a family experienced on a normal day. It was what he wanted, a normal day, whatever that was.

He heard the toilet flush and didn't mind it one bit. It beat the sound of gunfire, or explosions, or what it sounded like when pieces of a body landed at your feet or hit a rock in front of you. These were things he replaced with the little things like Ricardo taking a pee, and his wife running around trying to get him situated so she could sit and talk with her husband. He needed to hear these things from home to keep him feeling human after what he'd done and seen.

"Okay, okay. I'm here now. So sorry."

"No worries, Mia. I'm not going anywhere. Just sitting here biding my time, enjoying hearing you do the things you do well."

"Oh yea? Like what?"

He inhaled. *Game on.* God, he loved how quickly she could pick up what he was needing. "Well, for one thing, the way your little feet skip on the wooden floor at our house when you're barefoot and fully naked, your sweet little ass jiggling just out of my reach."

"Ah, you make a girl feel wanted."

"Oh, baby, you're wanted."

"How so? I mean, what would you do if you caught me?"

"First, I'd bend you over and just look at you."

"Really, I'd like that. I'm going to bend over right now. Can you see me?"

He heard her body move and had no doubt she was doing just that.

"Where are you?"

"In the bedroom."

"And Ricardo? I don't want him seeing you when we talk because I'm going to make you do things…"

"Not to worry, *mi amore*. He's watching TV right now. We have a few minutes, but you have to be quick."

"Quick?"

"Well, you usually like to take your time, but sweetheart, *mi amore*, I'm afraid I can't give you that."

"Then what can you give me?"

"It would have been nice with a snap chat or something."

"Not allowed, baby. You know that. And not smart, anyway."

"You should hear some of the girlfriends talk about it. Some of the guys are not so careful."

"I don't want to talk about any of that. What are you doing now?"

"Well, I am touching myself. If your hand was on mine, what would you make me do?"

"You just rub that nice little bud of yours."

"Ah, yes. I feel that. Sooooo nice."

"Man, this is making me hard, Mia."

"So pretend I'm going to put my lips on it. I can make it all better."

He heard her moan into the phone. "Nice, Mia."

"You taste good, sweetheart. I want you to come in my mouth."

"Come on Fredo, we gotta move!" Kyle's voice commanded and Fredo jumped so high he fell off the wicker chair onto the floor.

"Sorry. Okay, just one minute. Talking to my wife."

T.J. was behind Kyle, shaking his head as Fredo attempted to tell Mia he'd call her back. That is, if she could hear him. She was laughing so hard he wasn't sure what she was getting.

He hung up and placed the phone back in his vest and put the Kevlar back on.

"You were fuckin' your wife, weren't you?" T.J. grinned.

"Not possible, T.J. You know that."

"I'm telling you, that brain of yours is scrambled. Most men get serious when they get married. You were serious before. Now you're just scrambled."

"Speak for yourself."

"Fredo! Come!" Kyle shouted out to the veranda.

Coop handed him his duty bag. "You need water, I got an extra one."

"Thanks, Coop. What's up?"

"Little crowd down at the morgue. They can't get the bodies out."

The black Suburbans dashed down the little swale and back into the city center. The traffic was horrific. They were told there were only three traffic lights on the whole island, but today none of them were working, not that it would make any difference.

Kyle was trying to reach Cabrera. "Fuck it all to hell," he growled as he hung up.

The driver, one of Cabrera's men, was going to turn left and Kyle stopped him.

"Where the hell are you going? Morgue is over that way, isn't it?" Kyle barked.

"They didn't go to the hospital morgue. They were ordered to the morgue for Policia Nacionale."

"That's not what the plan was. Where's Cabrera?"

"He's trying to fix it. The Policia Nacionale diverted the transport."

Fredo leaned over the seat and asked the driver. "You mean each branch has their own morgue?"

"Yessir. At the house, we were working with the *Civil.* We think someone was tipped off, and the vans were taken over and ordered to the morgue at Nacionale. So sorry."

T.J., Coop, and Fredo all exchanged a look. Fredo knew this was going to cost someone something. Kyle was on the phone again. This time he was speaking with the Assistant Deputy in Morocco.

"I don't have a name, ma'am. But I'll be sure to put them on the line. What is the holdup?"

Fredo heard the high-pitched voice of Mrs. Nouri, but not what she said.

"How're we fuckin supposed to—sorry, ma'am—but how are we supposed to get that today?"

Kyle shook his head when he got the answer. "So what should I pay then?"

After waiting for another brief answer from her, he replied, "That's not a real answer, ma'am."

Kyle signed off after promising to keep her updated. Fredo's LPO turned to face the three amigos in the second seat.

"Well, not sure we could have known to have a plan B here, but it seems she has no jurisdiction on the Island. The consular office handling this jurisdiction is in Barcelona. She's going to try. She thinks the hang-up could be someone is looking to make some money over a death certificate."

"Which means a shit-pile of paperwork we don't wanna fill out," said Fredo.

"No kiddin'," said T.J.

"Kyle, we're gonna have to steal them away from the morgue, then," said Coop, cool and flat like it was no issue.

"We got twelve guys and three dead bodies, and who knows how many police. I wish I could get hold of Cabrera." Kyle looked at the driver. "You ready for a little fun? I got an idea."

The driver stiffened, suddenly aware of the fact he'd been conscripted to do something that was probably against a bunch of laws and would be impossible to explain.

"I am your driver."

"And Cabrera says to sit on us, right? Not to let us out of your sight, right?"

"Si, Senior. That is the case."

"So that's all you gotta do."

Fredo touched Kyle's shoulder. "What's the plan, boss?"

"We're going to play a little dress-up." He pointed to the driver. "In California we're used to dressing in drag for Halloween. You ever done that?"

"Drag?" The driver's expression was a deer-in-the-head-lights type of stare.

T.J. leaned back in his seat, crossed his arms and watched the passing traffic and people on bicycles. "This is gonna be fun." He finally broke out in a full smile.

"Hey, Lanny," asked Coop. "You do know that the Secretary is going to be rather odorous? I mean, he's already starting to bloat and, you know, the fluids and such."

"Coop, I think we need to find some adult diapers somewhere." He turned to the driver again. "Drug store or pharmacia? We need a big store that sells everything."

The second Suburban followed them to the edge of the local open-air market, surrounded by shops which sold everything known to man, including silks and shawls, even a used burqa in light grey. Kyle pointed, and Coop purchased everything he selected. T.J. found the adult diapers at one of the shops that had just re-opened after lunch. He pointed out words on the package, printed in red, *talla extra larga*.

Fredo followed Kyle and helped purchase several long saris and a used purse made of carpet fiber. On his own, Fredo purchased a huge brassier, which got a chuckle out of Coop.

The Suburban drivers were conferring while Carter and Danny ran over and asked what the stop was for and were told as much as Kyle had managed to figure out.

"Seriously, we're gonna take Robinson and dress him up as a woman? You gonna need lipstick and a wig and all that shit," said Carter.

"Then let it be so, but be quick about it," answered Kyle. Carter and Danny ran toward a booth that appeared to sell bright violet afros.

Cabrera telephoned Kyle and secured the location of the bodies. Without telling him too many details, Kyle advised they were on their way, and that Mrs. Nouri was trying to get hold of the embassy staff in Barcelona.

Their purchases in hand, everyone piled back into the black vehicles and sped the short distance to the Deposito De Cadaveres, a non-descript cinder block building with bars on the windows, but no glass. They pulled around the back side of the building to where there was a loading dock leading to a set of double metal doors that had seen several encounters with large vehicle bumpers and a couple of automatic rounds. Cabrera's vehicle and two ambulances were parked at odd angles in the back, both with their rear doors open and no contents inside.

The morgue rear doors were secured with chains running through two gaping holes in the metal.

"They don't exactly have the welcome mat out, so someone get the cutters," said Kyle with a sigh, "In case we gotta get out of Dodge in a hurry."

A set of glass doors were off to the right, near the corner of the building. Fredo guessed the bodies would have been brought in through that way. He turned and saw T.J. carefully cut the heavy chains on the rear entrance and stuff the cutters back in his medic's kit.

"You two," Kyle said to the drivers, "Stay here no matter what. When we say go, we go, understood? And you only take orders from me."

They both nodded agreement and looked scared to death. Fredo guessed they were new recruits and not long on Cabrera's force.

As soon as Kyle, Coop, T.J. and Fredo walked through the glass doors it was evident the Secretary was in residence.

The air ventilation system was nonexistent. Fredo wondered if he should have left the bags of goods they'd gotten at the market, but after looking at the crowd of officials, holding handkerchiefs over their noses, he realized no one would notice.

Cabrera spoke with Kyle. Beyond several officials sitting at a small table and two extremely large bodyguards behind them, and through an open doorway to the back of the morgue, were the three bodies. The Secretary was dripping, making a light brown puddle under the stainless steel table on wheels.

As Kyle spoke to him, Cabrera looked down at the bright pink plastic bag from the market. Fredo held it up and smiled.

Kyle dialed Mrs. Nouri and handed the phone to a small horse-faced man with a pencil thin moustache, his uniform impeccably pressed and boots polished to a high sheen. "*Si, Si Signora*. But no, that is not possible. We will have to execute the proper paperwork tomorrow."

The *general* returned Kyle's phone and made a call to one of his superiors, while Kyle and Cabrera conferred again. Several beefy guys waited behind the little "general" or who-ever he was. Fredo mentally called him *The Man In Charge Of The Dead Bodies.*

Fredo had seen morgues in many third world countries, and it was always a luxury if they contained a freezer or refrig-erated compartment for the bodies. This morgue had one, but it was being used to store file drawers. The four-inch thick steel-walled door was flung wide open.

"So much for preserving the evidence," he whispered to Coop.

The *general* continued to speak with his superior, when Cabrera interrupted him. They spoke in Spanish. The official looked over the crowd of SEALs standing before him and nodded.

Cabrera motioned for them to come inside the morgue but left his men outside to guard the entrance. It occurred to Fredo the *general* was not aware the rear doors had been breached, and hoped it would stay that way for a few minutes.

Secretary Harrison's expression looked even more frightening than before. His cheeks sunk in further, lips pulled back over his gumline in what could only be described as a grimace. The other two security detail had been placed with their arms crossing over their bodies.

The Team looked to Kyle for instructions.

Carter stepped forward. "Oh hell, let's do this!"

The team split into three groups, each one applying a diaper to their assigned security team member. Coop used his plastic tubing to puncture the bloated belly of Harrison so they could get the diaper on him snugly. The air that expelled was even worse than the air that had permeated the building.

The three bodies were wrapped in silk after Fredo installed the large white brassiere on Harrison, stuffing it full of rags from a folded stack nearby. Carter applied makeup he'd bought, ending with the lipstick. At last, he put the violet wig on Harrison, handing a black afro and another bright yellow one to the other two teams.

Cabrera's horrified expression was hidden behind the wet sterile wipe he had over his mouth and nose.

"You didn't see this," said Kyle as he attempted to pick up the torso of the Secretary. The man was stiff. Cooper massaged his hips and knees, bending them carefully to cheat the effects of rigor, helping Kyle to bring him to near-sitting position. They each wrapped an arm around their cadaver and lifted him off the table. The Secretary's head bobbed backward and the wig fell off.

Fredo brought one of the unused saris and wrapped his head and neck several times, crisscrossing his upper chest and fully encasing the wig. The man's grotesque makeup job had smeared, and Fredo could see there was no way he'd pass for being alive.

The other two bodies were completely stiff and were wrapped and wheeled behind Kyle and Coop's package. Fredo made sure the Secretary's head was braced and watched for leakage. The diaper appeared to be holding.

The drivers' expressions bore shock and horror as the three teams brought their packages out the gaping metal rear doors of the morgue. Cabrera motioned for them to help. They opened doors on both sides of the two second seats and watched as the SEALs sat their precious cargo between them. Kyle's van had the Secretary. T.J. sat in the rear seat, while the Secretary was wedged between Fredo and Coop in the second.

Their driver had already lost his lunch before he got the motor started. Fredo was having a hard time as well, but was buoyed by the sight of Cabrera giving the thumbs up to Kyle at the metal doors. They all knew there wasn't much time to get the bodies to the dock.

Kyle's phone rang just as they arrived in front of the Italian cruise line gate. "Gotcha. We're not going anywhere." He turned and held up his cell, telling them to cover their faces. He took one picture of Fredo and Coop with the Secretary between them. It was one of those photos that would never see the light of day, but might make its way to the bulletin board at the Scupper anonymously.

A handsome ship's captain walked down the dock in a starched and impeccable white suit. The guard at the gate opened the entry and allowed the vans to enter. The guard peered into the car, and then abruptly pulled back after getting a whiff of the Secretary.

The captain walked up to Coop's window and tapped it.

"Holy shit," mumbled Coop. "It's Teseo!" Coop rolled down the glass. "Careful, you might want to hold your nose a bit," he warned.

Fredo had never been so happy to see their Italian friend in his life. Teseo had helped them overcome the terrorists three years ago who threatened to hijack the cruise liner they had been vacationing on. Fredo was glad someone had kept in contact with the former Italian Special Forces commando.

"Way to go, Teseo. You got room for three additional passengers?" said Fredo with a salute.

"That's *Captain* Teseo Dominichello to you, Frodo," the handsome officer returned. "I have just the spot. A little on the cool side, but lucky for you, we're taking on food for the Atlantic crossing, so our freezer is fully stocked but we have an additional freezer in the cargo hold." He nodded to the Secretary.

"You heard from Nouri?"

"Yessir." Teseo came around to Kyle's side and as Kyle got out, the two embraced.

Two dark-skinned men brought a large stainless steel food storage container on wheels and opened the side doors.

The SEALs slipped the Secretary in first and then added the two from the second van under the worried eyes of the two ship's crew. The doors were closed and whisked away toward the body of the ship, the two crewmembers chattering and fully animated.

"I don't know how you did it, but thanks," said Kyle.

"No problem. I owe a lot to your boys, and besides, I'll be soon able to purchase one of those beautiful cherry red Ferraris we saw last cruise, remember?"

Kyle smiled and nodded. "Of course, how could I ever forget? Well, I can't think of a nicer bachelor to own it."

"Not for long!" Teseo winked. "Anyway, I like how generous my Uncle Sam is, and how appreciative he is of my many talents. Who knows? Perhaps someday I'll come to San Diego, and we'll have some fun."

Fredo watched as the handsome captain shouted after and chased his new cargo to the gangway. Tourists watched, leaning over balconies, some with umbrella drinks in their hands, the sounds of an on-deck Reggae band playing loudly behind them. Tourists, oblivious to what had just been loaded on board, waved, and the men of Kyle's SEAL Team 3 waved back.

Standing next to Cooper, Fredo heard him say, "Now that's not something you see every day, do you?" But the men kept waving and smiling.

They loaded up, said their farewell to the security guard, and headed back to the hotel.

"Holy Mother of God," Fredo quipped when they were halfway back. "I get the shower first."

"I'll start the laundry," said Coop, without an ounce of emotion in his voice. Kyle confirmed the injured Lyman had his rendezvous with the Naval vessel and informed Ms. Nouri that the Secretary of State would be steaming across the Atlantic for the next seven days, somewhere between the Canaries and Brazil.

Nope, no one would ever believe the day he'd had. No one. They were legends. The stuff of stories to be told for generations.

CHAPTER 22

Mia didn't answer her phone that evening. The Team had been given orders to stay sheltered in place at the hotel complex. They took turns watching the activity on top of the hill, the sirens and the police vehicles that populated the crime scene. No doubt, Cabrera was a very busy man.

Teseo's ship had left port, and since they weren't notified there'd been any difficulty, everyone assumed the Secretary would be chilling in the metal bin with two of his security detail until a safe rendezvous could be arranged with another Naval vessel. Kyle speculated it would have to be in international waters. He'd been in contact with Teseo by satellite phone.

"How they working that?" Cooper asked.

"Teseo said there would be a medical emergency on board, requiring the offloading of a family to the Naval vessel. It's being arranged now."

Armando looked out over the blue waters below. "You know, Kyle, I'm not thinking this is a terrorist group. I'm just thinking this is a bunch of thugs who botched a ransom."

"That's what Nouri thinks too," answered Kyle. "They were possibly related to some gangs here on the island who profit on both ends of the skirmish. They deal in guns, prostitution, human trafficking, anything really. Perhaps that's what started the jurisdictional feud between all the elements with the police forces. Who knows? But I agree, it just feels like criminals to me."

"I'd have a hard time thinking his Stanford friend would do that to him. The boys stayed in each other's houses. Their fathers were friends. I think someone found out about that and decided to try to profit from it. Just my take," said T.J. "We've seen those camps. They get in, they get out. They don't wait. That's what they're doing when they're waiting for a payment of some kind, don't you think Kyle?"

"I agree, T.J."

Coop had a question. "How did you know about Teseo?"

"It was a random email to Christy. He was thinking of coming to the States at Christmas. She had no idea exactly where we were headed, but she did know he'd try to contact me when he got to land, which was Gran Canaria. I didn't let on that's where we actually were. So I called him."

"Someone want to explain who Teseo is?" asked one of the newbie SEALs.

Fredo began. "Teseo was a junior officer on the ship nine of us took. Kyle, Coop, Armani, and Marc—a bunch of us and our ladies took this cruise from Italy to Brazil. We had Sanouk with us too, which reminds me—"

Kyle interrupted him, "There was this big deployment coming up, and we just wanted a little relaxation."

Coop and Kyle looked at each other and shook their heads, swearing.

Armando added, "Kid, this is a long story and you think this was crazy, what we did today? That was one helluva vacation, I can tell you!"

"We picked up some terrorists off the coast of Africa—actually, we think they came from our stop in Morocco," said Fredo. "But, hold on, Kyle. I just forgot about something—"

"Fuckin' snakes, too," added Coop. "There were cobras all over the engine room. I *hate* snakes."

Little details of the cruise were thrown in. Fredo could see the newbies were having some serious bouts of envy as various members of Kyle's team talked about the vacation that turned into a mission to save three thousand tourists and an Italian cruise ship.

"What happened to the ship?" the froglet asked.

"Oh, they blew it up, well part of it, anyway, man," answered Armando. "Had to bring us another ship, and then they towed that one back to, what, Mississippi? That where they took it to be fixed?"

"Yup," answered Coop.

"Wait. So who is Teseo?" another SEAL asked.

"Teseo was named after the human torpedo, Teseo Tesei, who invented some of the rebreather stuff we use today, kid." Coop bowed his head. "The guy was a real genius during World War II and was responsible for sinking a lot of British ships in the Med."

"Teseo's parents named him after the famous Naval officer. And he worked for the Italian Special Forces. We were so lucky he was on board. Really helped us get those assholes," said Armando.

"Holy cow. So you guys really see some duty."

Kyle inhaled, stuck his chest out, and said, "Yup. We get to do more than I think anyone else on the Teams. We got a little angel or a bright star following up overhead," he said as he pointed to the sky.

"We got some stories, kiddos," said Coop. "You will too. Trust me."

Fredo excused himself to try another call with Mia and there still was no answer. When he got back to the group, Kyle was getting instructions over his phone. He returned with a big smile on his face.

"Good news, ladies. We chill here for a day or so. Stay together, explore the village like tourists and the business men, our cover. But once Teseo's ship is in international waters, we're greenlighted to go home."

Fredo tried to adopt the casual banter and resume his smack talk from earlier, but as the group made their way around the little shops and frequented some bars as the evening came on them, he became increasingly concerned that he could not reach his wife. He decided to finally tell Coop.

"You talk to Libby?'

"Yessir. She's very excited and relieved we're coming home so quick. How about you?"

"Mia isn't answering her phone. And she knows I check in with her every day when I can. That's not right, Coop."

"You know, Fredo, I'm beginning to think you'll just die an old woman. You worry about everything."

"Seriously, Coop. That's not like her at all.

CHAPTER 23

Malmoud Suleimani was heavy of heart. He rode the bus down to the business district, past stores he'd not been inside and could never afford to shop. There was so much he didn't understand about this country, about these people. They could be a kind and loving people. They could also be so cruel.

But they are afraid. People, when they are afraid, react with meanness and hatred. He'd seen evidence in his own country. It had been the reason, when given the opportunity, to leave and perhaps find a place to spread the peace and love he felt in his heart. His way of life, his whole religion was completely misunderstood.

It would have been easier for him if he'd not ever confronted Sayid or knew what he was perhaps planning. The visit from the powerful Khan was not a good sign. The man was Wanted, and the authorities were looking for him in several states, not because he had done things against the law, but because he had inspired others to do so.

How he wished the burden could be taken from him, he thought as he watched people walking the Strand, eating ice cream and jogging with their dogs. It didn't take much for him to bring to mind the horrors he'd seen in parts of the Middle East. Even his pilgrimage had shown him a side of his religion that disturbed him.

He thought of himself as a quiet zealot. He read about being willing to die for one's beliefs, and indeed he was. But it was different than what Khan and now Sayid imagined. What if, instead of the bright and happy neighborhood he traveled, the buildings were bombed out? The children were screaming from loss of limbs or holding a dead parent? Soldiers roaming the streets indiscriminately shooting those whose appearance they did not like? The US population complained of this happening in their own cities, but what they'd seen was so small compared to what he'd seen. Lawlessness and fear drove those in charge to inflict desperate acts of violence *on their own peoples!*

It was insanity. And it was coming here. Creeping up on a careless or naïve peoples. They thought they could control it. They were so wrong. It would take a partnership of those willing to help to find and eradicate those fomenting the hatred and violence.

Sayid was playing in his own video game, Malmoud thought. No longer a gangly student, walking to class past green lawns and gardens of great beauty and enjoying the life of sunshine and privilege, but donning the fatigues of battle, causing death and destruction. He was following a hopelessly flawed and sick mindset.

So as he stepped off the bus, his sandals hitting the warm sidewalk, aware how everyone on the bus had stared at him with caution and hatred, he was going to do his patriotic duty. He didn't look like a patriot. But when he had raised his hand and joined the brotherhood of the diverse peoples of the United States, he'd also vowed to protect her in all her imperfections. Malmoud was used to being stared at. Used to being spit at. Used to women walking around him on the streets, or mothers hugging their children. He was an imposition in every grocery store line he stood in, the person who didn't have a right to be waited upon.

And yet, he was going to support them and their way of life. It was his word as a man and as a man of faith. It was who he was. Little did they suspect that a man like him would be the *real* wall, the *real* fence between their sunny way of life and the chaos that would descend upon them if he didn't act.

But his heart was heavy that many of his fellow-worshipers would never understand.

The bus took off in a blast of dust. He didn't have to turn around to find faces plastered in the windows watching where he was going. He could feel their eyes.

The steps to the police department were well swept. Vines covered the outside of the two-story stucco building built to copy a Spanish villa house. The pink bougainvillea vines with their hot purple blossoms were still covering the greenery, their papery leaves fluttering around like hot pink confetti from a wedding. Birds chirped from nests allowed to live amongst the vines and under the eaves of the building. Traffic buzzed around behind him, and he heard a jet overhead.

Inside the cool, dark foyer, he approached glass windows reminiscent of an old-time movie theater he'd seen in a picture book. The panes were thick, and two uniformed women were sitting side by side, awaiting visitors like ticket takers. Maybe he was getting his ticket to an action film he felt he'd want to walk out of halfway through. Maybe he wouldn't survive the full length feature. The larger woman with beautiful full cheeks and bright red lipstick smiled, lipstick on her large upper incisors.

"May I help you?"

"I am here to report a crime."

"Okay." She reached under the counter and slid a clipboard with a form on it under the bottom of the glass in the one inch space there. "You need to fill this incident report out, and then I'll summon a clerk to come speak to you about it. If you like, you can leave your telephone number so you don't have to wait."

"How long will it take?"

"We are very busy at the moment. If you waited, it could be an hour."

An hour? What amount of time was worth the cost of a human life or lives? Was that acceptable? Was there anything else more important right now that he could not wait an hour to be heard?

"I would like some help, please. This isn't a crime that has occurred yet. But I do believe it will be very soon. But not in an hour."

"So this hasn't happened yet?"

"No."

She began to pull the clipboard back inside her part of the cubicle, but Malmoud stopped her by putting his hand on it.

She sat up and tilted her head, narrowing her eyes. "What exactly are you wanting to report then? I'm confused."

Indeed. Malmoud was confused as well.

"I need to talk to someone who has worked with a terrorism task force of some kind. Someone who knows about such cases. I believe I have uncovered something that may be useful."

Everyone within earshot of the little hole in the glass window stopped and turned to face him. He decided he'd said the right thing.

He noticed a buzzing up on the ceiling to his right as a camera moved position, no doubt to examine if he was carrying something that could be dangerous or perhaps carrying a weapon. He smiled at the camera lens. It wasn't a big smile. Just enough not to look menacing.

The woman behind the counter backed away as did the woman next to her. She held her finger up and quickly departed stage right, as they said in Hollywood.

A woman and her young son entered the foyer behind him, walking up to the now empty window on his left. She eyed him carefully. Her child was crying and resisting her grip on his forearm. Malmoud decided the occupants inside the office might think he was a threat to the woman and child, so he bowed slightly, turned around and sat in one of the chairs in the waiting room, bringing the clipboard with him. In time, the other clerk appeared and the two women spoke in hushed tones.

A door opened in the paneled wall and an older gentleman stepped out wearing a suit and tie, but obviously also packing a gun at his waist. He did not wear a badge or nametag as did the uniformed personnel behind the window glass.

He waddled over to Malmoud, his shoes squeaking. And he did something extraordinary. He extended his hand.

"I'm Detective Clark Riverton of the Special Investigations unit."

"I am Malmoud Suleimani, cleric of the Free People's Center." He used the name they most often used when speaking with journalists and the public.

His hands were callused, but the handshake was firm and not afraid. "Let me take that from you, or have you filled it out?" Riverton extended his hand and Malmoud deposited the clipboard into his palm.

"No. She asked me to fill this out until she learned the crime has not been committed as of yet."

"I see. So you have a few minutes to talk in private, then?" he asked.

"Yes, please. This is why I came."

"Now I have to ask you, do you have a weapon?"

"No, sir."

"A knife or anything like needles or anything harmful?"

"No, sir."

"You'll be walked through a metal detector. Are you okay with that?"

"Yes. I'm fine with that."

"And when we get inside, you'll have to agree to a search and a pat down. I assure you, this is only a precaution."

"Yes, taken for people of my kind, I understand, Detective Riverton."

Riverton shrugged. "Would you stand, please?" He placed the clipboard on a chair nearby.

Malmoud did so. Riverton's deft hands worked down his front, both legs, slightly and carefully to his crotch and down the middle of his back as his arms extended to the sides as instructed. The woman and little boy watched with rapt attention.

"Come with me." Riverton picked up the clipboard, nodded and spoke to the woman on his way to the doorway inside, "Morning, ma'am."

She didn't have the words to answer him.

He banged twice on the paneled door and a buzzing sound signaled the door unlocking. The detective pulled it open and motioned by using the clipboard for Malmoud to walk through first.

Inside, two uniformed men, their hands on their sidearms, greeted him. He was searched again, just as the detective had done, and then sent through a large machine after he deposited his satchel to travel through the conveyor ahead of him.

"You will follow these gentlemen to the interview room, Mr.—you said your name was Malmoud Suleimani?"

"Yes, sir. Thank you."

As he followed one of the officers, the other walked behind him. Before they turned the corner to the right, Riverton shouted out, "You want something? A soda or coffee?"

"A water would be good," Malmoud answered.

"Coming right up. I'll be there in a couple of minutes. You just sit tight."

The room was small, containing a Formica table and three chairs. Both sides of the room were covered in a mirror-like one-way glass. Above and in two of the four corners, cameras with red blinking lights stood stoically, waiting.

He was ushered to the single chair across from two other chairs and was left alone. He examined his hands, knowing he was being watched by others on the opposite side of the glass. The room was very quiet, and sounds from outside were muted, blending voices. His heart pounded.

He thought about the conversation he'd had with Sayid and regretted not being given the opportunity to explain to him what life was like when he was a child, before everything got crazy and the whole region erupted. All the foreign intervention had done little to quell the violence, and the thugs who ran things were not the true believers they said they were. It was all a shame so many people had lost their property, their livelihood, and their lives, not to mention their country, now embroiled in something that would take hundreds of years to resolve. The zealots had even destroyed their history and evidence of a two-thousand-year-old culture. More of their civilization was found in museums all over the world than could be seen where it belonged, at the birthplace of civilization.

Unless calmer voices were heard, unless people could sit down and talk to one another with the desire to come to a common ground and agree to some measure of peace, it would continue to deteriorate until it was all gone.

He didn't know what this Detective had going for him, but he said a little prayer the man was strong and of good character. Otherwise, he'd just delivered himself and possibly his congregation into the belly of the lion.

It was so quiet, all he could hear was the buzzing of the overhead lights and the movement of the clock on the wall. He felt like he was back in school, back when the days seemed charmed and he felt safe.

The door abruptly opened, and it startled him. The heavyset detective walked inside, leaned over and handed him a refrigerated water bottle.

"Thank you."

"No problem. Now, before we get started, do you need to use the restroom?"

"No. I'm fine. Perhaps after I finish this?" He held the bottle up to his lips and drank the delicious cool elixir of pure water. Was there anything more wonderful in all the world than pure water in a clean bottle?

The Detective brought out a lined pad and a pen. He set that aside and then took out a small spiral notebook with a tiny pen attached to it. He pointed to the tablet. "In case you need to write something down, draw something or want to give me a statement. Let me know if you need to take notes, okay?"

"Sure."

"So tell me first how to spell your proper name."

Malmoud did so, and Riverton printed the letters in his spiral book.

"What brought you into the station this morning?"

"I spoke to one of my students yesterday, and that conversation bothered me. As I thought about it, I decided I needed to tell someone." He examined the puffy face of the man sitting across the table from him. He trusted him and hoped this feeling was reciprocated.

"Okay, good."

"First I want to tell you I consider myself a believer. I believe strongly in our religion, and for my people, it is a path, a blueprint to lead a better life. I also want to say I've been here over forty years, ministering to peoples from all over the Middle East. There's been a marked change in the population. Most have been very grateful to be able to come to America. Many have found it difficult to blend into your society. I am an American citizen, but I have to tell you I don't yet feel like an American. But I'm working on it."

"I understand. I think," Riverton said. He wasn't taking notes. They were just talking man-to-man.

"I have lost members of my family, both to radicalism and to the scourge of war. I am not here to judge what others have decided or what path they chose, but let's just say I have lost family on multiple sides of this conflict. Because, in case you were not aware, there are more than two sides."

"How many sides are there?"

"I'm guessing about a dozen."

The detective blinked and let his eyebrows raise in surprise.

Malmoud continued. "A discussion for another day, perhaps. Nothing is as simple as it seems, and yet, there are some very simple things that can be done to perhaps pour water on the flames of fear and hatred."

"On that we agree."

"So I'm here not only as a believer, but as an American citizen,"

"Who doesn't feel American yet."

"You are quite right. Who doesn't yet feel the embrace of my host country the way I should perhaps, the way I will one day perhaps. But in spite of the horrible things I'm aware of, I'm an optimist."

Riverton looked down at his notebook and idle hands. "I'm ready to listen. You've made your introduction. Now I'm sure you had something more to say than just explaining how you feel about living here. It's interesting and all, but my job is different than your job. You see, I don't minister to a flock of believers or teach people things. I try to wrest control from some very bad elements who prey on our society, particularly the innocent and defenseless. I try to be a shield. I don't have the luxury of thinking about it. So unless you have something specific to tell me about a crime that has been committed or is going to be committed, I'm afraid I am very busy."

"Yes. I understand." Malmoud chose his words carefully. "I have a student who has been radicalized by some elements overseas. I'm not sure where he went exactly, but I know he's been out of the country within the past year."

"Like a training camp?"

"Yes. He's been to one here in the US, in Oregon. But he's also been to one, I believe, in Syria. But that's just a guess. He has started to talk about things that concern me."

"What things?"

"Well, he has been associating with people I know to be Wanted men."

"Wanted where? Here?"

"Yes, Detective."

"Who?"

"One name is Amid Khan."

The detective didn't flinch. "What do you know about him?"

"Word has passed through my congregation that he has been hiding in the US from authorities. I believe if you check, you will find this to be true, but I have no first-hand knowledge of the man, only rumors."

Riverton was writing the name down. Malmoud realized that this was a new name for him and was a little surprised.

"And what does this have to do with your student?" the detective asked.

"He has informed me this teacher, Khan, is coming here to San Diego to visit him."

"When?"

"I assume soon. He wanted to ask if I knew a suitable girl to cook for him while the holy man is here. My student is single, you see."

"Will you allow me to check this out? Can you wait?"

"Sure."

"Do you want anything else?"

"Another cool bottle of water would be very nice. And a visit to your facilities."

"I'll have one sent in, and I'll send someone to escort you to the men's room."

"Thank you."

A very tall, dark-skinned officer escorted him to the men's lavatory, and pointed to one of three stalls.

"I'm gonna wait right here, but I'll be inside the door, making sure no one else comes in. Please," he pointed again to one of the stalls.

Suleimani did his business and washed his hands. He noticed how tired and very gray he had become. He looked older today. His joints ached. With his wife dead now three years, he kept to his stretching every morning and before sleeping at night, but didn't have any of the other usual exertions they'd had through sexual intercourse which used to calm him. But he wasn't complaining.

When he walked past the guard and into the hallway, a team of four men stood with Riverton. This meant they believed him. Good.

Riverton made some introductions, and they all returned to the little room. The men stood behind Riverton. The questioning was direct and an air of urgency had developed.

"How well do you know this student of yours, Sayid? Oh, and what's his last name?"

"Qabbani. I've only known him a little over a year. He moved here from Northern California to attend college, and I do not know anything about the family, except to know that my fellowship was recommended. I know he works while going to school."

One of the men standing beside Riverton asked, "Where does he work?"

"I don't know, but I believe it is in the landscaping business of some kind. That is his interest, in landscaping, growing and tending plants."

"So we've looked up your Mr. Khan. When have you met him?"

"I've never met him, only heard about him."

"And what have you heard? Please tell these men here what you began to tell me."

Malmoud finished the first water and opened and sipped from the second water bottle. The water was still as divine as before. All the men in the room watched him closely.

"He told me that the holy man was coming to see him. He wanted proper food to entertain him, so he asked me if I knew of a suitable girl to help him with the food preparation. That means the gentleman adheres to some sort of strict dietary regimen. From what I've heard, he is a bit of a fanatic."

They waited until he sipped more water.

"I told Sayid that I wasn't pleased he was coming under the influence of this teacher. I tried to explain it was perhaps dangerous to associate with him and that it showed a lack of respect for the peoples and country who took him and his family in as refugees." Malmoud swallowed. "He was unmoved. In fact, I'm thinking I may not hear from him again for some time."

"Do you know where this student of yours lives?" a man in black asked.

"Yes."

"Do you think you could show us?"

"I'm certain I could."

"You say he called you. Can you please give me his phone number?"

Malmoud lit the screen on his cell phone and passed it over to Riverton to copy the number down.

"And this is his address?" the detective asked, pointing to the details of the contact record.

"Yes."

Riverton wrote it down and then passed his note to the man beside him. The crowd left the room, but Riverton stayed behind, remaining seated in front of him.

"Okay. I'm going to tell you what's going to happen next. First of all, I want to thank you for coming in here today. That was a very brave and courageous thing to do."

"My concern is for the innocent loss of life." He slowly stared into the detective's grey-blue eyes. "I think you would do the same."

"Every day. I do it every day. Or try to."

"On behalf of those who do not thank you enough, I thank you."

"Okay then." Riverton brushed off the compliment as if it was something hot he didn't want to deal with. Malmoud wondered if compliments caused him pain.

"They're getting a team together and we're going to go over to your student's house. Hopefully, we'll find this guy." Riverton glanced up, assessing his reaction. "You have any indication he'll have weapons? Explosives? Accomplices?"

"I have no such knowledge. I am fairly certain my student doesn't own any weapons. It would surprise me. But the presence of this new teacher is worrisome to me."

"I understand. Have you overheard anything about their conversation? Or run across anyone who gave you a run down of what they might be planning?"

"No, I have not."

The door opened and an officer in a swat uniform nodded to Riverton.

"Well, my friend. If you would come with me."

CHAPTER 24

Fredo tried Mia again on her cell when their jets landed at the Avjet hangar in Morocco and still got no answer. They were waiting for the transport to arrive, and it was due at any minute.

"Maybe it's time we get someone to go check on her," said Coop.

Kyle and Armando were standing beside them both. Fredo looked up into his brother-in-law's face.

"Armani, you think any of her old gang, one of those guys could be messing with her? It's just not like her to not answer. And she didn't tell me she was going on a trip."

"I'm gonna call Mom. She must have seen her," said Armando.

Fredo had tried to put it out of his mind when he couldn't reach her just before they took off from the Canaries. He was sure he'd catch her or at least have a message from her when they landed three hours later. But now the angst was growing, and he had to do something.

"You want I get Christy to go check?" asked Kyle.

Fredo shook his head. "Let's listen to Armando."

"Hey, Gus," Armando started. "Say, you guys see Mia the last twenty-four hours or so?"

Fredo held his breath.

"Oh, she's not? When did she go over there?" Armando and Fredo made eye contact, and Fredo's spine began to tingle. He hated being so nervous, but this was a pattern he'd not seen with Mia. With Caesar getting out of prison after the holidays, his antennae was on full alert.

"Ask him to go check on them, then," Fredo whispered.

"When do you expect her home?"

Fredo waited for an answer.

"Well, Fredo's not been able to reach her, either. That's why we're calling because we're a little worried. Now, maybe he's missed her call or there's a simple explanation, but we're headed home, and he wanted her to know. We've been in some spotty places—no, sir, I can't tell you—but we'll be home tomorrow. Taking a red eye out of here. When we're on US soil, we'll text you guys."

Armando was listening to Gus Mayfield's conversation, while focusing on his shoe, drawing imaginary patterns on the dusty concrete floor of the private jet hangar.

"When did she last talk to Mia then?"

Armando nodded his head and spoke to Fredo. "He thinks he should go over there. Felicia was going to drop by some baby clothes she bought at a garage sale this morning.

He hasn't heard from either of them, and it's been a couple of hours."

"Tell him to get hold of Collins. That's not right, Armani," said Kyle. "I'm gonna try and reach Christy." He walked to the side to call his wife.

"Gus, you have our liaison's phone number, Collins?" Fredo handed his phone over with the contact number already recalled. "Here it is, Gus." Armando read the number to his step-dad. "Tell him something isn't right, and you're alerting him to the fact that Mom's late and Fredo can't get hold of Mia. We gotta catch a plane, and we sure as heck don't want too much time to go by while we're in the air—just in case something's wrong." After another pause, Armando signed off with, "Thanks, man. Keep us in the loop, and leave a message or update if we don't pick up."

"Shit, Fredo. I'm truly sorry. I accused you of being an old biddy who worried too much. I should go call Libby." Coop was as contrite as he could be.

"Christy's on her way over after she gets a sitter," said Kyle.

Fredo's heart was pounding in his chest. "I'm not thinking that's a good idea, Kyle. What if something's—I don't want her to go over without protection. Call it off, Kyle."

Armando's phone rang and everyone jumped.

"Gus?" He waited for information. "Okay, good. You let us know what you find out. You got any answer on Felicia's cell phone, or on Mia's, for that matter?"

Fredo turned to Kyle. "Christy shouldn't go over there alone. Seriously, Kyle, that's not a good idea."

"Okay, I'll let her know."

"Who are you calling, Armani?" Fredo asked.

"Gina. She might know who else to call." He left the area to have his private conversation.

Fredo knew Gina still had friends on the San Diego PD who would help in any way they were able, even bending the lines, if they were sure they wouldn't get caught.

Kyle returned and told everyone Christy was staying home.

"Should we be calling our ladies, warning them?" asked T.J. "I mean, they get together when we're gone. It wouldn't be uncommon for them to check on each other when we're overseas. I just hate to scare them unnecessarily. I'm thinking this is some kind of fluke. Mia goes off to the hospital because Ricardo gets into something, and her cell's dead or something."

"Hope to God you're right, T.J." whispered Fredo.

Armando walked back to the group. "Okay, Gina's gonna call the PD and talk to a couple of her former colleagues. We'll get a patrol to go by there."

"That helps some."

Their transport arrived. There was no mistaking the sounds of the lumbering jet that would be their home for the next fifteen hours. The good news was that they'd arrive directly at the San Diego airport, not an East Coast airport and then have to catch another flight home. The bad news was that they'd be out of communication that much longer.

Fredo tried one last time to reach Mia. "Babe, I'm going crazy here. If you can, just text me you're okay. I guess you're with your mom, and that's good. But we're worried sick. Please, baby. Leave me a message."

He was the last one to strap in and turn off his cell. He tried to think of anything he could do, but the only thing that would help was to get himself home, and now.

He started second-guessing everything he'd done the last few hours, from the argument with her about the baby to the little sexy phone call they'd had from the Canaries. Should he have called Collins the first time he couldn't reach her, or had someone check in on her after the landscaping guy fiasco?

But as the plane took off and droned on at cruising speed, he knew the only thing available to him was to fall asleep. Sleep would make him think better. It had been a long couple of days. These quick insertions always messed with a person's head. The jet lag and time zone differences and the distance between where he was and everything he held dear got to him, as it did many men.

So all he could do was relax, command himself to rest, and hopefully get some decent sleep. That's what he told his body to do.

He was hoping his brain would go along with it.

CHAPTER 25

The SWAT team arrived ahead of Riverton and Malmoud. The police radio had constant chatter, much of it in code Malmoud didn't understand. Riverton sat next to him in the back seat of the sedan driven by a uniformed officer.

"You said you've been here a long time? How long was it?"

"About forty years. I came as a young child with my parents. At that time, there were lots of Iranians coming to the States, and we came as part of that settlement group, though we were from Syria. My father was a physician there."

"So your whole family came, then?"

"Not all of us were able to come. My father's three brothers stayed behind, my grandfathers on both my father's and mother's sides stayed behind. Me, my sister and two brothers came together, and then we sponsored several others. But my uncles and both grandfathers died there, most of them in battle."

"I'm sorry about that. I truly am."

"Thank you." He examined the profile of the detective sitting next to him. "What about your family?"

"Who me?" The detective gave him a puzzled look. "I have a girlfriend, but no children, no wife. I'm not the family man type. This job is my family."

"So you sacrifice for what you believe in."

"I like to think I do some good in the world."

"You don't miss the companionship of a family?" Malmoud wanted to know.

Riverton chuckled. "Oh, I got companionship. No problem there, and don't get me confused with a saint, or a holy man as you put it. I'm just not the marrying kind. And I have little patience or tolerance for children."

"I would have liked to have children."

"None? You have none?"

"Back in Syria I could have taken on a second wife and had children. My wife couldn't have them because of something that happened to her as a girl."

"So she came from Syria as well?"

"Yes. But unlike me, she came as a young woman with her younger sister. Her parents had been killed. I met her at the Center when I first started. We married, but she was barren."

"So we have more than one thing in common," Riverton whispered, watching the action in front of him.

"Sir?"

"Well, we both want peace. We both want to protect the innocent. And we both don't have family—immediate family—so we're loners, you and I."

"You said you had companionship." Malmoud found he liked the detective and hoped the question wouldn't offend him.

"Yes." Riverton chuckled and shook his head as if to shake off an errant thought. "Different, very different from being married. I have a girlfriend, and that's all it's gonna be, trust me."

"Like they say, friends with benefits." Malmoud would never be able to explain his fondness for this crusty law enforcement individual to anyone he knew.

"In my case, I think it's more the *benefits* I seek. But do you have any idea how many women love law enforcement types? Maybe it's the guns and handcuffs and everything."

"Perhaps it is that they feel they can trust you."

"Well, they shouldn't."

"I think they know you'd sacrifice yourself to save them. That's what a hero does, right? There are lots of men, but men who stand up for a cause, to protect and make the world a better place, those men are rare."

The two didn't say anything for a few seconds. Malmoud mused on how strange the world was, and how difficult it was to see the black and white of solutions. But it was never hard to discover right from wrong. He knew this man knew the difference too.

"You know what I think, Malmoud?"

"No, what?"

"I think if there were more people like you and I there wouldn't be as much killing and heartache. Just imagine if we ran the whole damn world. What a place that would be."

"People would have to go to church, they would have to worship."

"That's okay. I can live with that, but they wouldn't yell as much or try to kill each other as much. Except at ball games and soccer matches."

Malmoud smiled.

"They would honor the children. Do everything to keep them safe."

"Yes. Odd, coming from the likes of us, right?"

"Bullies wouldn't be tolerated."

"Absolutely not. Maybe people would trust each other more."

"Or not be afraid to disagree." Malmoud was surprised he was feeling so good.

"Just imagine that." Riverton jerked, looking up as they both heard shouts coming from the second floor.

Malmoud watched as men in black quietly snuck up the stairway to the upper floor apartment where he knew Sayid lived. He watched in slow motion as someone knocked on the door, then waited. After a second knock and then a more forceful pounding of the door, they knocked it open with a metal pipe.

"Okay, I'm going to have to go see what they found. You stay put. Stuart here will watch out until I return." Riverton exited the car and ran across the yard and up the stairs and disappeared.

Malmoud wondered if perhaps the men had caught both individuals, and he hoped they caught them alive, since he didn't hear any gunfire. Riverton slipped inside the doorway with his gun drawn.

"Won't be long now." The voice from the driver startled Malmoud for a second. He'd been lost in thought. Wondering what he'd say to his student, what he'd say to the holy man, Khan.

"What?" He asked Stuart.

"Well, they just breached the door. Won't be long before it's all over. These things never last very long."

No one had come out of the apartment. Then he began to worry about the possibility of a bomb going off. He became concerned for Riverton's health, a man he now considered a friend.

He was relieved when the detective stood at the railing just outside the apartment doorway. He motioned for him to come up.

"Me?" asked Stuart.

"No, send him," Riverton boomed and pointed at Malmoud.

"Okay, fella, it's showtime. I guess they need you upstairs."

"Do you think it's safe? Do you think they have caught anyone?" Malmoud asked the driver.

"Come on, let's find out." He motioned for Malmoud to follow in front of him. Although not in police custody, the teacher wanted to cooperate fully. The narrow stairway had to be shared with a number of police and rescue crews coming down. At the top landing he poked his head into the apartment and found it buzzing with activity. Then he spotted Riverton, who came running over.

"They're not here. We're going through stuff. Come back here, I want to show you something." Riverton took his arm and led him to the bedroom.

Malmoud had never been inside Sayid's apartment. The walls were littered with posters and clippings he'd found and tacked to the walls everywhere. The place was barely furnished, with a futon type couch in the living room and a large screen TV by the wall in front of it. Several prayer rugs were laid on top of the carpeting. The galley kitchen he passed along the way to the back was nearly empty. A tea pot sat on the stove. A stack of water bottles still encased in packaging sat on the countertop, its contents ripped open and a dozen bottles missing. He didn't see anything of a suitcase or evidence the holy man, Khan, had been present.

But once in the back bedroom, Malmoud could see that this room was the epicenter of the student's life. A large screen sat on top of a desk along with a printer. Maps of San Diego were taped to the wall. Certain areas, including some parks and churches were circled in red. Houses were identified with red stars.

Malmoud was surprised at the level of industriousness the student demonstrated.

"You ever see this before?" Riverton asked, watching him warily.

"Never. I am shocked." It was a true statement. The amount of research and detail with all the districts of the San Diego area and the distances to parks and shopping, as well as schools and churches, was extraordinary. He'd spent quite a bit of time plotting out things.

"So, Malmoud. We see enough here to think he's got something big planned. Any idea what?"

"No. But I'm guessing this is all Sayid." He was distracted by some pictures on the wall of women, with X's written over them. They were pictures of models from magazines, in suggestive poses. There were also a few pictures taken with his cell phone and printed on a photo printer. "I think he must have followed some sort of instructions over the past few weeks. This couldn't be done in a day—even two people couldn't get this all done in a day." Malmoud was still at a loss for words.

"I agree. I wish his computer was here. Then we could tell what he was researching."

Malmoud was struck with how foreign all this seemed to him. He now understood he had no idea who Sayid really was or had become.

Riverton was shown some paperwork by one of the female officers. He took it to Malmoud. "It looks like this is a pay-stub. Do you know this business?"

He showed a stub from a Carlos Hernandez Landscaping Service.

"No."

Riverton spoke to the woman, handing her his cell phone. "Go find this guy, and when you get him on the phone, give it back to me. And bag this." He handed her the pay stub.

"Of course." The woman left.

Malmoud walked up to one of the maps. "Do you notice he puts numbers here?"

Riverton stood beside him as Malmoud pointed out the numbers following along red lines. "It appears to be a measurement."

"Between this apartment and these places. Between these places. Like he is calculating things."

The female officer handed Riverton the phone.

"This is Detective Clark Riverton of the San Diego PD. You have an employee, a Sayid Qabbani?"

"Ah, no. I have a Joel Qabbani. He's a landscaper of mine. Hired labor. Why, is he in some trouble? He didn't show up for work today."

"We just want to talk to him. Where are you working?"

"Over off Clover & Sunset. We just finished two houses down the street. Why?"

"Is that the only job you are doing right now?"

"Well, at the present time, yes. We're working in and around the rain. Mostly cleanup. Our big stuff happens in the early Spring."

"So he didn't show up. Did he call?"

"No. Wish he would have. We're short-handed now and I'm not going to finish today."

"So any idea where he is? It's urgent we talk to him."

"I'm sorry. I wish I could help you. Should I have him call you if I hear from him?"

"Yes. Call this number. By the way, did he work on the last job there, those two houses down the street?"

"Yes, he did."

"So that was yesterday?"

'Yes. And didn't say anything to me about not showing up, either."

"Okay, thank you. Can I ask you, what kind of a car does he drive?"

"Oh, he doesn't drive. He walks. He doesn't live too far away from the last job, either. I dropped him off a couple of times. But he walks everywhere. I see him most days, even when we're not working."

"You have any trouble with him?"

"Oh no, not a bit."

Riverton came over to the map and looked at it again, tapping it several times. "You see him, please don't mention we talked. Just get in touch with me personally, okay?"

"Sure. Um. Is he dangerous?"

"At this point, I don't want to scare you, but, yes. I wouldn't have him working around you or your men or your customers. You see him, do not try to talk to him. Get in touch with us first."

"No problem."

"Wait a minute." Riverton peered at the map again. "Where was the last job? What was the cross street?"

"Like I said, it was Clover between Sunset and Pacifico. We're just five houses down, if you want to stop by."

"Thanks for your help."

Riverton turned his phone off and placed it in his belt holder. "Steps, Malmoud," he said as he tapped the map for the third time. "He's marked how many steps it takes to walk between these places. He's got it all lined out in steps."

That made sense to Malmoud.

Riverton's cell rang again.

"Hi, Gina. What a pleasant surprise. Say, I'm in the middle of something, but if it's important, I'm all ears."

Riverton listened. All of a sudden his expression turned dark. "How long since anyone's seen them?" Then he nodded. "Give me the address and I'll try to stop by."

He got only partially done writing the address down when Malmoud saw Riverton drop his pen and his notebook on the floor at his feet.

CHAPTER 26

Fredo told himself he'd sleep. He repeated this over and over again in a chanted mantra, willing himself to close his eyes and rest, but it wasn't working. He stared up at the red lights in the ceiling, noticing they fluctuated slightly. He'd never realized that before. Carter was reading on his iPhone, grinning and licking his lips. The light from the screen illuminating his face as if he was some apparition. Cooper was leaned against him, and with his long torso, part of the top of his wiry hair prickled against Fredo's cheek and annoyed him, so he shoved the farm boy to the side so he could lean on Danny. Armando looked like he was in perfect repose, a sly smile on his face. Ever in control, there wasn't a hair out of place, and even unconscious, Fredo could see he was lethal.

Kyle was seated across the aisle from him, and like everyone else, his headphones were covering his ears. Although his LPOs eyes were closed and he bounced around like the rest of them, Fredo got the impression he was still watching him through careful slits.

Fredo needed the rest, but he just couldn't shut everything off. He began to dread landing, especially if he battled all the remaining twelve hours of the flight and then dozed off just before they touched down. That would be his luck.

Like sheep, he counted his mistakes going all the way back to high school. His grades were shit. But he was kept around because he was the best wrestler in the district. He'd found this little trick he felt ashamed of now, tapping a guy's anus discreetly, which would make him flinch. Then he'd get the takedown. It wasn't fair, but then Fredo was all about winning because wrestling was all he had. He was a one-trick pony. Nobody told on him because they were too embarrassed to admit what had happened.

The girls didn't gravitate to a stocky guy with horrible acne. He'd gotten teased so often in school he wore his unibrow like a badge of honor, he was so totally comfortable with it. Nothing anyone could say now would make him tweeze it. Even Mia had asked him, but stopped after she saw he was resolute. Funny how he could be so firm about that and not about other things.

With a rock hard strong body, he knew he was destined for the military and wanted to travel, so decided the Navy would be his ticket out of East LA. Besides, all the pretty girls were in San Diego anyhow. When he saw the training course at Coronado, he knew the SEALs were his destiny. Fredo had never regretted the decision. He'd never wanted to be a hero, just wanted to be the best at what he did and to protect as many innocents as he could until his ticket got punched. There was always someone handsomer, faster, taller, a better swimmer, but nobody could beat him at wrestling. And he didn't even have to cheat anymore to win. He just strapped on them and wouldn't let go until they understood they didn't have a chance and quit.

And that's how he got Mia. She'd been busy throwing her life away. Even her brother couldn't stop her from running with the wrong guys, jerks who treated her with total neglect and disrespect. He knew why. She was so freaking beautiful she didn't feel she deserved it. His wife needed someone to worship the ground she walked on, give her confidence she was worthy of love. Fredo didn't care how much he had to grovel, he was just like that high school wrestler. He would never quit. He'd never quit on Mia, or stop trying to bring joy to her life.

It was so long ago, and yet it was only days really, since they'd had that big fight and he'd questioned her faithfulness. But this was more where *he* was coming from than her. He often wondered what she saw in him. He'd totally understand if she wanted to be with someone handsome, a guy all the girls would fall over. Especially a guy who could give her children.

But she was in many ways just like Fredo. Mia wouldn't give up on him. He knew that now. He'd been such a stupid fool for letting that matter. If she'd stay with him, who cared? If he made her happy, if he made her laugh and she seemed to enjoy living with him, raising little Ricardo as his own son, what was one more?

Now, in light of everything else he'd seen these past two days, how little it all mattered. The world was a pretty dangerous and crummy place sometimes. If they could carve out their little piece of heaven, it could all go to hell. Just leave his little fantasy life with Mia alone. She wanted that, too.

If anything happened to her, he wouldn't stop until he got those responsible for it and put them in an oily grave and set it ablaze. He'd make sure they suffered the flames of hell, and he'd suffer right along side them if it meant they'd pay the ultimate price for harming one hair on her head. Even if she told him she wanted to leave him, even if he was forced to watch her leave, he would never ever give up hope in his heart. He'd always be there, just in case she changed her mind. Just in case she saw the error of her ways.

As deals went, his wasn't such a bad one. He got the most beautiful wife in the world, one beautiful toddler and another baby he'd love just as much. He had a job he loved and men he worked with who would take a bullet for him at any time. And they were *needed*. They weren't the best of the best of course because there were a lot of incredibly talented and strong warriors in the brotherhood of the military. But as a group, there was none better, none more trained, and none who had consistently the right combination of skill, mental prep and dumb luck to get the impossible done. Those things that others wouldn't or couldn't do.

For all these things, he was grateful.

And here he'd been moping away, whining about his life and his fears, leaving Mia alone with that asshole that wanted to plant flowers next to her. Who could blame him? But that wasn't Mia's fault. It was Fredo's. He'd left her alone. He'd gone off because he couldn't emotionally reel himself in and had left her unprotected and exposed.

If that asshole had anything to do with harming Mia, or was even part of the reason she wasn't answering her phone, he'd willingly saw off every body part of his and feed it to Coop's dog. Or slice him up and drop him off the pier and let the sharks get him. He just couldn't get that guy's picture out of his head for some reason.

He thought about Julio, the kid with the blue eyes. The kid who saved his life. just because he'd known his older brother.

If he wanted to feel sorry for someone, he should feel sorry for Julio. Bright kid, lots of potential, but stuck in a neighborhood with nothing. The Center would help, but he'd have to stay clean long enough so they could get him trained and get him into a BUD/S class. If he could get in, he'd make it, Fredo knew that. And they'd do it in honor of his brother, Ephron.

Ephron was perfect SEAL material. Tall, handsome, hell of an athlete, but with one little flaw: he hated swimming. That was it. He would have made one awesome warrior. It was such a shame his blood had been wasted on the dirty streets Fredo and the other men of SEAL Team 3 were trying to clean up. Now that wasn't a fair shake. A pregnant girl without a husband, baby without a father, mother without a son, little brother without his older brother to protect him.

And here he'd been so caught up in his own little dented head sperm he hadn't thought about any of them. What a selfish prick he was.

He got up and used the lavatory. The transport didn't have attendants, but someone had thought to bring them an ice chest full of waters and a basket with small packets of pretzels, potato chips, fig bars, and trail mix. He sat at the end of the row, three seats down from the next Team guy, strapped in, and drank his water in silence. He needed a shower. Something hot and steaming.

"Fredo," she called him. When he opened his eyes, the room was filled with steam. "Come here and take a shower with me." Mia's red nail polish was easily recognizable. He was confused. Wasn't he on the airplane coming home to her? Had he missed the whole drama? The reunion? The touchdown? How had he gotten home?

"Hey, Mia. Where were you?"

His clothes were already shed. The steam shower was warm and inviting. Her body was more curvaceous than he'd remembered her before, but then she was pregnant. She smiled, her red lips inviting, her teeth so white and straight.

"Poor Fredo. You've had a rough couple of days. You need to put your life back in Mia's hands, huh, *mi amore*?"

She drew him into her, and soon he melted into her slick, wet, bulbous body. Her arms were up over his shoulders, laced at the back of his neck. Her breasts rested against his chest as she leaned and squeezed her tiny body against his. Her belly pressed into his. She turned back and forth, her nipples dragging over his chest, her thighs massaging his. "No more worry. No more long faces, *mi amore*. You're here now, with me."

He knew it must be a dream, but he surrendered to her anyway. His hands eagerly rubbed the warm water over her body, smoothing down shower gel. Everywhere he touched her, she arched and moaned. He turned her, suddenly urgent to be inside her without their long foreplay. The tiles were cool to his forearms as he pinned hers beneath him, clutching her fingers in his. Bending his knees, he spread her thighs. Then he bent lower still and angled up, catching her just right, rooting deep inside and nearly taking her off her feet. She pushed against the wall into him as he balanced her on his cock. He found the fine hairs behind her ears and at the base of her neck and got lost. He pressed her upper torso into the cool tile as he whispered love poems, pressing inside and up deep again and again. He couldn't fill her enough. He held her thighs under her knees, careful to give her belly room as he pumped against her.

He had barely caught his breath when he opened his eyes again and she was on him in bed. With her large belly in front, she carefully rocked her torso on him, squeezing her breasts, her nipples dark and huge. Mia leaned forward, closing her eyes as his thrusts sent her some place wonderful. She balanced her forearms on his shoulders enough to raise her hips up and down on his shaft. The long strokes made him grow, and he worried he'd soon be too big for her. She suddenly stopped, letting him feel the spasms milking his shaft as she shattered into orgasm and they came together perfectly.

With one arm under his head, he just lay back and looked at this beautiful creature who brought him so much pleasure, who loved him just as hard and as intensely now as the very first time they made love in the cramped cabin of the cruise ship. His Mia. She always would be his Mia. He lived for her. He would gladly endure anything for her. Maybe it was real after all. Maybe he was really there in his bed, the sizzle of their lovemaking hanging in the air, her beautiful light brown body glistening in the moonlight. Even sweaty, Mia was beautiful, like she was covered with tiny crystals of sugar.

He had dribbled on himself, thinking about tasting all the places and body parts that had been dipped into sugar. He brushed his mouth with the back of his sleeve, and it broke the dream. Opening his eyes, he saw the back of a plane, an eerie red light pulsing, the equipment jiggling, and heard the drone of the engines, deafening, even with earphones.

He examined the row of men he'd done battle with. Not a one was awake now. Yet he was still here.

He closed his eyes, trying to get back into the dream. He envisioned the shower, all the ways they'd made love under the water, all the ways they'd made love in their bed. He pretended he was an angel or bird above her while she slept. He held her every morning before she awoke, his fingers on her bare body, claiming her anew each and every day. He wanted to do that until the day he died, and even on that day, he wanted to touch her. He would always touch her.

The plane jolted onto the runway, and the tires screeched as they landed. Fredo was instantly awake and alert. He had slept after all. He could hardly wait to be home, and now he was close.

The rest of the team began to stir, some putting away reading devices or powering up cell phones to check for messages. Fredo looked at the screen on his, hoping for something and found it blank. Not one.

But as they began to taxi to the gate, several phones beeped and two phones rang. Both Kyle and Armando had their devices to their ears. Fredo watched, holding his breath. Both of them looked sternly back at him, and he knew something had happened. Something he didn't want to know about.

CHAPTER 27

The house had been surrounded. Riverton was standing beside Malmoud while the technician connected a headset to a computer device and place it on his head. "We're gonna want you to try to talk to Sayid, if he'll let you."

All he could do was nod. He had no words. His tongue was stuck to the roof of his mouth. His gut was doing flip-flops.

The drone they'd sent in was tiny, smaller than a bird, but had a powerful camera. Inside the house, they could see the women handcuffed to chairs. A toddler screamed, his face red and terrified. The man he didn't recognize, who was probably Khan, had lost his temper and was about to strike the child with a backhand. What terrified the child even more was that he saw what could be coming his way.

To his credit, Sayid stopped the teacher from striking the child.

They'd watched as Sayid and Khan had previously been on the telephone, making calls, then yelling to people on the other end of the line. The dark-haired younger woman was now screaming, then yelling at Sayid. Mahmoud braced himself for some violent act on his part, but he turned, spoke to Khan and untied the baby from the high chair where he was restrained, and gave the child to the woman. That left her with one wrist connected to the chair and the other around the child's waist, but more importantly, reduced the decibel of tension in the room. She was talking to him, trying to soothe him, calm his nerves, for the good of them all.

The older woman stared back defiantly, hatred brewing in her eyes. Malmoud didn't think this was wise, and wished he was there to protect her.

"Try the number again," Riverton said to the technician.

Everyone listened for a ring, and there was none. The police couldn't figure out what had happened to the telephone they knew was in the house.

"We should try her cell again."

"Try Sayid's. I will talk with him," whispered Malmoud.

Riverton looked down at his feet for a minute. "Only if you're talking to *him*, not Khan. You tell him that we have surrounded the house and there isn't any escape. Tell him to somehow incapacitate Khan."

"What if he won't?"

Riverton shrugged. "We're running out of time. That baby is going to be a problem. They've been trying to call people now for the past two hours. I think Khan will tire of this soon. He's already lost his temper once."

"Let me try first."

"Do it," Riverton said to the technician. He adjusted the headset on Malmoud's head and listened in through an earpiece spliced in by a phone jack.

"We've got only another five minutes on the drone," someone told Riverton.

"You got backup?"

"We only bring one. In five minutes, it will do an automatic homing for a recharge."

"Let's hope he picks up."

They could see, though the screen was becoming wavy and cutting out in bursts of blackness, Sayid looking through a square satchel, probably for his phone. He glanced to the other room before he answered it.

"Hallo?"

"Sayid, this is teacher Suliemani. I have urgent news for you. The police have surrounded this building. You are in danger. Can you disable Khan?"

Sayid laughed. While he yelled in Arabic, Malmoud translated. "He's getting Khan. He's unmoved, telling him the police have surrounded the area."

Riverton swore. He signaled the SWAT commander, "Go."

Sayid spewed a load of epithets into the phone.

"Losing signal," the tech shouted to Riverton.

The picture was getting very grainy, breaking up. And then it went black. After several other choice sentences, the line went dead.

Malmoud removed his head set. "I'm afraid I'm the son of a goat whore and a snake and various other things, including traitor and that I have condemned my family to death."

Riverton put his hand on Malmoud's shoulder. "I've been called worse."

He could see someone had affixed a white package to the front door. Within seconds the explosion was deafening, setting off car alarms nearby. The front door was completely shattered, and men began pouring inside, to a hail of automatic gunfire.

CHAPTER 28

Coop and Armando escorted Fredo from the airport while Kyle and several others brought their own vehicles. Though they tried to talk him out of it, Fredo insisted on driving his own truck. The whole group headed to Fredo's home, running red lights discretely. It was a short freeway hop and then down into the neighborhood where so many of them lived.

As they came upon the street, the whole area was blocked off with flashing red lights. A large SWAT van was the first thing Fredo noticed. Two red rescue vehicles were standing idly by. Smoke was coming from the interior of his home and the front door had been blown off, residue from the blast still wafting up into the early evening sky.

Fredo ran right past the first police guard, a woman, who had been preoccupied. But she stopped Cooper, Kyle and T.J. and wouldn't let them pass, even summoning backup. Fredo continued running through the maze of vehicles and came around the rear of one of the red rescue trucks. A yellow jacket was hanging in the back of the open van, and Fredo grabbed it as he heard a "Hey" coming from his left. He didn't have time to check out who might be trying to stop him.

The jacket was huge on him, the sleeves extending two inches past his fingers, but he didn't care. He wove his way around groups of police and paramedics, scanning the crime scene for a stretcher, for someone injured and being treated. He stopped one of the paramedics.

"Are they all still inside?"

"Yes. No one's come out yet."

"Casualties?"

"One, that we know of."

"A hostage or—?"

"We don't know. They said to be prepared for one."

Fredo continued to scoot closer to the front door's opening. He slowed down, took a deep breath, and started to cough. He heard Ricardo wailing, and was never so grateful for the sound of his distress.

He's alive!

He slipped inside, walking slow and deliberately. The jacket had a clipboard in the large pocket on his right side, so he took it out as if he was examining something. As he entered his living room, a body lay to the left, having taken several rounds to the chest. It was an older man he didn't recognize. Sitting on the couch, in handcuffs, was the landscape helper, Joel. Fredo wanted to run over and up the body count to two. The kid's eyes got wide.

"I told you, kid," Fredo blurted out.

The uniformed officer guarding Joel—if that was his name—objected.

"Hey, you're not authorized to be here."

"Fredo!" He heard Mia's scream. "Oh. My. God. It's Fredo!"

He ran in the direction of the back bedroom pushing past two navy-uniformed paramedics. At last he saw his beautiful wife break through a crowd of people surrounding her. She was in his arms before anyone could stop her.

"Oh, Fredo. Thank God you're here. It was awful, *mi amore.*"

All he could do was soak up the moment he feared would never happen. He loved this woman more than he loved his own life. Her shaking body clung to him, her hair wild and her scent filling his chest as he inhaled the beauty that was Mia. It was the answer to everything he'd hoped for and dared to believe.

She kept trying to explain, and he just wanted to hold her.

"Shhh. Shhh. Enough. We'll talk about all of it later. You need to relax, Mia. I've got you. Never letting you go, sweetheart. I'm here."

Oblivious to the discussions going on around them, he buried his nose in her hair. His fingers found the back of her neck, stroking her and holding her against him as tight as he could. He could feel her soften to him. He knew she wanted to talk, to get something out, so he asked her.

"Tell me what happened."

"You were right. You were right about all of this."

Detective Clark Riverton appeared seconds before several large officers restrained Fredo, which began a struggle that drew attention quickly. The two were separated and Mia screamed. "I want my husband. That's my husband!"

Riverton nodded, and both Fredo and Mia were released. They were instantly in each other's arms again. Felicia Guzman was holding Ricardo, who was crying and reaching out for Fredo, shouting, "Papa!"

It melted Fredo's heart to see that Ricardo wanted to come to him first, and not his mother. With one arm around his wife, he took the toddler in his arms, lost his balance, and fell to his knees, taking Mia with him. That set off another flurry of activity.

"I'm fine. I just had to sit down!" he shouted to the crowd, still on his knees. He soothed Ricardo, whispering in his ear until the boy stopped screaming and began to whimper. He hugged the two most precious people in the whole world. Felicia Guzman walked over, hugged Fredo by the neck, and kissed the top of his head.

"Now she'll be fine. She worried the most about you, Fredo. But now my daughter will be fine." She kissed him again.

"Thank you, Mama," he said to his mother-in-law while peering over at his wife. "And you? Are you feeling better now?"

"Yes, Fredo. Everything is as it should be now."

"The baby?"

"The baby is strong. I think she gave me strength. We are so happy to see you, my love. I am so happy you got back home safe."

Gus Mayfield burst into the room, took his wife in his arms and then addressed Fredo. "Geez, man, I saw you come streaking by. I couldn't believe you got through all those people. I tried to follow behind, but they snagged me."

"I think Kyle and Coop got delayed out at the perimeter."

Amid Khan was pronounced dead at the scene. Sayid Qabbanni was taken into custody. Mia and Felicia answered questions, and their statements were taken. Ricardo fell asleep in Fredo's arms.

Riverton told them they would have to do some evidence collection at the house. He suggested the three of them find another place to stay for the night and assured them someone would come over to board up the front door and be on guard to preserve the scene until they could return the next day.

Fredo's mind was sifting through ideas about where they could spend the night in privacy. Though Felicia and Gus offered their second bedroom, Fredo needed to be alone with his family. When they offered to take Ricardo for the night, Mia agreed.

"Let him get spoiled on pancakes and hot chocolate by his grandparents. We can sleep in, Fredo." Her warm brown eyes smiled back at him, and his heart began to unthaw.

"I know a place by the beach. Not too expensive. Not the Hotel Del, but it's vacant, and I just cleaned it before we left for the Canaries." Coop stood behind them and held up keys to the Babemobile. Coop leaned into Fredo's ear, "And no flowers or room spray to make you sneeze. Honest. But, sorry, I got the scented dryer packets for the sheets. Just couldn't help myself."

CHAPTER 29

Moonlight shone on the bay as it always did. Sounds of sea birds playing in the salty night air were calming. Being close to the water was his kind of therapy, listening to the little waves kicking up sand and moving shells, tiny rocks and the creatures that lived in the surf.

"In all the months I've known you guys, I've never been inside," whispered Mia as she spooned into his back while he unlocked the door.

"I'll warn you. They don't call it a Babemobile for nothing." He chuckled. "I used to give—still do give—Coop such a hard time. Libby agreed at first to let it be parked down the street but she told Coop one day she didn't like to drive past it anymore, knowing what Coop used to do here."

"He was a player, like my man, Fredo?" She giggled and slid her palms under his shirt, then around to his front, and hugged him from behind.

"Well, not sure about that." He didn't want to talk about the past. "Coop was the one they always wanted." He turned and took her face in his rough hands, thumbing over her soft lips. He was still amazed at her beauty at midnight under the stars. "I was just waiting for that one special girl. I never looked for anyone but you, Mia." He kissed her, felt her form her curvaceous body around his. "Once I met you, it was all over for me. I was done. Cooked and done."

She sifted through the hair at his temples. "Ah, *mi amore*. I put you through so much. I regret all the days we didn't have while I was being a stupid, selfish girl. And so grateful you waited for me to come around."

They kissed again, the passion flaring. He picked her up with one arm under her shoulders and the other under her knees, flipped the metal plate down with his foot, and stepped inside with her. He dropped her to her feet slowly, feeling her body melt against him on the way.

After picking up their bags, he closed the door before flipping the small retro light switch next to the rounded space-age opening. The yellow glow of aging plastic lamp covers was romantic, he thought. The wood paneling, which had been freshly polished, shone with a dull patina. The Babemobile had undergone a redecoration with palm trees and hula girls wearing flowered leis covering buxom tops the dominant theme on the pillows, the coverlet over the couch, and the curtains. Coop had added some retro appliances to match the decor, including a thirties-style teapot and an old blender with a turquoise base.

He turned on the stereo, located in a panel above the step-down to the driver and passenger seats of the vehicle.

Mia was walking down the hallway, opening up closets and drawers and peering into the bathroom on her way to the rear bedroom.

"This place is wonderful! What a love wagon. You can just feel it, can't you?"

Yes, he had to admit, the aura of the place used to hit him between the eyes every time he was inside, and it used to piss him off. Coop, he always felt, had been the lucky one. Fredo always felt like the comic relief.

But tonight he would be the main event. He left the channel on a light jazz program broadcast from UC San Diego and turned to find his beautiful wife sitting on the edge of the bed. Her legs were crossed, but she'd removed her shoes.

"I think we need a shower. Don't you agree, *mi amore*?"

He definitely agreed with that. "Let me see if I can figure it out." He was hoping he didn't have to light a pilot to warm the shower water, but was rewarded with the sounds of an instant hot water heater gurgling in the cabinet below the sink. When he exited the tiny stainless steel cell of a bathroom stall, Mia was already naked. He noticed immediately her breasts had enlarged. It was probably his imagination, but she did appear to have a very tiny belly.

"Look at you, Mia!" he said as she approached him.

"I like how you look at me, Fredo. It makes me feel so hot and sexy."

"You are sexy." He could barely get the words out before she covered his mouth with hers, twisting her body against his, rubbing her mound against his thigh. Her hands roamed under his shirt and then down the front of his pants.

"Off. These come off now," she whispered as he bent to kiss her long neck and shoulder. She undid his cargo pants and slid them off his hips, kneeled, and took him into her mouth.

Fredo sucked in air as her lips and tongue worked over his member, elongating him, one hand fondling his balls and pulling down on his sac. He quickly removed his shirt and tossed it toward the kitchen.

He didn't want her to stop, but he wanted to clean himself for her. The long plane ride and the ordeal she'd been under all had to be washed off. He didn't want any of the fear and sweat from the unknown to remain. He guided her to stand, lifting her gently under the elbows. "Come, Mia. Let's wash each other."

The warm water felt heavenly against his back as he pressed her into the metal side of the stall, savoring a long, languid kiss. Her nipples stiffened against him, her mound urgently sought his limbs. The space was so small that every movement she made touched him somewhere. She brought the shower gel bottle between them and drizzled the lemon soap all over both their fronts. Her hands explored his chest, and his did the same, as if lovingly sculpting his statuesque beauty, squeezing her breasts and enjoying the feel of her muscles beneath his fingers.

She turned him around and massaged his back, washing up around his shoulders and his neck, squeezing the tension out of him, working down his spine to end at his thighs. Her warm body cupped him, her knees matching behind his knees, thighs against the backs of his, her hands moving around to rub gel all over his manhood, giving him a firm squeeze. She pressed her forehead against his shoulders and sighed. "*Mi amore.* I missed you so much. I would die without you."

His heart leapt. He quickly wiggled his way to face her, their naked bodies resting against each other as the warm water sluiced between them. In the steam of the hot shower, he found her red lips, plunged inside her, and devoured her mouth. He felt her breath go ragged as he kissed her neck, biting the creamy smooth flesh, running his teeth down to her breast, and taking her nipple roughly. At this, she seemed to explode. Her nipple was sensitive as he tasted her, biting and rubbing his tongue over the stiff areola.

Looking into her eyes, he could now touch her place of need. His fingers slid down her belly until he found her opening, and he waited. Her hungry expression spurred him on, and then she placed her palm over his and helped guide him deep inside her. She rolled her head back and moaned at his touch, exposing her long graceful neck begging to be kissed.

She was his completely. There was no hesitation. There never was. Their bodies found and explored each other until the water grew cold. Even then they played, kissed and relished the foreplay. There wasn't room to fuck properly, since tonight he wanted her splayed all over the bed, begging for more. He was mad with desire.

Fredo turned off the water and let the droplets pour off them as the steam dissipated in a hush, and then silence. He thought for sure she could hear his heart beating, and perhaps she did, because her palm pressed against it, and then she followed it with a kiss to his breast. He held her hand there, holding it against his chest so she could feel how he loved her. He knew she could. He saw it in her eyes.

Her coy smile turned up the sides of her mouth playfully. "Come. Fredo, my love. I need to show you how much I've missed you."

His libido spiked at the thought. Joy sparked and ignited every cell in his body. Every nerve ending was open and waiting for her.

She took his hand, and dabbed him off quickly with a white fluffy towel she'd gotten from the closet. She then presented it to him to do the same. He couldn't. He let the towel slip to the floor, took her in his arms and walked her back to the bed where he placed her. She scrambled to the pillows, begging him to follow her.

At last, he was on top of her, kissing her neck and shoulders, loving to suck and taste her body, massaging her opening with his fingers and then following up with his mouth. Her juices were sweet on his tongue as she writhed beneath him.

But she needed him inside because she pulled his arms, begging him to crawl up her body and angle himself. As he pressed the tip of his cock into her, she squeezed his butt cheeks into her fists, forcing him inside her. Her legs wrapped around his waist, her pelvis angled and desperately giving him full access to her, giving him a longer penetration. Beads of water on her chest rolled to the sides, and her perfumed hair was full of silver droplets, making her look like an angel beneath him. Her fingers threaded his hair, drawing him down to kiss her hard.

He palmed her butt checks, raising her pelvis slightly as his hands grabbed her hips. In long strokes, he pumped, then became furious with desire to own every piece of her body. He pulled her up against him, beginning to feel her shattering, the pulsation from her sex sending little ripples throughout his body.

And then, this finely tuned, delicate body of hers exploded. She bit his shoulder, clawed at his back, and held him tight against her cervix. She released him and then drew him in again deep. She began a long moan as her orgasm coiled and struck them both.

He'd planned to make love to her all night long, but he needed to thoroughly satisfy her first. He desired to push her over the edge, have her lose control and pull him down with her. He'd match every step she took, every movement with a counter of his own. He'd give her back what she was giving him and more. Anything she wanted, he would be there for her, ride her down into the fall.

Spilling inside her brought a smile to her face, her eyes full of dreamy lust, feeding off his orgasm, and holding him tight against her womb, where he belonged.

They fell asleep while still connected. He slipped the coverlet up over them both and gave her a good night kiss.

Now he could sleep. The world was right where it should be. He was headed into complete oblivion to rest, to recharge, to soak up as much love generated between the two of them as was humanly possible.

They went out for breakfast to the Golden Bear grill down by the wharf. Griz was glad to see them and had two lattes ready for them quickly. He served up an oyster scramble, the specialty of the day.

"And why not?" Fredo said as he shared the plate with her.

"I love them this way," she said.

They went for a walk along the beach before returning to the Babemobile. He was thinking about the upcoming rotation plans for the team and needed to mention they might be on deployment during her due date.

"Fredo, if you can, you must do a mobile chat so you can see your new son."

"A son? You think it's a boy?"

"I do. Something is very strong with this child. I don't know what it is, but this is all different, not at all how it felt before."

"You were under a lot of stress before, Mia. Perhaps that is it?"

"No, Fredo something about this baby. I feel it. I don't know what it is, but I feel different."

"Should we make sure everything is okay? The paramedics last night said you should get checked out, just to be sure."

"Already scheduled. I must be nearly a month along. Not yet time for a heartbeat, but they can do an ultrasound and measure the size of the baby. That will confirm our due dates."

Back at Coop's motorhome, they changed the sheets and brought everything they'd used back with them in the truck to wash and return later.

Ricardo was pleased to see them when they got to Gus and Felicia's. He ran up to Fredo, who carried him on his shoulders. Mayfield told Fredo privately that Felicia hadn't slept well, and although they'd offered to take Ricardo for another day, he thought it was too much for her to handle.

"I completely understand."

"We're thinking of taking a road trip up north, go see what you guys started in Sonoma County."

Fredo gave him Nick and Devon's number as well as Zak and Amy's. "And make them introduce you to their neighbor. Gus, you'll love Zapparelli."

With Ricardo in tow, they said their goodbyes. Fredo thanked Felicia for the gift of her daughter. "I'm eternally grateful to you for bringing me my Mia." He followed up the words with a firm kiss on both her cheeks.

Felicia burst into tears and could barely respond. "You saved her life, Fredo. It is I who is grateful. You did what I could not do."

Ricardo's things were packed in several cloth bags. "God, Ricardo, you travel heavier than your mother," said Fredo.

Ricardo was in a very active mood as they waited at Mia's obstetrician's office. She had tried to get him interested in the puzzles and other small toys left in the center of the room for children, but he was quickly bored, fussy, and needed constant holding, which seemed new.

Fredo noticed in him the fear he'd seen with children overseas in the war-torn areas. He would have to monitor this since he knew the stress of the last two days events could leave a lasting mark. He vowed to spend some private time with Ricardo, doing some focused activity and free play. He also wondered if he was somehow jealous of the new baby. Deployments, even short ones, would now start taking their toll since he was old enough to experience it.

They were called and ushered into a room. Fredo held the squirming Ricardo, who wanted to lie down next to Mia on the table, but had to be talked out of it. He watched as the ultrasound wand was placed over Mia's belly and moved back and forth in the gel placed there for conduction. Dr. Feldman smiled.

"Ah, there he is."

"He? You can tell it's a boy?" asked Fredo.

"No, we just say whatever comes to mind. But it appears—" he moved the scope back and forth again, "we have some additional news." He tapped on the screen, and Fredo saw a small outline in white of a dark gray round object. "That's your baby there, and everything looks nice and normal."

Fredo was relieved.

"And that?" The probe moved over another section of Mia's belly. "That's another one. Let me see if we have a third, aaand no."

Fredo blinked at Mia, in shock.

"Twins? You are sure?" gasped Mia.

"No denying it. I think we're a bit early to detect heartbeats, but next visit we can confirm. You see it there? One, two?"

Fredo thought about his dream, all the toddlers and babies being born that evening. Part of it was coming true. He needed to talk to the doctor in private. He was ready to face the paternity of these children. While Mia was taking Ricardo to the restroom, he cornered the doctor.

"Sorry, Doc, but there's something bothering me."

"Okay. You wouldn't be the first father to walk out of this office in shock. Twins can be a life-altering event."

"That's not what I'm wondering. I was tested a few months ago." He inhaled and then decided to just come out with it. "Doc, I'm sterile. I saw it with my own eyes."

"You want me to do a followup?"

"Well, I had one, and they told me my sperm—" Fredo leaned in to whisper in the doctor's ear—"had dented heads and did not move."

Dr. Feldman smiled. "It's rare, but in some cases this can be reversed. Were you on any medication you've now stopped or changed your lifestyle any?"

"No. Not really."

"Well," he opened a drawer under the counter, brought out a small plastic cup with a cardboard lid on it for urine samples. "Get me a specimen, and I'll take a look. I got a microscope back in the lab. It's an easy one to check."

"Thanks." Fredo took the cup and retreated to the restroom. A short time later he brought out the cup and waited in the hallway.

"Your wife's in the waiting room, Mr. Chavez," one of the staff whispered to him.

Doctor Feldman motioned for him to follow him back to the lab. He smeared Fredo's semen sample onto a slide with a swab stick, placed it under the microscope and turned on the bright light. He flipped off the room lights and then examined through the lens.

"Hmm."

"What is it?"

"Well, see for yourself."

Fredo leaned over, squeezing his fingers together into fists. He peered down the barrel of the lighted contraption. While he did see several sperm with dented heads that were completely motionless, he also saw a few very active ones moving all over the place.

"Holy crap," he said and hugged the doctor, causing him to drop his glasses. Fredo scooped them up, presented them back to him, then he gave the man a big kiss on his cheek. "Thank you!"

He ran down the hallway, ready to tell Mia the news. And on the way home, he was going to buy some more tofu, get one of those vegetable drinks for the whole family, plus buy more broccoli and beets and whatever else green he could find.

* * *

SERIES OVERVIEW

SEAL BROTHERHOOD
SEAL Encounter (Book .5)
Accidental SEAL (Book 1)
Fallen SEAL Legacy (Book 2)
SEAL Under Covers (Book 3)
SEAL The Deal (Book 4)
Cruisin' For A SEAL (Book 5)
SEAL My Destiny (Book 6)
SEAL Of My Heart (Book 7)

BAD BOYS OF SEAL TEAM 3
SEAL's Promise (Book 1)
SEAL My Home (Book 2)
SEAL's Code (Book 3)

BAND OF BACHELORS
Lucas (Book 1)
Alex (Book 2)
Jake (Book 3)

TRUE BLUE SEALS
True Navy Blue (prequel to Zak)
Zak

NASHVILLE SEAL
Nashville SEAL (Book 1)
Jameson (Book 2)

FREDO
Fredo's Secret (novella) Book 1
Fredo's Dream (Book 2)

NOVELLAS

SEAL Encounter
SEAL Endeavor
True Navy Blue (prequel to Zak)
Fredo's Secret
Nashville SEAL
SEAL You In My Dreams (4/19/17)
SEAL Of Time (Trident Legacy) (3/28/17)

BOXED SETS

SEAL Brotherhood Box Set 1 (SEALs)
SEAL Brotherhood Box Set 2 (SEALs)
Ultimate SEAL Collection Vol. 1 (SEALs)
Ultimate SEAL Collection Vol. 2 (SEALs)
Big Bad Boys Bundle (SEALs)
Immortal Valentines (Paranormal)

FALL FROM GRACE SERIES

Gideon: Heavenly Fall

GOLDEN VAMPIRES OF TUSCANY

Honeymoon Bite (Book 1)
Mortal Bite (Book 2)

THE GUARDIANS

Heavenly Lover (Book 1)
Underworld Lover (Book 2)
Underworld Queen (Book 3)

PRAISE FOR THE
SEAL BROTHERHOOD SERIES

"Fans of Navy SEAL romance, I found a new author to feed your addiction. Finely written and loaded delicious with moments, Sharon Hamilton's storytelling satisfies like a thick bar of chocolate."—Marliss Melton, bestselling author of the *Team Twelve* Navy SEALs series

"Sharon Hamilton does an EXCELLENT job of fitting all the characters into a brotherhood of SEALS that may not be real but sure makes you feel that you have entered the circle and security of their world. The stories intertwine with each book before…and each book after and THAT is what makes Sharon Hamilton's SEAL Brotherhood Series so very interesting. You won't want to put down ANY of her books and they will keep you reading into the night when you should be sleeping. Start with this book…and you will not want to stop until you've read the whole series and then…you will be waiting for Sharon to write the next one." (5 Star Review)

"Kyle and Christy explode all over the pages in this first book, *[Accidental SEAL],* in a whole new series of SEALs. If the twist and turns don't get your heart jumping, then maybe the suspense will. This is a must read for those that are looking for love and adventure with a little sloppy love thrown in for good measure." (5 Star Review)

PRAISE FOR THE
BAD BOYS OF SEAL TEAM 3 SERIES

"I love reading this series! Once you start these books, you can hardly put them down. The mix of romance and suspense keeps you turning the pages one right after another! Can't wait until the next book!" (5 Star Review)

"I love all of Sharon's Seal books, but *[SEAL's Code]* may just be her best to date. Danny and Luci's journey is filled with a wonderful insight into the Native American life. It is a love story that will fill you with warmth and contentment. You will enjoy Danny's journey to become a SEAL and his reasons for it. Good job Sharon!" (5 Star Review)

PRAISE FOR THE
BAND OF BACHELORS SERIES

"[Lucas] was the first book in the Band of Bachelors series and it was a phenomenal start. I loved how we got to see the other SEALs we all love and we got a look at Lucas and Marcy. They had an instant attraction, and their love was very intense. This book had it all, suspense, steamy romance, humor, everything you want in a riveting, outstanding read. I can't wait to read the next book in this series." (5 Star Review)

PRAISE FOR THE
TRUE BLUE SEALS SERIES

"Keep the tissues box nearby as you read *True Blue SEALs: Zak* by Sharon Hamilton. I imagine more than I wish to that the circumstances surrounding Zak and Amy are all too real for returning military personnel and their families. Ms. Hamilton has put us right in the middle of struggles and successes that these two high school sweethearts endure. I have read several of Sharon Hamilton's military romances but will say this is the most emotionally intense of the ones that I have read. This is a well-written, realistic story with authentic characters that will have you rooting for them and proud of those who serve to keep us safe. This is an author who writes amazing stories that you love and cry with the characters. Fans of Jessica Scott and Marliss Melton will want to add Sharon Hamilton to their list of realistic military romance writers." (5 Star Review)

ABOUT THE AUTHOR

NYT and USA/Today and Amazon Top 100 Bestselling Author Sharon Hamilton's SEAL Brotherhood series have earned her Amazon author rankings of #1 in Romantic Suspense, Military Romance and Contemporary Romance. Her characters follow a sometimes rocky road to redemption through passion and true love. Her Golden Vampires of Tuscany earned her a #1 Amazon author ranking in Gothic Romance.

A lifelong organic vegetable and flower gardener, Sharon and her husband live in the Wine Country of Northern California, where most of her stories take place.

Connect with Author Sharon Hamilton!

www www.authorsharonhamilton.com

f facebook.com/AuthorSharonHamilton

@sharonlhamilton

http://authorsharonhamilton.com/contact

Made in the USA
Columbia, SC
11 October 2021